OATH OF FIDELITY

A DARK MAFIA ROMANCE

JANE HENRY

SYNOPSIS

Oath of Fidelity: A Dark Mafia Romance
Deviant Doms

Synopsis:

She'll pay the price for her betrayal... as my bride.

Elise Regazza is beautiful.

She's also a liar.

A schemer.

A woman who betrayed The Family.

And she owes her life for what she's done.

When she begs for mercy, I offer her a single choice: Marry me.

Solidify my power in The Family.

And she agrees.

But make no mistake, little Elise will never be free.

Now our vows will be her shackles.

My rules will be her collar.

And disloyalty will not be tolerated.

The traitor will learn to honor and obey the man she hates...

For better or for worse.

Until death do us part.

CHAPTER 1

Tavi

I stare at the cracked tile that leads to the altar of Saint Anthony's and remember how it broke. I wonder if anyone else here does. Not everyone can say they recall the way their father body slammed the alter server on their first Communion day.

Why'd he do it? Who the hell knows. The kid probably looked at him funny or showed my father what he thought was a form of disrespect.

I can still see the way my mother's face grew cold and impassive, her typical response to my father's fits of rage. Unless his fury was aimed at one of *us*. Then, we saw another Tosca Rossi, one whose own face and body bore the brunt of his fury and anger when she came between him and us. My father was, after all, a psychopath. He bled out over a year ago on the very property where I was born.

We didn't try to save him. It was time.

I wonder sometimes if mental illness is genetic. I wonder if it knocks on my own door, but I refuse to answer it. It's the age-old question I think most men ask themselves at one point in their lives.

Will I become my father?

I fold my hands and listen to the gospel readings, chosen by my sister-in-law Angelina for the special occasion of her son's baptism. My niece Natalia fidgets uncomfortably in her seat, and when she looks at me, I put my finger to my lips to remind her to be quiet. I soften the correction with a wink to show her I'm as bored as she is. With a sigh, she turns around and obeys.

Elise catches my eye. I feel my body go rigid, a coldness suffusing my limbs. She blinks and starts as if struck, then turns to Angelina and whispers something. Angelina hands her the sleeping baby dressed in the traditional white gown used for every Rossi family baptism.

Elise is my betrothed.

Elise and I didn't choose this. Few of us in The Family ever do.

I think of every sacrament we endured within the walls of this church. While I was way too young to remember my own baptism, I remember Mario and Marialena's, my younger brother's and sister's. I remember how Mama bought us small, matching tuxedos, and how my father made us polish our shoes. I remember my older brother Romeo making me and Orlando sit still when we fidgeted. I remember first Communions, a few of my cousins' weddings, and the somber funeral for my father, probably the only funeral I've attended where not one person shed a tear. Romeo ordered champagne for the funeral brunch.

As I remember the sacraments we've celebrated here… I know why that broken tile's never been replaced. Romeo himself probably ordered it kept there, since he's the church's largest benefactor and has a say in all repairs and projects. But that tile… it's a stark yet subtle reminder of the power the Rossi family holds.

I've looked over my family's bookkeeping for years. We singlehandedly support this church. There's a reason why Saint Anthony's is the most affluent in all of Massachusetts.

My brother Orlando clears his throat and wiggles his eyebrows at me. The whole church is silent, expectant, even the organ still as he waits for me. I'm baby Nicolo's godfather. It's time.

I stand and join Orlando, who beams as he walks to the altar beside his beautiful wife Angelina. They both smile at me, but I don't share their joy. Angelina nearly threw my family into ruin. She forced my hand in ordering the execution of a man I never wanted to kill. It's because of her I'm marrying the woman beside her.

"Come, godfather," my future wife murmurs. "You're supposed to stand beside me." I don't like her telling me what to do in even the most innocuous way, so when I give her a look that seems to startle her, she softens her tone. "Please."

She bends her head toward the baby and nuzzles Nicolo's soft, fuzzy head. His white satin bonnet has fallen to the side, attached loosely to the traditional gown with a matching satin ribbon. I watch as she kisses the baby and still doesn't meet my eyes.

Beautiful, proud Elise Regazza walks by my side to the altar. A foreshadowing of things to come? We'll walk this same path in only four weeks. But today, we're the chosen godparents for Orlando and Angelina's baby, so we take our place where we belong.

Elise Regazza may be many things—spoiled, headstrong, and materialistic, to name just a few—but the woman is lovely. Stunning, really. Shorter than me by about six inches, she still stands tall in chunky heels. She has the same light brown hair as Angelina, the one character trait that allowed them to pull a temporary identity switch at one time. Now, however, Angelina's highlighted her hair lighter, making Elise's look slightly darker in comparison.

Her hair is long and straight, and hangs well past her shoulders. Her beautiful, deep amber eyes, framed in thick lashes, catch my attention. I know she wears contacts mostly but occasionally glasses, though she's never let me see her wearing them. She hides the fact that she does, but I know everything about her.

I'd like to see them on her. I imagine she'd have the sexy librarian look going on, but she's too proud.

Her gently rounded face would make her look almost girlish, if not for the wild defiance in her deep amber eyes, the color of a shot of amaretto. A gentle smattering of freckles and a dimple in her chin complete the fetching, nearly girlish look, but her full, light pink lips and curvy, hourglass figure are *all woman.*

What my family knows, that no one else sitting in this church does, is that Elise Regazza is my prisoner.

I allow her some freedom, at Orlando's suggestion, because his wife Angelina is her best friend. But I don't trust either of them. Those two were, after all, guilty of conspiring against my family.

They've paid their dues, some would say—Angelina is now married to my brother, after a lengthy imprisonment of her own. Because of their marriage, she's now a full-fledged member of our family. And Elise has been under lock and key for months.

She's allowed to take walks, and to travel to the shops within ten miles of here, but I track her every move and insist she have three high-ranking bodyguards on her at all times. It's nothing short of walking confinement. I don't regret it.

I don't think she's dangerous. She'd like to think I do. But no, I don't keep a tight leash on her because I fear her escape. I want her to remember she's my prisoner and will be until we take our vows and consummate our marriage.

I had a GPS tracker embedded under the skin of her left upper arm, the exact place where one would implant birth control. I know wherever she is when she's not directly in my line of vision.

She also wears a thick, gold cuff bracelet fitted with GPS as well, one connected to the apps on my phone. It heats and generates a warming sensation across her wrist, when I want to issue her a warning. It also shows me her constant whereabouts, as well as her vital signs—her heartbeat, her body temperature, and even when she's waking or sleeping.

I know when she's doing yoga, when she's jogging, or when she's resting. I watch her more closely than most wardens monitor prisoners.

But Elise has behaved herself. She's comported herself with the dignity befitting a mafia princess, just as she was raised, and as she'll soon learn to become once more.

"Welcome," Father Richard says, smiling benevolently at the large, well-dressed group of family members that have come after mass to witness Nicolo's baptism. Nonna and Mama sit up front, Mama dressed in a form-fitting black dress, and Nonna wearing her own traditional black dress and sensible shoes as well. But among those in the congregation are my sisters, my brothers, the sworn brothers of The Family and their own loved ones, as well as my cousins, aunts, and uncles. Nearly every pew in the church is occupied with someone dressed in black or gold, like an Italian mafia photo shoot for a travel guide.

"We've come to witness the sacred ritual of baptism," the priest continues. "What name have you given your child?"

"Nicolo Lorenzo Rossi," Orlando says without hesitation, his chest nearly swelling with pride. Angelina beams at the baby, and as Nicolo begins to sniff and fuss, Elise automatically begins to sway from side to side to soothe him.

The priest begins the ritual of anointing, first making the sign of the cross on the baby's forehead, then leading Elise and the baby to the solid marble baptismal font that stands in front of our semi-circle. He lifts a small golden cup, Elise holds the baby over the font, and with the ritualistic prayers, Father Richard pours water over Nicolo's head.

The baby starts, opens his mouth, and wails so loudly you'd think he was being tortured. Undeterred, Elise smiles and holds him steady while Father completes the baptism. Her pretty, dainty hand, adorned with several slender gold rings, her nails manicured and painted a bold, vivid red, cups the baby's head gently.

"Here, Uncle," she says, handing me the baby after the last sprinkling of water. I reach for him, gathering him up in the miles of satin, while he continues to wail his heart out. "Why don't you hold your godson?"

I hold him up to my shoulder and tuck one hand against his bottom, and imitate her swaying from side to side. I have lots of younger siblings and a niece, as well as tons of cousins, so I'm not new to this. The baby nuzzles my shoulder and begins to quiet.

Elise's lips gently part and her eyes widen as she watches me, but the look only lasts a few seconds before her gaze shutters and she looks away.

I don't know what the look means. I don't much care, either. We're following the steps laid out to us from our fathers before us and their fathers before them, from generation to generation.

"Come, Elise. Follow me."

She mutters something under her breath that sounds like *as if I have a choice*. She's right. She knows I've set her bracelet to close proximity, and if she's more than ten feet away from me her wrist will begin to heat. It won't heat to burning, but it won't be pleasant.

"What was that?" I ask in a low voice out of the side of my mouth, still smiling for the flashing cameras all around the church. The smell of incense envelops us so strongly it's nearly cloying.

"Oh, nothing," she says in a voice as sickly sweet as the incense. "I said exactly what you want to hear. *Yes, Tavi.* That's what you want to hear, isn't it?"

Ah, so she's decided to toy with being smug. We'll see if she's still smiling when I get her alone.

"Good girl," I say, in a tone as mocking as hers. "That's exactly what I want to hear."

Among other things. We'll get there.

Four weeks. Four weeks until we take our own place at the altar, when we both take vows to each other. Orlando and Angelina will be the only ones in our wedding party, but we've caved and allowed Mama and Nonna to plan the huge, lavish wedding that's our custom, the wedding Romeo and Orlando never had with their wives. They've waited long enough. It's our turn now.

Four more weeks until we consummate our marriage. When our obligations will be complete.

In theory, anyway.

I've watched my brothers grow soft with marriage and brides, allowing their wives to basically do what they want. They think they're in charge, that they're the heads of their houses, but I've seen how lenient they've become.

That won't happen with me.

I won't have a wife that doesn't know her place.

And even though Elise has been kept prisoner, she's nowhere near done paying the price for what she's done.

Elise will be my wife, and she'll learn exactly what that means.

CHAPTER 2

Elise

I hate him. I hate his beautiful, arrogant face. Those full lips that smirk in mockery. Those eyes that only scorn, that large, muscled body of his that he's worked to strengthen so he can intimidate and over-power, and those ruthless, *ruthless* hands of his that do *not* know how to treat a lady at *all*.

He's everything Piero never was and stands for everything I hate.

My heart aches at the fleeting memory of Piero, the bodyguard I knew from childhood, the only man I've ever loved and ever will. The man now dead because of me. But the ache is brief, quickly passing when I shove it away. I won't dwell on Piero. I can't bring him back.

Instead, I focus on Tavi. Ottavio Rossi. The man I'll be essentially *shackled* to for the rest of my life. The thought alone makes a lump form in my throat. I swallow and look away, blinking back tears.

I knew from childhood that I'd never marry a man I loved. But it didn't stop me from dreaming. I wish I never had. I wish I'd found joy in other parts of life and resigned myself to a future with a man I don't love, but instead I let myself fall. I let myself hope.

I hate Tavi, but I have to marry him. It was the only way I was able to save my life and Angelina's. I feared they'd kill her once they knew who she was, when we switched places. I feared she'd bear the brunt of the punishment we'd earned for defying the most powerful mob in New England.

So I came to The Castle, the family home north of Boston on the North Shore. I allowed myself to be taken and imprisoned. It was a choice I willingly made.

And here I am.

Four weeks until I bear the final yoke that will make me a full-fledged Rossi.

Yeah, you could say mine is a classic case of leaping from the frying pan straight into the goddamn fire.

I sigh and look to Angelina and Orlando, the happily married couple walking hand in hand beside Tavi. That was supposed to be me, if Angelina and I hadn't decided to change the course of fate. You could say our plans didn't work the way they were supposed to, and now my best friend is married to one of Boston's most dangerous.

Next up? Me.

They might call it marriage, but we all know what it really is.

Incarceration.

Modern-day slavery.

Call it what you will, but I know exactly what I'm getting into.

Before my mother and father were estranged, I knew enough to witness their loveless marriage. I knew what marriage meant to them, to my aunts, and to my uncles. I'm an only child, so I knew from an early age what was expected of me.

And now it's my turn.

"Shh, baby." I startle at the sound of Tavi's voice. My cheeks flush, and my heart does a strange little leap. But when I look to him, he's only crooning at the baby. I turn away quickly so he doesn't see my reddened cheeks.

I thought for a moment he was talking to me, but I should've known better. He wouldn't use that gentle voice, and he definitely, *definitely,* wouldn't use a term of endearment. Seems the only soft spot in his whole damn heart belongs to his niece and nephew.

I have to remind myself who Tavi is, because it almost softened me to see him holding his godson. But he scowls every time he looks at me, those dark blue eyes of his narrowed and angry. His muscles tense. While the others laugh freely, and some are even jovial, Tavi never cracks a smile. But when he holds his godson… when he holds that precious little baby to his chest, his eyes begin to soften a little, and I begin to wonder if maybe, just maybe—

No. Love isn't for us. This man imprisoned me. He's taking me as his bride out of a sense of duty. No more, no less. I turn my back to him, searching the crowd for Angelina, since she's been swallowed up in the cousins and aunts and uncles that have just met her for the first time.

From an outsider's perspective, it looks like the most close-knit family you could imagine. Gorgeous, stunning women dressed in designer clothes embrace Angelina and kiss both her cheeks, the Italian custom. Angelina glows beside Orlando, her face flushed pink. I know the real truth, though. I know who these people are. They're no better than the family I grew up with myself.

Ruthless. Selfish. And the men that lead this family? *Monsters.*

I hold my head high and walk to the edge of the small garden that surrounds the church. It's late April in the north of Boston, a bit cloudy but otherwise warm. A scattering of green buds raising their bold little faces upward border the little garden with statues of saints and the Virgin Mary. Someone's gardened recently, welcoming the advent of spring.

"April showers bring May flowers," I whisper to myself as I reach a paved pathway that leads to a bench. It's rained steadily for days. Today's the first dry day we've had in ages.

I sit on the bench, and my wrist begins to heat.

Goddammit.

I've strayed too far from *His Fucking Highness,* and this medieval contraption he's configured for my wrist has begun to warn me. I reach for the clasp, even though I know it won't yield to me. It's locked, and he has the key.

Some twisted, lonely women might find that hot. Like he's possessive of me? Yeah, no. I find it controlling and manipulative.

Something inside me seems to snap. I hate that I'm his prisoner. I hate that he thinks he owns me. He hasn't even married me yet, and he already acts like he's my husband.

I begin to claw at the bracelet, my fingers digging into the skin around it until it's red and swollen. "You fucking thing," I mutter, close to tears. "Fuck you." The warmth increases, as if it can hear me, just as the bracelet seems to suddenly loosen.

I watch in astonishment as the clasp falls open, and the bracelet falls down my hand to my lap. I gasp, and my eyes quickly scan the crowd to find Tavi.

He'd punish me for this, I know he would.

I fold my hand and hide the bracelet on my lap when I see him, then quickly slide it, unlocked, back on my wrist. He stares at me, still holding the baby, but he's a good distance away from me at this point. I smile at him and wriggle my fingers. He blinks in surprise. It takes me a minute to realize why. I've definitely never been friendly to him before.

"Hey, there, beautiful."

I look up, startled, to see Ottavio's youngest sister Marialena heading my way. She smiles broadly, revealing perfectly straight, white teeth, and her gorgeous hazel eyes light up. With her light brown hair that hangs almost to her waist, those large eyes framed with thick, exotic lashes, and her slender figure, the woman could seriously model. All the Rossis could, really. And she's calling *me* beautiful?

"Oh, hey. You should consider modeling."

Eh, why pull punches.

She smiles even broader. "Me? But my face isn't all *symmetrical*. Don't you need a perfectly symmetrical face to model?"

"Looks good to me, but I guess you could model your hands or something."

"Say it." She stands in front of me and wiggles her butt. "It's the ass I should model."

I laugh out loud. "Definitely the ass, but don't tell Tavi I was checking you out."

She rolls her eyes and waves her hand in the general direction of her brothers. "Oh, what-*fucking*-ever," she says with a sound of disgust. "You can check my ass out all you want, babe. Anyway, saw you waving to me, thought I'd come over and say hi." She sits down beside me on the bench and pulls out her phone. "My family will be here forever chatting about nothing, before they go back to The Castle for food. So help me, Tavi better have brought three boxes of those cannolis or we'll have World War Three on our hands." She frowns, flipping through notifications on her phone. "Three unfollows. What's that all about?"

"Why is Tavi in charge of the pastries? Is that his job?"

She blinks at me in surprise and drops her phone to her lap. "Don't you know? He owns pastry shops in the North End."

"*Really?*" I'm intrigued. I've always heard the North End was like Boston's Little Italy, with all the imported Italian food and the rich heritage of Italy on every corner, cobblestoned streets and all.

"Wow," she says, back scrolling on her phone. "There's a lot you need to learn about your future husband before you marry him, huh?"

I inwardly cringe and outwardly shrug. "I guess."

Why? Why does it matter? We'll be married because we have to be. He won't be my lover, and I won't be his. We'll be little more than a strange concoction of roommate and fuck buddy, I guess.

I hope he knows how to move those powerful hips of his. A girl could forgive a lot from a man who fucks well.

"Well. So for starters..." she taps her chin thoughtfully before grinning, taking a selfie, then sending it out with a swipe of her phone. "Tonight's a full moon. You know what they say about reading Tarot cards and a full moon?"

I snort. "No, why don't you tell me."

I know she's super into things like Tarot cards and astrology and crystals. I like tangible, real things, things I can touch and see.

"Elise," she says, rolling her eyes at me. "Listen, babe. Reading Tarot cards during a full moon is the *most optimal* time to read them, and most especially when you're *right* on the verge of a major life change."

Major life change? My major life change was when Piero died. Getting married to Tavi will only be a matter of course.

"Yeah." I shrug. "Okay. Does Angelina do it with you?"

Marialena nods her head eagerly. "Yup. Loves them. Rosa, she couldn't care less and Mama thinks they're the work of the Devil." She shrugs. "But the clearest answers are always during a full moon, because it reflects the improved intuition of your diviner..." She points both thumbs at herself.

"Which is *me*, by the way. The most compelling Tarot reading you could get is during the full moon cycle."

"So… why don't you read yours?" I ask, stifling a laugh.

"Oh, honey, I so will. Trust me. Hey, that's a pretty gold bracelet you've got there."

Pretty? Ha. She can have the damn thing. "Thanks." I slide it gently along my wrist, afraid it's magically fastened itself back together, and give a little sigh of relief when I feel it still loose and unlocked. I'd give it to her if the possessed little torture device didn't heat on its own. I don't want to surprise her or hurt her in any way.

"So what do you say, Elise? Come with Angelina and let me read your cards tonight."

I shrug. "If Tavi will let me."

She stands and gives me a bold wink. "He will. Trust me. I'll talk with him." She does seem to have some sway over her brothers. How much, I have no idea.

When she walks away, I look down at the bracelet and back to Tavi. He's got his back to me. Occasionally, he glances over his shoulder, but he seems more preoccupied than he was before.

I stand with my back to him. He's oblivious to the fact that the bracelet's no longer locked on me. With my heart hammering against my chest, I walk quickly to the edge of the garden, close enough to him so as not to alert him right away.

I drop the bracelet. It makes a soft thumping sound when it hits the ground, and a little puff of dirt rises into the air. Quickly, I kick it as hard as I can under a bush. With my back to the crowd, I run my fingers along the bare skin at my wrist. It feels so good. *So good.*

I know I'll get in trouble for this. He'll find out eventually, and I'll probably deal with his anger as a result, but right now? I don't care. I don't.

I tell myself I've grown used to his anger. A thrill of exhilaration runs through me. *Point one, Elise.*

"Hey, what's up, girlfriend?" I look up to see Angelina walking over to me. I grin at her. She's glowing as if lit from within, a happy mother and happy wife.

I look to see Tavi and Orlando are chatting at the edge of the garden.

"Oh, hey. How are you? That baptism was beautiful."

"Thank you," she says warmly, then sidles up beside me. "So I'm told we're reading Tarot cards tonight?"

"Ha, supposedly. Who's got the baby?"

She snorts. "Your future husband, of course. Seriously, Elise, he's going to be a fantastic dad. Did you see how adorable he is with Nicolo?"

Has she been brainwashed or something? I don't respond at first, but after a minute passes, her face grows suspicious.

"Elise… what's going on?"

I turn away from her. Angelina's the only real friend I have here so far. I don't want to push her away.

"It's hard to imagine the guy who's imprisoned me as a *good dad* or *good husband*, you know?" I ignore the pang that hits my chest. I thought I could share my reticence and anger with her, but I don't know if she gets it anymore. I can't share it with Marialena, or any of the other women here. Vittoria's married to Romeo, and she looks at him with the same starry eyes as Angelina has for Orlando. Tosca, the matriarch of the family, has been kind to me, but her adherence to Family laws supersedes all else.

And there are no other friends for me outside the Rossi circle, nor will there ever be. The Rossi family keeps things so close to the vest, they even have a family doctor who does house calls. It's practically a damn cult.

Angelina smiles. "I know, babe. I do. I thought the same thing at first, but you'll see… they have a strong moral code. And yeah, they don't do things the way you and I do, or did, but they're loyal. So loyal." Her voice gets a faraway sound to it and her eyes grow distant. I have the strange, unshakable feeling she isn't telling me everything.

Maybe she's only mulling over her own unexpected foray into love. I watch her absentmindedly finger her necklace, the "riot of flowers" Orlando paid a small fortune for. I've been jealous of that stunning piece since I first saw it.

Angelina continues. "You know, I didn't think I'd come to fall in love, but I did."

I snort. "Love? Yeah, no."

I look back at Tavi. The beautiful, handsome-as-sin, *diabolical* Tavi.

I will not love this man.

"We'll see," Angelina says softly. "We're going back to the house, and girl, wait until you see that spread they've got for us. And let's see what the cards say tonight, okay?"

Back at The Castle, I realize Angelina was absolutely right about at least one thing. The entire Great Hall's been transformed into something out of a fantasy, which doesn't take much because it's already magnificent. Huge tables covered in silvery tablecloths bear large platters of fruit cut into works of art, another table hosts crackers and cheese from all over the world, and another a fondue station that has my mouth watering. One made of cheese with an array of things to dip into it, another with a chocolate fountain. *Yum.* Chocolate's my obsession.

Uniformed staff bear trays with flutes of champagne, while still others have platters of appetizers and finger sandwiches. Round tables are set with fabric tablecloths and water glasses. Carafes, mugs for coffee and overflowing baskets of bread with little pats of butter in the shape of rose petals wait at every table.

Okay, so my family never did *anything* like this, most especially for a child who'll never even remember it. A sudden realization hits me straight in the solar plexus.

I draw in a sharp breath. If this is how they do a baptism, the wedding's going to be *epic*. I cringe at the very thought.

I've kept close to Tavi on purpose, so he knows I'm still nearby, and I've managed to hide my bare wrist from him. I had a member of staff fetch me a long-sleeved cardigan and donned it as soon as we got home. If he knows, he hasn't let on. I suspect he doesn't, not yet.

I feel my upper arm through the sweater. He's embedded something there, though, I know he has, and I know he's enabled my phone with air tags as well.

I'm not going to try to escape. First, I have nowhere to escape *to*, and I wouldn't want to put any more of a burden on my best friend than I already have.

But a girl can have a little fun.

I take a large plate of food and walk over to the table where Angelina and Marialena sit, easily thirty feet from Tavi. My wrist should be on fire by now. I swing it freely for one gleeful second before I hide it again. I'm hardly *free*, but I do have the momentary upper hand. Heh.

I set my plate on the table and flag down a waiter with a tray of drinks.

"A glass of champagne, miss?"

I smile and take one in each hand.

CHAPTER 3

Tavi

She's up to something. I know she is.

Elise has glanced my way more times this afternoon than she has since she came here. I've had enough people I've interrogated and questioned under my watch to know the look of a guilty conscience.

Like I fucking care if she's up to anything. I've tracked her every move, and she knows it. There's nothing she's going to get away with. Still, I pull Orlando aside.

"Angelina say anything to you?" I ask. He's drinking his third flute of champagne and has a pastry in his free hand. Brother's been bodybuilding with me for the past four months.

"Cheat day?" I ask, eying the cannoli with envy. My cheat day's on Friday, a long fucking way away.

He opens his mouth and polishes off the whole damn cannoli in one bite. "What?" he asks around a mouthful of food.

"Jesus, man. You'd think married life would make a guy grow the fuck up already. You look like a twelve-year-old."

He rolls his eyes, wipes the back of his hand across his mouth, and flags down a waitress. "Grab that tray of cannoli you put in the kitchen, will you?"

"Yes, sir."

He grins at me.

"You've got powdered sugar in your beard, asshole."

He brushes it off and shrugs. "You're just jealous it isn't your cheat day."

"Fuck off."

So what if I am.

He grabs four shrimp cocktail from the nearby table, skewers them all at once, and opens his mouth. I grab the skewer from his fingers and plop them into my own mouth.

"Son of a bitch," he says reverently. Normally he'd deck me for stealing food, or try to anyway. But today he's in a good mood.

"Shrimp ain't cheatin'," I mutter. "Good clean protein."

He grabs another stack and eats them before I inhale those, too. "So what were you asking me about? Something about Angelina?"

"Yeah. Elise looks like she's up to something."

Orlando looks across the room where Elise sits with Marialena and Angelina. Marialena holds the baby on her knee and says something that makes Angelina and Elise burst into laughter.

"Looks like she's just sitting and eating, man. Relax. She's almost your wife. You've got, what, six weeks left?"

I drink my champagne. "Four."

"Ah, perfect. You gonna take a honeymoon?"

"I don't know yet."

A honeymoon is a celebration. This is nothing to celebrate.

A honeymoon gives you space to sleep in and fuck all day long. I don't need an excuse for that. She'll be mine, to use however I want, whenever I want.

I don't know why that knowledge feels so hollow, void of any joy it should bring me. Instead, knowing that I'll have her as my ready-made fuck toy feels like nothing more than an obligation.

I shrug it off.

I shrug everything off.

Romeo walks over with Mario, our youngest brother. "Alright, boys. We've got two, soon to be three, of the Rossi boys married." Romeo's voice is louder than usual and his cheeks flushed. Someone's been in the limoncello again. "What're we gonna do about this player?" He slaps Mario's back affectionately. Mario laughs and tucks his head, clearly taking this as a compliment.

"You ain't gonna do *nothing* about this playa," he says in his best Boston gangster accent. "This playa fuckin' loves tappin' tail he doesn't have to *provide* for and all that." He gives us a shit-eating grin and sips his drink.

Santo saunters over, his gaze cold and calculating as always.

"You boys hear about Regazza's property?"

"Fucking Regazza," I mutter. Elise's late father, who drove his family to near ruin, died right here in The Castle after double-crossing us, something she doesn't seem to hold against us.

Yet, anyway. The jury's still out.

The Regazzas didn't seek retaliation after the truth was outed, but relocated to Tuscany, as far away from our family home in the Italian city as possible. Last I heard, they'd relocated again to Lombardy, east of Milan and as far North from Tuscany as possible.

"Squatters taking it over, man," he says. "It's a fucking dump."

"Which property?"

"He owned a few retail locations near Copley."

"No shit?" Romeo mutters, his eyes half-glazed. Romeo oversees operations and calls every final shot. Orlando's the group heavy, the one who closes deals and takes lives, whenever the situation calls for it. I'm the group strategist, the one who makes business decisions and advises The Family.

So all eyes come to me.

"You'll inherit that property, Tavi," Santo says coolly. He takes a joint out of his pocket and rolls it between his fingers, but knows better than to light it. Mario will join him out by the garden. They'll get high before they take a woman—or women—for the night.

I don't touch the stuff and barely drink except on special occasions. I like to be in absolute control of myself.

"We move in, clear them out tomorrow. Copley's prime location. They use it for retail, you said?"

Santo nods. "Yeah. Imported Italian shit. Leather bags, shoes, scarves."

"Anything left?"

Santo shrugs. "No idea. We'll have to find out. Heard this from one of our suppliers."

Romeo frowns and puts his glass to his lips, his eyes traveling across the room to where his wife Vittoria sits. She looks his way and winks. He grins at her.

Fucking sickening.

"We should've known this before now," Romeo says with a shake of his head. He hates being taken by surprise by anything. "Tavi, tomorrow, let's run a full scan of everything and anything we can find on Regazza."

"On it." I already questioned his Underboss before he relocated to Tuscany, then Lombardo, a town in Lombardy. I thought he told me everything he knew, goddammit. "May need to fly to Italy."

"Smart," Romeo says, nodding sagely as if I've just explained the miracle of the Great Pyramids to him.

"We should get you tipsy more often," Orlando says. "Jesus, man, you've lost your edge."

Romeo gives him a lopsided grin. "Outside, right now, Orlando, let's see who's lost his fucking edge." Romeo hands his empty glass to Santo and cracks his knuckles.

"Ah, no," Orlando says with a snort. He won't take the bait. "I love my wife way too much to get my nose busted on our son's day of baptism. Plus, you know I can't hit you, man. You're too pretty. You'd win in a landslide."

And he knows hitting the Boss would get him killed. I pulled a gun on him once for doing exactly that, and I'm under vows to do it again.

"Don't make me kill you, Orlando," I mutter, shaking my head. But Romeo doesn't wanna let it go.

Orlando sees the blow coming and ducks Romeo's fist, then does a little dance like a boxer in a ring before he belts out a laugh. In the corner of the room, I see Mama roll her eyes heavenward. Orlando grins. "Gettin' old, man. Lettin' your Capos fight too many for ya, huh?"

"Fuckin' asshole," Romeo says with a grin of his own. He swipes another shot from a waitress and saunters over to Vittoria. Seconds later, she's sitting on his lap and he's whispering things in her ear that make her blush beet red.

I look away, but only for a second. I swing my gaze back to the table where the girls sit.

Elise isn't there. I whip out my phone and look at the tracking app. Air tag's right here in the room. Embedded tracker's got her right here in this room as well.

But her bracelet? It's at *the fucking church.*

I narrow my eyes and look around the small room, but I don't see her in the melee of people. I walk the perimeter. I'm well versed in the art of finding someone who's hiding. Skirt the perimeter, lock down exits. There are two exits out of this room. I signal to two nearby guards, who promptly come to my side.

"Man the exits. You see Elise, you lock her down and alert me."

They leave swiftly and silently.

She isn't here. How could it lie, though? That fucking tracker's in her *arm*. She could lose the bracelet, she could lose her phone, but that damn tracker would mean cutting her own flesh to remove it. Still, I can't find her no matter where I look.

I go to the exit and call Orlando.

"Yeah, man?"

"You seen Elise?"

"You lost her with three motherfuckin' trackers on her, bro?"

I curse under my breath. "Have you seen her?" I repeat.

I can hear him talking to Angelina, Romeo, and Vittoria. "Nah, man. The girls say she was here just a few minutes ago then excused herself. Check the restrooms?"

The Castle is fucking *huge*, with over twelve bathrooms. Plus I already know. She didn't go to the bathroom. She's pulling a fast one on me.

"Thanks."

I hang up.

I know that the bracelet at the church was her doing. She isn't there, but the tracking app says she never left the church. I saw her with my own eyes, so she somehow got the tracker off herself. But if she's in this room... she's hiding.

And I don't play games.

I once waited eight hours for a traitor to surface on the waterfront, huddled in a small sailboat in the dead of winter because I knew he was coming. I found him, alright, and damn near got frostbite, but we brought down a whole insidious cartel with his intel.

I'll stay right fucking here until she shows herself.

This time, I can wait here, in the privacy of my home, with staff I can order to bring me whatever I need.

I place my phone down on the table, app open, signal for a waiter, and order myself a cocktail. She can't hide for long. Like someone hiding underwater, she'll have to resurface for air. I'll stay in this room until the last guest leaves.

And while I sit, I plan how I'll punish her when I find her, before I truss her up and drag her back to Tuscany. My pretty, willful fiancée will learn that she hasn't even begun her punishment for the betrayal she inflicted on my family. She's changed the entire course of my life with her deception.

No more.

We'll start with a good, long spanking. I don't know if she's ever been spanked before. A part of me hopes she hasn't. I'd like the novelty of it all to be on my terms.

I adjust myself, hard from the image I conjure of her over my lap, squirming and begging for mercy.

Tears don't sway me, or mournful pleas.

Guests begin to dwindle until the only people left are my immediate family and Marialena's best friend, redheaded Sassy.

"Hey, Tavi," Sassy says, sitting down beside me.

"Hey." I take another sip of my drink.

"You waiting on something?"

"Yep."

When I don't offer more details, she rolls her eyes. "Like pulling goddamn teeth," she mutters, before she says in a louder voice, "Who are you waiting for, Ottavio?"

I place my cup down on the table. "My betrothed, *Sassy.*"

"Ooh," she mutters, pursing her lips. "Touchy, aren't we?"

I grunt under my breath. "Have you seen her?"

Sassy smirks at me and examines her fingers. Goddammit, we need more brothers in this family. This girl needs a firm hand just like they all fucking do. "Maybe I did, maybe I didn't. What do I get if I tell you?"

"The chance to come back here?"

Sassy blows out a breath and rolls her eyes. "You can't kick me out of here, Tavi, you know that."

"Wanna test that theory?"

She holds my gaze.

"Fine," I mutter. "What do you want?"

"I want Marialena to go with me to Tuscany on spring break."

I roll my eyes and blow out a breath, as if she's asking a lot. Romeo already told me he'd allow it. I think he feels bad he nearly exiled Marialena in a fit of rage recently. Got a bit of a hot temper.

"You know that's Romeo's call, not mine."

She shakes her head. "Now, Tavi, I've been here long enough I'm practically a member of this family."

True.

"And you know as well as I do that Romeo might call the shots, but *you* are the Underboss. You're his right hand man. You ask him to let us go and he'll let her. Guaranteed."

I pretend to think this over. "Fine, I'll talk to him, but I want you to tell me where Elise is, and you owe me another favor, too."

"What's that?"

"Don't know yet, but I'll let you know, when I need it."

She rolls her eyes. Sassy alright. "Okay, fine. Deal. I'll let it go only because I know you're getting married so the terms won't involve sexual favors."

As if the fact that any of us were getting married would impact that at all. My father had a fucking harem.

Leaning closer to me, Sassy lowers her voice. "I'd check the coat room if I were you."

The coat room. What's she doing in the fucking coat room?

Standing, Sassy beckons to Marialena, and the two of them head out.

I polish off my drink and slide it onto a nearby tray to be taken to the kitchen. I'm grateful I wore soft-soled shoes today, Italian leather. They make no noise when I head to the coat room, adjacent to where I am now.

The guards at either exit watch me, but I signal for them to stay.

Not far from the reception room, between the Great Hall and the main entrance, lies the small coat room. We hid there when we were younger, a favorite place for hide-and-seek, but we took cover when my father was on a rampage as well. I don't know why he never sought us in the coat room, but it was the one place he never looked.

The house is usually bustling with servants, family, and guests, but it's quieter now that evening's fallen.

With the Great Hall at my back, I walk past the sun room with its large, arched windows now darkened after sunset. The rocking chairs strewn with quilts sit idle in shadows as I make my way to the small coat room adjacent to the main entrance.

During parties it's a forest of jackets, furs, and leather in here but only a few coats remain right now, stored during the warmer months until the colder weather returns. It's old-fashioned to have one of these, but it's useful. Guests have a harder time concealing weapons when they're required to check their coats.

I don't see Elise at first, but I doubt that Sassy's bluffing. She might be a tease and sarcastic as fuck, but I've never known her to be a liar. Quietly, I glance around the small, darkened room.

I see her shoes before I see her. In the far corner of the room, three heavy woolen coats conceal her, but the toes give her away. They're pointed inward as if she's grown tired or relaxed instead of sitting upright and watchful. She hasn't heard me, then, or she's fallen asleep.

I shove the coats aside. Elise jumps, startled, as if I just woke her. She sits on a tiny stool that barely accommodates her. Her eyes blink blearily, and she balls her fists and rubs them in the sockets, like a child just waking from a nap.

Ah. She tried to hide, but fell fast asleep. The coat room's still connected to the Great Hall, so the tracker showed her still in the room. The Castle's not a good place to track anyone—too many tunnels, turrets, and hidden passageways.

I won't make that mistake again.

The anger I feel at finding her, at the nerve she has in hiding in the first place, fades a little when I see how vulnerable and small she is.

Only a little.

"There you are."

I watch as color rises in her cheeks, and she gives me a little shrug. "Here I am."

Her arm's angry and red where I've embedded the tracker. Did she try to get it out? She'd need more than sharp fingernails to do that.

I crouch in front of her so we're eye to eye, my forearms resting on my knees. She doesn't move but sits perfectly still. "I hope you were comfortable in here, sweetheart."

Her brows draw together, though she tries to look brave. She juts her chin out, but can't hide the way her voice wobbles.

"I-I was. Why?"

I rest my hand on her thigh. I've barely touched the woman except to drag her to her imprisonment. I haven't punished her, not yet. That will change now.

"Because you won't be comfortable for long."

I stand and don't even give her the chance to stand for herself. I reach for her. My hands fit around her waist. It's the most physical contact I've had with her. She's slight and warm, soft in all the right places, but I don't dwell on that. It's important she know exactly who she's dealing with.

I won't go soft like my brothers have. I fucking *won't*.

I lift her off of the stool and plunk her down in front of me. If she's afraid, she hides it well.

She'll learn.

"Hold my hand, Elise," I say quietly. I won't cause a scene. Not here, not now. "And come with me."

CHAPTER 4

Elise

I didn't mean to hide that long.

The sun's set outside the windows as we walk to the stairway.

The Castle's huge, but I've only seen a part of it. As prisoner, I've never gotten the tour, and can only mentally sketch the layout of the parts of The Castle I haven't been in from what Angelina's told me. I have a blueprint of it in my mind, though, from what I've gathered. That's how I knew the coat room was here.

I know I'm in trouble. I know I damn near asked for this. And even though I didn't *plan* on getting in trouble, I did want to rattle him a little. Remind him that he isn't omnipotent like he thinks he is.

But I decided I would handle whatever he did to me for the sake of showing him he doesn't own me.

I wonder, though, if my plan was faulty. The imbalance of power between the two of us is nearly laughable.

As we walk hand in hand, staff parts and nearly hides, walking as far away from us as they can get. Two stern, uniformed guards wait for his signal, and when he nods—a sharp jerk of his head—they flee as well.

If I could, would I?

Or would I rather face the tempest and know what I'm dealing with?

We don't walk toward the Great Hall but to the front of the house, and I stifle a sigh of relief. I've spent time in the cold, dark dungeon, just like a medieval torture chamber, that's still *fully functional* and reserved for what one might call *special occasions*. Angelina's visited there herself and told me it's at the back of The Castle, so we'd have to walk toward the courtyard and kitchen.

Tavi hides his anger well, but I know by the way his nostrils flare and his grip on my hand that he's furious. I'm not surprised.

From the coat room, we walk toward the lobby and reception room and the large, ornate main entrance where Tosca greets her guests. Here, in the main entry hall, there's a spiral staircase that takes us to the second floor.

Each of the men in the inner circle of The Family has private chambers on the second floor. Though they all have homes elsewhere as well—Boston, Tuscany, and a few other places—all call The Castle their home.

I've never been to his private chambers.

I'm going to be married to this man. We're going to take vows in four weeks. I'm going to spend *the rest of my life* with him, and I've never even seen the inside of his room.

The irony isn't lost on me.

It's no surprise, though. We don't have a relationship. I'm only a check mark on a list of to-dos for him—no more, no less.

I'm used to it, though.

I didn't mean anything to my father or mother. You get used to lowered expectations after a while. Piero, however…

I shove the memory away, stuff it into a box, and slam the lid shut. I won't raise those ghosts, not now.

I blink away tears and turn my head so he doesn't see. Instead, I try to observe our surroundings and add it to the mental map I have of The Castle.

My feet are noiseless on the carpeted stairs, like muffled hiccups. Each step brings me closer to whatever it is he'll make me face.

The second floor is home to the private rooms,

elegantly outfitted with thick, luxurious carpet. Everything's immaculate and stunning, like a mansion centerfold in a home and garden magazine. The smell of spring flowers lingers in the air. At the landing, I see why—a huge vase overflowing with flowers sits on a gleaming tabletop.

When I catch a glimpse of his face, I'm not surprised he looks impassive. He holds his temper better than most men I've known. I wonder if it's because Tavi's so angry all the time, it's almost his *default*. He rarely smiles, and when his family's gathered together, he's the quietest of the bunch.

"Where are we going?" I ask, not because I really care, but because I don't like the silence.

"Quiet."

Well, that was super effective.

I wonder where everyone is. It's so still here. Is anyone else home?

They must be. I know Angelina and Orlando are spending the night before traveling back to Boston, his sisters Marialena and Rosa are here, and Romeo and Vittoria as well. Tosca and Nonna have their own rooms somewhere, and staff resides on the first floor. But it's silent here, like a church when everyone's gone home. I hear nothing but the gentle ticking of a clock somewhere on another floor.

At the top of the stairs, I get a view of the ground floor, and my heart leaps with excitement. I can see the entryway, the reception room, a hallway that leads away from the main entrance to another part of the house I've never seen before. Someday, I'll be more than a prisoner here, and I'll explore every inch of this magnificent castle. Even though I didn't choose to be here, I've always harbored a few romantic notions, and a little part of me now can't help but imagine I'm Beauty, locked in the Beast's chambers to pay her due, but soon I'll be mistress of this castle.

My imagination never did help me. It only ever got me in trouble.

I grew up with a father who had a furious temper, so Tavi's anger doesn't worry me... that much. I suppose the unpredictable nature is what unnerves me more than anything, but I'm still determined to make the most of this.

I'm going to be his wife. He can't hurt me *too* bad. I mean, the others all seem pretty happy here? No one smiles as much as Marialena, unless it's Mario. The two of them are like rays of sunshine wherever they go.

Surely Tavi inherited *some* of that warmth and light.

Maybe?

"Those flowers are gorgeous," I murmur to myself. In an instant, I'm pressed to the wall in front of me. His hand is at my throat, trapping me in, my whole body caged by his as if I've flicked a switch and brought on his wrath.

"I told you to be quiet," he says.

Oh. Right.

I draw in a deep breath, reluctantly inhaling his clean, masculine scent. My pulse races against his fingers. His rough hand gives me an inexplicable sense of protection, which makes no sense at all because he's basically threatening me. And yet… it does. Maybe it's because I can feel the restraint in his grip. A girl could get lost in his embrace.

I blink hard and force myself to smile. "You did, didn't you?"

I watch as his dark blue eyes narrow on me. Slowly, he shakes his head from side to side.

"I thought a woman raised Regazza would know better."

Jerk. My own anger fizzes and boils, threatening to explode. "Know better about what?"

He shakes his head from side to side. Caged in his grip, I take the opportunity to look at him. Really *look* at him.

He's tall like all of them, much larger than I am. While not quite as big as Orlando, Tavi's features are rougher, sterner. He's ruggedly handsome with the shadow of a beard on his square jaw, full lips cast downward in a perpetual frown, and not a trace of humor in the glacial blue of his eyes. It isn't his classically sexy Italian looks that get my attention, though. No, any handsome man from Italy knows the art of seduction from the cradle, but this guy… there's something almost regal about him, something almost cruel that should terrify me, but it doesn't. I'm intrigued.

As he holds me in place, I'm vividly aware of the way his muscles ripple under the shirt he wears, the way his broad shoulders fill his suit coat. It doesn't take much to imagine being pinned under him, while he—

"I'd think Regazza's daughter would know better than to mouth off to someone who's bigger, stronger, and more powerful than she is."

Oh fuck *off*.

"Bigger, yes. How nice of you to point that out. Some of you like to chew bricks for breakfast and spit them out, but I'm not much of a breakfast eater. Stronger, of course, you have biology on your side, don't you?" The skin on my face tightens when his fingers constrict my windpipe by a sliver, enough to make it harder to breathe. I draw in a staggering breath. "But more powerful? Don't fool yourself, handsome. Those who need to brag about their power aren't as strong as they think, are they?" I gasp, my voice high and reedy, but I press on. "Machiavelli once said the measure of a man is what he does with power."

If there was anything I learned while observing my father, it was that people who are powerful don't need to *call* themselves powerful.

Asshole.

A cold smile plays on his lips so briefly, I wonder if I imagine it.

"Aren't you clever. Machiavelli, is it? He also said that never was anything great achieved without danger. So you learned nothing from your father? Perfect. Just what I needed. A wife I need to train from the ground up."

Ooooh, he knows how to push *those* buttons good and hard. I want to slap his beautiful, arrogant face and teach him what male chauvinism gets him.

"I learned how to buck up, buttercup," I snap, barely containing my rage. "I learned—" I can't talk anymore. The air in my lungs freezes when his hand clenches harder. I gasp for breath and smack at his hands. Stars blur my vision, the room spins, and I have the stark, terrifying realization that he's choking me to death just seconds before he releases my throat. He holds me pinned in place, gasping for air.

His mouth comes to my ear. "When I tell you to be quiet, I fucking mean it. Do that again, and I'll gag you all motherfucking day. Now take my hand and walk with me, like we're two lovers going to bed, and not a prisoner about to face punishment from her captor. Got it?"

I nod, still unable to speak. When he releases my throat, I stagger. Tears spill onto my cheeks, but I turn away and swipe at them angrily so he doesn't see. I stand and walk with him, my head hung low.

I hate him so much it makes me cry.

Somehow, he opens the door. I don't watch. There's a series of codes and locks and clicks, but I don't pay attention. It doesn't matter.

Nothing matters.

The door slams behind us.

"Strip," he grates. "Take all your fucking clothes off and leave them by the door."

Right, like I don't know what *strip* means. He continues, seemingly oblivious to the vitriol I'm mentally castigating him with. "When I come back out here, I want you bent over the arm of that couch, hands in front of you, palms down. You have sixty seconds."

And then he's gone. I turn in the direction of a door that just clicked shut and blink.

Where am I?

Where did he just go?

I glance around, acutely conscious of the downward clicking of the timeline he just gave me.

I'm in a sitting room of sorts, and beyond where I'm standing there's a kitchenette, a desk and bookcase, and several closed doors. The one on the left is the one he just entered, and the one on the right is still shut.

Bathroom? Bedroom? Office?

But why would he have an office if the desk and bookcase are out here…

48

I remember with a sudden tripping of my heart that he gave me sixty seconds. I probably have thirty left, and I think this is *probably* not a hill to die on.

I tear off my clothes and leave them in a heap by the door. Whatever.

There's a dark, chocolate-brown leather sofa and matching armchair in the living room. He wants me bent over the arm of the couch.

Lovely.

He could do damn near anything to me in that position and he probably will.

Before today, he's barely touched me. I doubt he'll fuck me, not now, not when there are four weeks left to the wedding. Traditionally, in an Italian mafia wedding the marriage is consummated on the wedding night, or is supposed to be, anyway.

I flounce naked over to the couch, glad that at least Tavi can't take my virginity.

It's the one thing I gave Piero that could've killed him even before his betrayal did, the one act of treachery my father never found out about. It's my secret. My dirty, painful secret.

I shove the memory away again and mentally count to sixty.

Then I count again.

Where is he?

I don't hear a thing, but I'm wide awake, vividly

aware of my naked body on display. My breasts are small but pert, pressed up against the smooth, cool leather. My hands are splayed out like he commanded, palms down on the soft leather, my forehead pressed between them. My legs are parted, cool air kissing my naked sex and ass while I wait for him.

And wait.

And wait.

My back begins to ache like this. My belly and breasts nearly fall asleep, all tingly pressed up against the couch. I try to roll my neck, but it's too awkward a position to really move at all.

I close my eyes, but this is too uncomfortable to really fall asleep. All I can think about is what the next decades of my life will look like, married to a man like him. I want to sob. I'd rather be a nobody on the street than shackled to a guy who commands my every goddamn move.

I start when a door opens behind me.

"Good girl."

I don't expect his praise, and I don't expect the way I react to his words.

Nobody has ever called me a good girl before. Ever.

I like it.

I wish that I didn't. I wish I wasn't relieved he's finally here.

I wish I didn't want him to touch me.

"You did exactly what I said for once." Noiselessly, he walks up behind me. My pulse races when I feel his hands spanning my hips possessively, his rough, calloused palms gliding up my sensitive skin. I close my eyes, not surprised to feel his hardened length pressed up against my ass. It isn't the silky fabric of his pants that keeps me from touching bare skin, though. I turn my head to the side.

He's wrapped in an ivory towel. The bastard had me strip and lay over the couch while he took a *shower*.

The terry cloth is thick and soft but slightly damp, and he's naked from the waist up.

I want to observe every detail. I want to run my eyes along his tattooed arms and neck and chest, the curve of his biceps, the tight abs and strapping shoulders. If he's to be mine, at least I should get to play a little.

When I was a little girl, my Nonna used to tell me a good luck fairy would smack babies with her magic wand to make them handsome or beautiful. I thought it an odd Italian tradition, but accepted it. And now all I can think is, Tavi got whacked good and hard.

I turn my head and look back at the couch.

"I like you in this position." He gently grinds himself against me. Heat suffuses my core.

"Am I allowed to respond or are we still doing that silent thing?"

A pause before he responds. "Depends. What were you going to say?"

"Just that I'm not surprised you like me in this position."

"A pointless observation."

"A pointless position."

Without warning, his palm slams against my ass so hard I lose my breath. I come up on my toes as pain explodes along my skin, and he smacks me again. And *again*.

Fuck.

Prelude to my punishment, or is this the punishment itself?

I hiss in a breath and brace my hands on the couch when he pauses, unwraps the towel from his waist, and twists it into a rope. I know what he's going to do right before he steps back, flicks his wrist, and sends the wet end of the towel curling toward me like a whip.

The *whack* resounds in the room. The pain is deep, it *burns*. I hold my breath when he wraps it around his fist, spins it, and whips it again, then again, each flick more painful than the last, the crack against my ass deafening.

"Ow! God, that fucking *hurts*."

I imagine locker-room jocks whack each other with towels, but I've never been struck by one. I've never been struck by *anything*. It hurts a *lot* more than I would have anticipated, probably like an actual whip.

"Of course it does. Don't you ever fucking hide from me again."

Whap.

Tears blur my vision, but I blink them back. I won't cry, not from this.

The towel hisses through the air and whips me again.

I nod. "Fine," I manage to hiss out. "I won't."

I gasp when he grips my hips again. The towel falls to the floor, the goddamn traitorous thing. His hard cock juts against my ass, unencumbered with the towel between us. "Why did you?"

"Hide?" My voice is choked, my whole body tense as I don't know what he's going to do next.

"Yeah, Elise. *Hide*."

After taking that spanking, I feel like he's torn away a layer between my mouth and brain. I couldn't lie to him now if I wanted to. And what benefit is there to hiding the truth?

"I wanted you to pay attention. I feel like I'm nothing but an object to you. I wanted to rattle you." It's the bald truth and sounds so stupid when I say it out loud.

"Yeah?" he asks, as he lays his body down over mine. "Is this enough attention for you?" My ass throbs, and deep, deep in my core, my sex pulses from his nearness, his scent, and if I'm honest, the spanking he just gave me. It hurt like hell, but it doesn't mean I'm not all kinds of aroused because of it.

I nod. "I guess, yeah."

"You fucking played my family." His fingers splay me open, and I gasp at the rough, unabashed feel of them. He spreads me wide before he teases my slit. "I won't allow that."

I nod mutely. "It's more complicated." My clit throbs, but he's circling the edge of my channel, teasing me harder. He spreads my juices up my ass. It's filthy and sensual and so deeply erotic I'm breathless. I've never been violated like this before, never been treated like a sex object, and damn if it doesn't make me feel wanton and sexy. "It had nothing to do with your family and everything to do with mine."

His fingers work their magic, slicking my ass. I feel the very tip of his cock right there, circling the tight ring of muscle. I hold my breath, my whole body tense.

Will he?

"I should fuck you, right here, right now," he says in an angry, furious whisper. "I should fuck you into submission."

He could. We both know he could. We also both know that it isn't allowed, that we consummate our marriage on our wedding night.

But I'm not allowed to come to the wedding bed "defiled," either. I didn't bring my virginity here, and he likely knows it. I haven't followed the rules. Any of them.

It's the only saving grace. If I'd come to him traditionally and he found I wasn't a virgin, he'd have the right to cast me back to my father, and I'd pay dearly. I've heard of such things happening before, but didn't care in the heat of the moment with Piero. But I have no father to take me back, and my family's disowned me. They want as little to do with the Rossis as possible, so here I am, whether he likes it or not.

I can sense that he's warring with himself. I don't reply.

If he wants to fuck me right here, he can. If he wants to toy with me, he can. I can't stop him. All I can do is make the most of this, seek pleasure where he'll let me.

To my surprise, he falls to his knees behind me.

"*Bellissima,*" he murmurs, before he curses up a blue streak.

"*Grazie,*" I reply before I think my answer through.

I don't expect his snort, like an almost-laugh. I'm so shocked, I jump. I bite my lip when I feel his mouth on my ass, kissing the skin he just whipped.

"Why are you laughing?" I whisper, my voice husky, a surprise even to me. I almost convinced myself he wasn't capable.

"Because I didn't expect you to respond so graciously. You're naked and welted."

Welted!

His tongue licks the welts on my ass, before he kisses them again. I close my eyes against the rush of heat in my chest. I feel it cascade over my cheeks, tendrils licking my core. "You're so wild and willful, yet you pull out the Italian delicacies like fine china."

I shrug. I'm used to being treated like a second-class citizen, though he's definitely the first to ever get a cock involved.

"Le ragazze spiritose—sono sempre ottime spose," I say in perfect Italian.

"Ah, you speak Italian."

I nod. Of course I do. It was expected of me.

"You think humor makes for a good wife?" Of course he knows Italian, too.

"I think many things make for a good wife, but I doubt a good wife is important to you."

He kisses me again, but I don't trust his gentle caresses. No, he has a purpose in this. I know from my upbringing never to trust an Italian man. They seduce anything with breasts and a pussy as easily as they walk.

Piero was the exception to the rule.

All others used a play of kindness like flattery, an Italian man's easiest tool to get in your pants. And I've been around here long enough to know his brothers are no different from the men I grew up with. Mario especially flatters his next lay with the ease of an angel.

I know better. I know a devil in disguise.

"Hmm," he says almost thoughtfully. "Now why would you think a good wife wasn't important to me?"

"Because you took *me* for your own." He didn't know who I was. He could've had his pick of women he chose, but instead, he took the first one owed to his family as an act of retribution. "You took me for retribution. A payoff. I'm no more than loot from war or a stack of bills. You didn't weigh your options or do your research. I'm no fool, Ottavio."

"You were foolish enough to hide from me today, knowing you'd be punished and that I'd only watch you more closely."

I shrug a bare shoulder, keenly aware of how close he is to me, his mouth and his tongue and his fingers.

Keenly aware of how easily this could turn.

"You call it foolish. I call it intentional."

From my peripheral vision, I watch him shake his head from side to side. "Ah, lovely. You make a mockery of me? After I've whipped and humiliated you?" I don't think I imagine the warning in his tone, but how much more could he do to me?

He can whip and humiliate me all he wants. It won't faze me. Whereas other women may be scared of the tactics of a man like him, I've known them from the cradle.

"Not a mockery, no," I say honestly.

"Then what?" He stands and grabs the towel from the floor and fists it in his palm.

I don't respond. I'm not sure how to. I'm not sure why I did it, but it wasn't to mock him. This is far too serious a venture for me to treat it so lightly.

"You wanted my attention, Elise? That's what you wanted?"

I did. Reluctantly, I nod, even though I already recognize the danger in his voice.

"Stand up, then."

I stand, slowly uncurling myself like I'm waking from a dream. My breasts feel strangely full and tingly, and my skin feels heated and alive.

"Turn around."

I turn around unhurriedly, apprehension flooding my limbs. I stare at my future husband. My strapping, furious fiancé.

I take in all of him. His sturdy shoulders decorated with ink, the Rossi rose on his inner forearm. The flourish of tattoos along his neck and chest, the smattering of dark black hair. Though he has the Rossi family dark blue eyes, there's a coldness to his that distinguishes him from the rest. Whereas Romeo's the Boss, Orlando the group Enforcer, Tavi's the brains behind everything they do, I know it.

And that might make him the most dangerous of them all.

He crooks a finger at me.

I face him squarely, unblinking, as I walk to him. I've got nothing to lose.

When we're standing so close our toes touch, I have to tip my head back to look up at him. We're both stripped. Naked. My family would castigate us for this before our wedding night, but here, it doesn't matter. We've broken so many rules we've rewritten the script.

His cock juts in front of him at full mast, and my pussy clenches in response. We could be Adam and Eve in Eden for all our bodies know. I don't care right then who he is or what he's done. My body's on fire with primal need.

"You want me to watch you? You want my attention?" His voice is hoarse and rough, just like him. "You've got it, baby." I hear the mockery in his tone, but it doesn't stop me from liking it.

"Touch yourself," he orders.

I don't need to be asked twice. I obey immediately, grateful for the pressure of my fingers on my slick folds. But the truth is, I don't want to be the one touching myself. I want his rough fingers again. I want that stern glare in his eyes to soften when he makes me come. I want—

His phone blares in the silence, a resounding sound like a siren. Still watching me, he turns and fetches it from the table beside the door, then walks back to me as he answers it. I freeze when he takes the call, but he quickly mouths, "Don't fucking stop."

My mouth partly opens as I touch myself and he takes his call.

"Yeah?" He listens, but his eyes are on me. I work myself faster and harder, and when I reach for my nipples to squeeze them, bliss floods my limbs, the first shock shuddering through me. He reaches for his own thick cock and gives a languid stroke.

"Jesus," he mutters.

I pause only for a split second before I start stroking again. I need this. I want the release. He's told me to touch myself and worked me this far, I'm not stopping now. A little sliver of fear warns me that he could command me to stop at any minute, but God, it will be worth another punishment just to defy him and make myself come.

I close my eyes, lost to sensation, stroking myself faster, circling my clit and pinching my nipples. I don't even stop when he reaches for me and sits on a stool by the kitchen. He tugs me onto his lap while I work my climax, muttering in Italian and English, grunting answers and asking questions.

I'm right on the edge but can't bring myself there. I whimper and tense, so close I want to lose all control, but I'm frozen on the edge of release, when he sinks his teeth into the muscle at the base of my neck and shoulder and bites.

I shatter. I burst into flames. Stars blind my vision and I gasp and moan, bliss flooding me in a sudden vicious torrent.

He mutters into the phone. "Be there in ten. I'm bringing the girl with me."

I open my eyes and see an unfamiliar shade. I blink, but don't move. After what I've been through in the past few months, I'm used to waking in a place I don't remember right away. I've learned it's better to come to your senses while lying totally still.

I feel around me on instinct to see if I'm alone in the bed, and find my wrists are not secured as they have been. I can move my arms freely. I pat behind me and all around. I'm alone in a large, cavernous bed, one of the biggest I've ever seen, and definitely the biggest I've ever slept in.

Definitely alone.

A wave of grief hits me so hard I close my eyes, immediate tears blurring my vision. My nose stings and my throat burns. There was a time not that long ago when I'd feel Piero's warm, comforting body beside me. I bury my face in my pillow and stifle my cries. I don't know where I am, and don't yet remember how I got here, but I know I don't have the luxury of dwelling in grief right now.

And then I remember.

Tavi brought me here last night. Tavi, my enemy.

My future husband.

The tears start afresh.

I sit up, oblivious to the time or where exactly I am, but when I open the shade, I see Tuscany's singular landscape giving way to rolling hills that lead to mountaintops, nature's border between Tuscany and the southern regions of Italy. Tuscany any time of year is beautiful. In April, it's simply breathtaking.

I go to lift the window, because I long to fill my lungs with the warm, fresh air of an early Tuscan spring, but find it locked. I frown and flick the lock, as if something so simple would make a difference. *Of course* I'm locked in here. That I can walk freely is a miracle in and of itself.

Still, I can see for miles outside this window, a luxury I haven't had in months.

From here, I can see a vineyard, though I don't know which one. There are as many vineyards as there are gardens here in my homeland, the place my heart longs to live. Here in Tuscany, I learned to read with the help of tutors. Here, my father had a lover who kept him occupied and left me mostly to my own devices, unlike when we went home to America. In America, I was like a pesky scab he liked to pick until it bled.

Tuscany, though... here, I breathe more freely. There's a relaxed sort of measure to life here, more like an ambling stroll than the American trot and sprint. Known for its stunning panorama of land-scapes, rich history, and the arts, most consider Tuscany the home of the Italian Renaissance. One of my favorite things to do, especially in the warmer months of April before the sweltering heat of summer, is to stroll the city streets and shop.

It's very easy to spend money in Tuscany. I'll enjoy spending Tavi's.

With my luck, he probably won't even care.

I pause in my musings when I hear footsteps outside my door. For a moment, my return home helped me forget my grief, but now I remember who I am and why I'm here.

I'm under the watchful eye of my enemy. I can't let myself forget that.

There's a preliminary knock at the door only as a matter of formality, for a moment later, it swings open. My future husband fills the whole doorway, the light behind him casting him in a dark silhouette. I turn away. I don't want to see his beautiful face right now. Not when the memory of Piero still burns in my mind like the fading brilliance of a sunset.

"*Buongiorno*, Elise," Tavi says as he enters my room.

I respond while looking out at the countryside. "*Buongiorno*." My voice is a little husky from sleep. We arrived late last night or early this morning, and it will take a few days for me to adjust to the time difference, if we're even here that long. He didn't tell me why we were coming. I didn't ask, because I don't much care.

"Look at me when you speak to me, please," he says in a deceptively calm voice. The effects of the punishment he administered still linger, and my skin tingles at the memory of his hand on my throat when he threatened me. I'm under no delusion about who he is or what he's capable of.

Piero lies dead because of men just like him.

Still, I obey. I'll pick my battles.

I turn back to him and stare at him, unblinking. "I said good morning."

He stands only paces away from me, fully clothed in dress pants and a sophisticated button-down shirt, but the collar's unbuttoned and he wears no tie. I'm still wearing a T-shirt I wore to bed last night. We packed hastily, so I have very little with me, but it doesn't matter. I can get whatever I want here.

64

"You hungry?"

I shrug. I'm not a big breakfast eater. "Not really, but I'd like some coffee, please."

"Of course. I'll have it sent right up."

He looks over my shoulder at the countryside. "If you behave yourself, I'll unlock the window."

"Very nice of you," I mutter. "And maybe if I'm really good you'll let me dress myself, too."

I don't expect the smack of his hand to my ass, harsh and punitive, or his mirthless chuckle. I didn't mean to snap back, but it's in my nature.

"Watch it, lovely."

I bite my tongue to keep from giving him another scathing response. I don't flinch from the hard smack, but glance back at him. His gaze dares me to disobey or talk back again. Here, deep in the countryside, no one would hear me if I called for help, and I'm confident he's got a team of guards and staff ready to assist him.

It doesn't matter anyway.

Nothing matters.

I turn to face him and hold his gaze when I talk to him. I don't know if he'll demand it every time, but I can stroke his ego once in a while.

"Can you tell me why we came here?"

He looks past me, out at the landscape, as something catches his eye. I glance out the window where he looks, as a hawk dive-bombs from the pretty blue sky straight to the earth below. I gasp when it grabs something—a small rodent?—in its vicious beak before soaring back upward. Tavi, however, doesn't move.

"Amazing creatures, aren't they?"

"Hawks?" They make my skin crawl.

"They can use all their senses at once, you know. They're ruthless and flexible, and miss nothing with those eyes of theirs."

"Charming," I say, unimpressed, and not the least surprised a man like him admires such a predator.

Not missing a beat, he continues. "To answer your question, we're here because I need to identify a body."

Is there no end to the violence? Just when I think I'm used to it...

"Oh?"

With a nod, he doesn't offer any more information.

"Was someone killed then?"

He shakes his head, still staring out past me at the rolling landscape. "Not sure. A cousin of mine died in a car crash. A friend of the family tipped us off." He frowns. "No family nearby to identify the body, and things are looking pretty dicey."

He's come to identify a rotting corpse.

Accounting, the most boring job I can think of, is starting to look pretty damn good.

"Don't you have other people to do that sort of thing for you?"

For some reason, the question's enough to bring his gaze back to mine. He looks at me curiously, his mouth, as usual, curved downward in a frown.

I wish he wasn't so handsome when he's angry.

"We do. But Romeo sent me, so here I am."

That's curious. "Why do you think he sent you?"

He looks away again and goes back to sit on the bed. Resigned?

"Because Romeo's the Boss, and I do what he tells me to."

"Ah, so I'm too female to know what the Big Men know?" I nod and keep my voice nonchalant, because I'm being cheeky as fuck and know how he is.

The floorboards creak when he takes a step toward me, his large body simultaneously blocking sunlight and heating my skin. I shiver when his warm, rough palms skim up my naked arms before his fingers wrap around me, shackling me in place.

"I won't have a wife who doesn't know her place, Elise."

I swallow hard, fighting anger and arousal. Anger at his high-handedness, arousal at his dominance.

Anger at my lust.

"How medieval of you. Fitting, here in this ancient city, isn't it?"

His mouth comes to my ear and he nibbles the lobe, sending a shockwave down my spine, before he whispers, "I think you liked being spanked by me. Didn't you?"

I shake my head.

"You little liar," he breathes. "You want me to take you over my knee. You want to feel my hand on your ass." Heat rises to my cheeks, and my skin feels all prickly and hot. "You want me to make it hurt." My heart skips a beat. "Don't lie to me, lovely. You *like* it rough."

I do. Gentleness sometimes feels like an insult, like a whisper of passion when I want to hear a scream. Whether I like it or not, the edge of violence makes me feel *alive*.

"Of course I don't," I lie through my teeth. I'm so wet it's mortifying.

"No?"

I shake my head. I won't give in to him, I won't. He's my enemy. And I don't care if I'll be married to him, the only way to save any semblance of dignity is to steel myself against him, to fight him even as a part of me whispers, *please*.

He holds me to his chest, as hard and unyielding as a wall, a visceral reminder of his strength and fortitude. He's everything I shouldn't want, but I can't help craving his inflexibility and strength. If I meant something to him... if I truly, *honestly* meant something to him, I'd be... safe.

Like I once was, before Piero was ripped from me. I swallow my pain and shove it back to the dark burial place in my mind.

Tavi kisses my cheek. It feels like betrayal. A soft, teasing, seductive betrayal.

"Then if you don't like being punished, Elise, you'd better watch that mouth of yours."

I nod, because I want to cry. I hate how little control I have in any of this.

To my surprise, he draws in a deep breath, as if imbibing my scent or gathering his strength. I don't always understand him. Hell, I *rarely* understand him.

Without warning, he releases me and turns away.

Okay, that was intense.

"It doesn't matter if you eat breakfast or not. It's nearly lunchtime."

Wait, *lunchtime?*

I stretch my arms up over my head, and don't realize how far the T-shirt I wear travels until I see his hungry eyes on my ass. I quickly put my arms down.

69

"Do you have any workout equipment here?" I ask. Maybe if I bring us back to the mundane, we can ignore the sexual tension that coats us like velvet, deep and sensual. "I miss my morning workout. But after I get some movement in, I'd probably like some lunch, thank you."

I think of simple, real things. Gardens and dresses, sunsets and boats. I won't think of being dominated. I won't think of the wedding night that looms in my future.

I won't think of Piero.

"We have excellent staff here, or I can take you out to eat if you'd like." The velvet curtain begins to rise.

I really have missed the food in Tuscany. Even though the Rossi family's Nonna cooks beautifully, it isn't the same without the Tuscan backdrop.

"We do, yes, and I'll have an escort bring you down there, but not until I've gotten you proper workout gear. You'll wait for tomorrow, then."

I nod. Not a point to argue on.

"Then if you don't mind, I'd like a shower, and can you assign someone to take me for a walk? I love walking outside this time of year."

He shoves his hands in his pockets. "The coroner won't be ready until three, so I can take you for a walk."

Great. Another chance to be near him. Just what I didn't want.

I'm staring out the window at the way the leaves gently dance in the wind and can almost feel the breeze on my bare skin, when I hear the bed gently creak under his weight. "Go get your bag, Elise. Do you remember where it was?"

My pulse races when he commands me, at the way edicts flow off his tongue with ease, a natural leader if ever there was one. I shake my head.

"Check the closet."

I look around the large room to locate the closet. Wow, is it gorgeous here. The room is big and airy, especially for Tuscany. Even though I grew up wealthy, my family's homes in Tuscany were small and fairly cramped compared to America. This room's decorated in authentic, timeless, beautiful Tuscan style—rustic but elegant and feminine, a mixture of wood and white. From the arched door-way, I can see a sitting room, and in here, visible wooden beams above me, streaked white as if a painter thought to soften the harshness with casual strokes of his brush. A small desk sits in one corner with an ornate pillow-topped seat, and instead of overhead lighting, elegantly curved lampshades complete the look. White shelves built into the walls adorn either side of the bed.

I take this all in briefly, as I don't think it smart to keep Tavi waiting.

The closet's tucked far in the corner.

"Wow," I say softly, as I walk to the closet. "This room is beautiful."

He nods formally. "Thank you. I hope you like it. This will be one of the rooms you stay in until we're married."

Until we're married.

My heart skips a beat. I swallow, my throat and mouth dry, either from travel or nerves or both. I'll share a room and a bed with him after we take our vows, my thoughts turning to our wedding night and his dark promises of rough sex. I turn my head so he doesn't see my heated cheeks and change the subject.

"Do you know if I still have family in Tuscany?"

I hate that I don't know. I've been so removed from everything that mattered in my life before my escape with Piero. In my mind, there are only two seasons of my life I've lived—life before Piero and after.

He doesn't answer at first. When I see my luggage in the closet, I tug the wheeled suitcase out.

"I would've had staff unpack for you when we arrived, but you were so tired. And to answer your question, no. The Regazza family's relocated to Lombardo."

"Why?"

"They wanted distance from the Rossis."

The stark feeling of being utterly alone hits me again. My family's left me to keep distance from the Rossis, yet I'm as entrenched with them as possible. I have no siblings, my father's dead and my mother's long gone, but I did have aunts and uncles and cousins. Some of them meant something to me.

"You have a new family now, Elise." There's an edge to his voice that challenges me to defy him, to push against his absolute ownership of who I am.

I do have a new family now. I don't know how I feel about that.

I don't hate them. I don't think I do, anyway. Angelina, my very best friend in the world, will be my sister-in-law, the man she loves, my brother-in-law. I like Vittoria, Romeo's wife, and Tavi's sisters. His mother is aloof, but there's a certain strength to her I can't help but admire. I know the other women adore her, but I don't yet know why. I'm willing to find out.

And who doesn't love portly, jovial, rosy-cheeked Nonna, with her wiseass cracks and broken English and incessant need to feed and nourish her brood. She's the only woman the men defer to. Even Tosca doesn't have the sway she does.

I never had the benefit of close companionship with women like me. I had nannies, and a few friends, but no sisters. When my father took a third mistress, my mother asked for a place of her own. On his insistence, she stayed married to him, but it's only a formality.

The Rossi family's different, though. Ruthless. Cruel, even. But they have something my family never had—the unbreakable bonds of family. They're ride or die like no one I've ever met, for better or for worse.

I push the suitcase toward him and don't respond. When he leans forward on the bed casually, his scent lingers like bottled sex. I'd bet money he buys his scent from Italy. Only Italian cologne could make a woman forfeit her panties, though the French are close contenders.

A girl could fall for a guy like him just by the way he smells.

I wonder what he's up to.

"Open it up, and lay it all out." His fingers lace together like he's praying, but if he believes in God, I doubt they're on good terms.

Obediently, I do what he says. I don't remember what I packed, but he tossed a few things in here. I open the luxury case, revealing neat, pretty clothes, folded almost into little packets. I pull out a few pairs of jeans, some short-sleeved tops, some under-garments. On the right, I remove my flat iron and a bag of makeup, some flats, low-heeled boots, and silver sandals with a thick wedge heel. No workout clothes or bras. No sneakers. *Dammit.*

"I'll need sneakers and a sports bra when you get the workout gear," I tell him.

His eyes meet mine, sardonic and a little cruel. "Do that hot yoga thing. I hear you can do it naked."

That he dismisses something that's important to me pisses me off.

"Fine," I snap. I reach for the hem of the T-shirt and go to yank it off when he grabs my wrist. My pulse heats, remembering how he pinned me against the wall in the hallway. Remembering the punishment he administered only hours before.

"From now on, I'll be the one to undress you."

I place my hands on my hips. "Fine." Seems my vocabulary's taken a nosedive.

A part of me wants to ruffle him, wants to stoke that anger in his eyes until he ignites, because only then do I have control over him. But he's not that easily provoked. Maybe it's because he dwells daily in a simmering temper, or he's learned to only let his temper flare when it behooves him. He only smirks at me, reaches for me, and yanks me between his legs.

Standing before him like this, I feel like a little girl dressed in borrowed clothing. With one quick tug of the fabric, he eviscerates that feeling. Standing before him naked, there isn't a trace of me that feels like a child. Every inch of me feels all woman, from the messy bun at the nape of my neck to my toenails painted hot pink.

"You're beautiful, even when you're angry."

I huff out a breath, but only to hide the way I inhale

sharply when his thumbs graze my nipples. "You bring out the best in me." My words are tight, nearly swallowed with a gasp. He stares, mesmerized, as he traces the blunt edge of one finger across the valley between my breasts, under the low swell, then back again, before he angles it downward and swirls across my bellybutton.

"Careful, Elise," he whispers, as he bends his mouth closer to my naked skin. His hot breath ghosts across my breasts. I stifle a moan when his warm, rough hands cup my ass and hold me closer to him.

"Why?" My own breath is no more than a whisper. He's barely touched me, and I already feel the quickening pulse between my thighs, a growing ache of need. My sex clenches, longing to be filled by him. He may be my enemy, but my body may be the most traitorous of all.

"Because no matter what you say, your body tells me you like this."

Traitor.

"Like what?" I don't even recognize my voice. I moan, my head falling back, when he traces the edge of my nipple with the warm, sensual heat of his tongue.

"All of it, lovely. This," he says, a prelude to a quick suckle of my nipple. Sparks of arousal shoot through my limbs. "This," he continues, while he tickles the hardened bud with his tongue and squeezes my ass. "This," he breathes, before he bites me. Fear quickly melds to desire when he kneads my ass.

Jesus.

"If you're a good girl today, I'll reward you when we get home tonight," he says, moving one hand from my ass to my inner thighs. I part my legs on instinct, and a ghost of a smile flashes across his lips before he's sober again. "And if you're a bad little girl, no reward for you." He scolds me like he's speaking to an errant child, and something about the authority in his tone excites me. "I'll send you to bed with no dessert, after a good trip over my lap."

I want that. I imagine myself over his lap, his sturdy thighs beneath my belly. Even the thought makes me part my legs further.

I realize that what he threatens as punishment excites me. He can't wield that power over me if I lean into it. My heart races with the knowledge of this newfound control.

"Wear the black jeans and pink top," he says, as he presses the heel of his hand to my throbbing pussy. "And I'll take you to lunch. We'll buy you some workout clothes and sneakers later, but we've got business to tend to first. Dress, now. I'll dress you often, but you will dress yourself when I command you to so I can watch." Ah, the games he plays.

I almost whimper when he stops touching me. I'm so turned on, I can barely think straight. But I do what he says. My stomach growls with hunger.

I dress slowly, the last vestige of control I have over this man that commands my breath, my pulse, and everything that gives me life.

It isn't until we're in one of his cars with him driving, the warm Tuscan wind in my hair and the sun on my face, that I realize.

The entire time he touched me, I didn't think of Piero.

CHAPTER 5

Tavi

I've told myself that I wouldn't fall for a woman. *Any* woman. Definitely not the woman who betrayed my family and nearly sent us into ruin.

But maybe I could enjoy being with her.

She sits beside me in the car, as I take her into town. There's one thing Elise and I have in common: we both love Tuscany.

I love my family and would lay down my life for my brothers, any of them. But here in Tuscany, life slows for a little while. Without the trappings of my family, I feel a little more like... well, *me*.

Here, I'm not just Ottavio Rossi, Underboss to Romeo Rossi, second in command to The Family. I'm not just a made man. When I drive down the long, winding roads that lead me to the heart of the city, the sunroof open, while low streams of music in Italian are swallowed by the breeze, I'm just me. The guy who loves books and football, who wore glasses when I was a kid and got a perfect 4.0 in high school, who passed on a free ride to Harvard in favor of working for The Family.

To some, I'm the guy with the reputation for being undefeated in a fight, or the guy who's known for bringing down some of the most powerful cartels in our time, or the one who's managed to convert some of our most lethal dirty cops.

But here, in Tuscany, when I shed the skin of family life... when I'm alone... I'm just me.

"Where are we going?"

"You got a favorite?"

Elise twirls a piece of her hair thoughtfully. She looks sad. I shouldn't care that she does, but I want to know why.

"No," she says, but her voice is hollow. She's lying.

I reach for her thigh. I mean to put my hand on her leg to remind her not to lie to me, but instead of gripping her painfully, or giving her a reminder to obey, I run my hand up her jean-clad leg and down again. Thoughtfully. My dick jerks.

She's fucking gorgeous.

"You're lying."

She tries to scoot away from me, but that only

makes me grip her harder. "You're gonna be in my bed, Elise. You'll have my babies and take my name, and not too long from now. *No* lies."

She turns her face from me, and my eyes focus back on the road. But I don't miss the way she swipes under her eyes, or the colder tone her voice takes. "I had a favorite once, but I don't anymore. It lost its appeal to me. You?"

Interesting.

I shrug. "I like anything I don't have to cook."

"That's interesting for a guy that owns restaurants."

I shake my head. "I own pastry shops, not restaurants. Orlando's the restaurant owner."

"Ah. You don't like cooking?"

I shake my head. "Nah. I've got plenty that would do it for me anyway."

"Orlando likes cooking."

"Yeah." It's like she's taking notes on who does what, so she can catalog us in her mind. Fair enough.

"Well, that works. I do like cooking. And I like everything here," she says. "I'm literally starving, so anything and everything goes."

I find a quiet trattoria I know well, far off the beaten path. They know who I am, and quickly secure the most secluded table for us before they bring us the wine menu. I order *ribollita*, a thick stew with vegetables, potatoes, and beans, *panzanella*, a dish made with bread and seasonal vegetables, and *pistecca alla fiorentina*, a simple but hearty steak dish. We finish our meal with a light ensalata.

Elise holds herself erect and answers everything I ask her politely, but doesn't initiate any conversation herself. She wipes her mouth with the corners of her white napkin, thanks me, and smiles at the end of the meal, but the smile doesn't reach her eyes.

She's doing everything right, but she isn't here, isn't really with me. In the distance, sad music plays, the lilt of a violin and a sad, mourning thrum of strings. A soundtrack to our story.

I shouldn't care about her pain that she can't help but show, but I do. I'm finally here in Tuscany, with the woman who's going to take my ring, but she's only here physically.

I know that look in a woman's eyes. I've seen it before in my mother and my sister Rosa.

She's mourning.

Why?

Does she mourn for her father? He was a filthy, conniving, traitorous asshole and I doubt he treated her well, but blood runs thicker than water. Even *I* miss my old man once in a while.

Maybe she mourns her past life that she's said goodbye to.

Does she mourn the death of her bodyguard?

I remember when I called the hit that ended his life. Orlando's Angelina railed at me for what I did. She sobbed, telling me that I'd killed the only man Elise had ever loved.

She only confirmed for me then that I'd done the right thing. Elise had no business loving her bodyguard. She was a betrothed woman from birth and knew that. Though she didn't know who she'd marry, it was no secret that one day she'd be chosen for marriage by her father to someone suited for her. That someone was supposed to be my brother.

Still, I can't logic my guilt away. I've learned to mute it after what I've done, because of who I am.

It's best if Elise never finds out I had anything to do with Piero.

"Why are you staring at me?" she asks, a faint color painting her cheeks when I catch her eyes. "Do I have something in my teeth?"

I shake my head and look away.

I can't care about this. It doesn't matter. Life in the mob for both of us means a life of resignation. We find joy when we can, which is why my brothers and I eat well, drink heartily, and fuck often and hard. Sometimes, pure carnal indulgence is a good distraction.

It's the least we can do.

Fucking hell, I wish I didn't have to wait that much longer to be with her.

Maybe we don't have to. Maybe I want to fuck her before then. What happens in Tuscany...

I haven't fucked a woman in goddamn months. Mario's tried to persuade me, and even Romeo urged me to go with Santo into Boston and pick up a girl. Said it'd take the edge off.

Nothing takes the edge off.

I get the check and pay for our food when my phone rings.

"Yeah?"

Uncle Leo. "Tavi, the morgue's ready for you."

I glance at the time. "They're two hours early."

"Opened up especially for you."

Jesus.

I didn't want to take her with me to do this errand. I wanted to shop with her, get her what she fucking needs, then keep her under surveillance nearby when I did the dirty work. Something simple, mundane. But now, we're too far away for me to follow those plans. "I'll have to take her with me."

"She's a fucking Regazza," Leo knows immediately who I'm referring to. Of course. "Nothin' she ain't seen before."

Yeah. I just spent a hundred euro on lunch I hope she doesn't lose.

I hang up with Leo. "Looks like we have to do that errand sooner than planned."

She winces and wrinkles up her nose. "Oh, yuck. I'm sorry."

I'm surprised by her sympathy. I didn't expect it.

I only shrug. "It's alright."

It isn't, though. I'm here to identify one of Leo's brother's sons. His nephew, my cousin. Leo hardly knew him, but Jenoah and I went way back.

"Did you know him?"

I swallow the weird lump that rises in my throat and takes me by surprise. "Yeah."

Why's my vision all blurred? I blink in surprise and take a left onto the freeway.

Elise sighs. "That really sucks. It's miserable work." She shakes her head. "I had to identify a body once."

"Did you?" That surprises me. We usually shelter the women in The Family from death, at the very least.

"Yeah. Fire to a home when I was younger. My nanny was killed. I was unscathed. My father thought that I was the target, so he went off on this rampage and made me go identify her. Back then, you remember how rudimentary things were in Italy."

I huff out a laugh. "Some things never change." I'm

on my way to identify a body that's rotting because it's sat in a morgue for way too long.

"I didn't really know her well. I'd only just met her. So that didn't bother me so much as actually going into the morgue, you know? So cold. So scary. I imagined dead people walking the halls, and ghosts coming to claim their souls."

"I don't think it works that way."

"Do any of us really know how it works?"

I don't answer. We don't. Plenty make a good case for exactly what she fears.

I park at the furthest end of the lot to prolong our walk inside, but once indoors, I'm greeted as if I'm a king. Sometimes my status comes in handy. Sometimes, it fucking grates.

"Mr. Rossi." An older, staid woman in a burgundy pantsuit meets me at the door. She speaks to me in Italian, and I answer her. Elise watches us, understanding every word. I'm welcomed to the morgue, I'm their honored guest, anything I need, blah blah blah. Seems an odd place to be treated so well.

"This way, sir," she says in Italian, gesturing for me to follow her.

When she gives Elise a curious look, I nod. "She's with me."

Saying that feels oddly familiar, something I'm not used to.

Even the cool air and clean interior doesn't hide the

stench of rotting flesh. Our guide hands me and Elise scented cloths to hold up to our noses as we enter. "You can sit outside," I tell her. There's nowhere for her to go, and my staff's outside the door. They follow me everywhere.

"No," she says, shaking her head, then pleads with me as if to soften telling me no. "Please, Tavi. I want to see."

I hold her gaze for a moment before I nod my consent. I want to know why, but I don't ask. She wants to see, so I'll let her.

It feels oddly nice having her here. For once... for goddamn once, I'm not alone.

When they roll out the body, my body tenses. Elise wordlessly reaches for my hand.

I don't deserve this. I don't deserve her kindness or her gentleness. I should be her owner, her master, not someone who cares for her.

But I take her hand.

I'm not prepared for the wave of emotion that washes over me when I see my cousin's pale, lifeless face. I don't see my cousin lying on the bed before me. I see so much more, like demonic visions come to haunt me in my sleep.

The faces of everyone I ever loved—Romeo, Orlando, Marialena and Mario, Rosa and Santo, Mama and Rosa's little daughter Natalia, even baby Nicolo, flood my vision. Each lifeless face is cold and pallid and still. I flinch at every image, accosted by the nearness of death. The scent is overwhelming.

"Yeah. It's him. Jenoah," I say, and my voice sounds strange, as if it isn't my own.

"Thank you, sir," the woman says in Italian. She goes to cover the body, but something makes me stop her.

I reach my hand out in front of her, my voice hoarse. "Stop. *Fermare,*" I say, my voice hoarse. The two women watch me as I peer closer at the decaying body and swallow the bile that burns my throat.

This was no mere accident.

I trace a reluctant finger at his throat, covered in lacerations. The cuts and bruises and swollen skin aren't enough to hide the telltale signs of strangulation.

I take out my phone and snap pictures.

My words roll out, harsh and cold, in clipped Italian. I want to see the coroner.

"Si, signore," she nods, her eyes wide and panicked. "Si."

She tells me that he's gone home for the day but she'll get me his number. I nod and allow her to wheel the body away.

Something's wrong. This was no mere accident. I was brought here for a reason.

I check in with my guards. "Anything out of place?" I ask, but everything's kosher. Nothing out of place at all. I have to call Romeo, as soon as I can. He'll have to make the call to Jenoah's father. It's his place, not mine, but I'll take a higher rank beside him when I marry Elise.

Cold rage burns in my belly. Someone killed my cousin. Someone made it look like an accident, then had his body sent to the morgue so his flesh would rot before he was claimed and given a proper burial.

The faces of the people I love, cold and dead, still plague me. I stand in a sort of stupor, the rancid scent of death enveloping me.

"Tavi," Elise says gently. "It's over. They have a waiting room. Let's go."

She's wrong. It isn't over at all.

Still, when she tugs my hand and leads me to the door, I let her. My eyes sting and my nose burns at the impotent rage that powers through me, the fury that damn near chokes me. Fuck it, I haven't cried since I was a child. I hate that I feel like this. I hate all of it.

I broke my leg in three places during a football game when I was a senior in high school. I was there the night my cousin Nicolo died and left a wife and children. I buried my father, my grandfather, and countless other made men.

I learned to take my father's anger and rage. I learned how to throw my body between my younger siblings and his fists or belt.

Not once did I cry.

I won't cry now.

But I let her take my hand. I follow her when she leads me out of the room. I sink onto the chair and bury my face in my hands.

CHAPTER 6

Elise

I'd bet everything I own that Tavi never meant to show his humanity in that cold, dark room. I'd bet everything I know that he meant to keep up the stoic face, to treat the identification of the dead body like nothing more than a business transaction.

He can tell himself that. Men like him think they're impervious, that they can wall themselves off against actual human feeling. I've seen it with my own eyes.

He can't, though. He can try, but there's too much loyalty in Tavi to be fully immune to death and pain. Only the truly selfish are alone.

That isn't him. He might be cruel. He might be heartless. But his blood thrums hot in his veins, and his heart beats still. I know because I've seen the way he is with his family. I know that these men value loyalty above all. They all do.

He isn't the callous creature he wants me to believe he is.

Sometimes I wish he was.

It would be easier to hate him.

I don't know what happened to him, what trauma he's experienced, but I know a part of him is broken. Just like me. I can't ever forget the depravity I've witnessed with my own eyes and imagine he's not much different. I spent so much time staring at the cold floor of his family's dungeon, stained in blood, that I imagined the echoes of the screams of the ghosts that haunt that place still linger. And I know he's had a hand in all of it since becoming a made man.

Despite my knowledge that he's dangerous, that I need to protect myself from him because he *will* hurt me—hell, he already has—I can't help but soften toward him. I feel as if I see the smallest flicker of a burning ember where others see only ash. If I fan that flame…

Who am I to think I can influence who he is at all?

He sits in front of me, his face buried in his hands, but his shoulders don't move, and no tears squeeze between his fingers.

They don't bother to make the waiting room in an Italian morgue welcoming. A small, circular folding table and metal chairs sit on a concrete floor. This is where you sign paperwork, make a phone call. Shake hands. Do whatever else it is that's required before you bury your dead.

I watch as he inhales, and I feel every sharp intake of breath as if it was my own. Shards of ice stab my lungs. I stand, tentatively at first, then decide I don't care if he pushes me away.

I mentally brace for him to dismiss me. I reach my arms around him. I don't know if it's him I want to comfort, or me.

My heart aches. I want to cry for him.

Wordlessly, he takes his hands from his face, his beautiful, tortured, perfect face, and reaches for me. With one sharp tug, he yanks me onto his lap.

"It's fucking brutal," I tell him, my voice surprisingly strong and loud in the barren room. They should warm this place. This isn't a room for the dead but for the living.

"What is?" he asks, his gaze tortured and broken. My frigid heart melts a bit more.

I shake my head. "All of it."

The lies, deception, and manipulation. Violence, threats, and bullying. Anger and sadness and death. Every bit of it's depraved, and he knows it. You forfeit a childhood and peace for security and wealth, yes, but it's a choice most of us would rather not make. I'm not sure if anyone outside mob life would ever really, truly understand how he's been raised, what it does to you.

But I do.

"Yeah," is all he says, shaking his head. When I meet his gaze, his serious, stern eyes that flicker with the hint of warmth, he reaches his hands to my waist and yanks me even closer to him, his grip painful and hard.

I gasp when he arranges me so that my legs straddle either side of him. My shoes slip off my feet and click on the concrete floor.

I know he can't control much of this... *but he can control me*.

I know before his mouth touches mine that he's going to kiss me.

If I let him.

My heartbeat throbs when his hands slide up either side of my face, framing me. "It is fucking brutal," he echoes, his eyes on mine cold and angry, but the warmth in his hands belies his frigid gaze. "All of it's fucking brutal." His hands press harder, tighter, before he wrenches my mouth to his.

He doesn't even try to tame the ferocity in his lips as he takes what he wants.

This isn't a kiss but an ultimatum. His tongue plunders my mouth, invading me, as his grip on my face tightens to nearly painful.

I gasp in a breath, and breathe his in. My own hands reach for him and land on his shoulders, then snake around his neck as if to save myself from falling.

Every breath melds with his. My gasps are swallowed whole. I'm consumed in fire as if burned by a dragon's flame. And still, he kisses me, claims me.

I lick his tongue and knead his shoulders, craving the sensual touch of skin to skin. A thread of desire weaves its way between us. His responsive moan only encourages me to do more.

I want to touch his skin. I want to feel his naked flesh. I want so much more than this.

I've forgotten where I am or why we're here. Still kissing him, I reach for the top button of his shirt and fumble to unbutton it. I'm still broken, still scarred from what I've been through, but I don't want to think about that, not now. I don't want to be *defined* by my past or my pain.

I want to live in the here and now. This, after all, is the only reality I can control. *We* control.

His hands travel down my face to my waist, and my heart flips in response. He grants me access.

Now I can touch him.

I slide my fingers under his collar, while he threads his hands under my ass and scoots me closer to him. When his buttons fall open, I eagerly scratch my fingers along the column of his neck. The feel of his hot muscle and sinew is all male, so potent it's exhilarating.

He's *all mine*.

My pulse throbs between my legs.

He bites my lips and licks my tongue. I slowly begin to melt on his lap. I feel his hardened length beneath me, as my hands knead his shoulders. I reach the flat of my hand to his neck and skate my hand down his T-shirt to where his naked chest is dotted with dark, coarse hair.

I whimper when he pulls his mouth off mine.

"Not here," he grates, his voice hoarse. "Jesus Christ, woman."

I drop my head to his shoulder and don't bother to hide my disappointment.

He's right. We're in a goddamn *morgue*.

We don't need to talk. I don't need to clarify. I *know*.

He may be brutal and cold, but Ottavio Rossi knows who I am. He knows every thread that's knit me together. He knows what I fear and what I hope for, not because he's known me for long, but because the two of us were forged by the same fire.

Tuscany always brought out the romantic in me.

We're both panting and hot, and a little disheveled, like two lovers caught in the beam of an officer's flashlight in the back of a parked car.

"You started it," I breathe.

"Fucking hell, I didn't," he says in an almost boyish tone that's at once endearing and a bit unnerving. "You were the one that undid my buttons and touched me."

"Oh. Right." I did. "But you were sad and I wanted to make you feel better."

I don't expect the look of shock on his face as his eyebrows rise. "Did you, now?"

I bite back a smile. Bemusement softens his hard angles a little. It becomes him.

"Listen," he says, gentling his voice to a register I didn't know he was capable of. "Fuck the mob rules. Fuck what's expected of us. They can go fuck themselves if they think I'm gonna wait until our wedding night to have you."

"You should tell me how you really feel, and no need to censor your language."

He gives me a lopsided smile, the first I've ever seen from him. It's honey and sunlight, so sweet and warm it makes my toes curl. I'd cross hot coals to see him smile like that again.

A thread of hope blooms in my heart. "Who?" I breathe, excited.

"All of 'em."

I nod. "Mhm. Agreed. What are they gonna do, anyway? Give me back? Pretty sure there's a no-return policy."

His lips tip upward in an *almost* smile again.

Me. I did that to him.

I've melted the Ice King.

My heart does a little somersault in my chest.

And then my mind catches up with my body.

Wait.

Wait.

He said he *isn't going to wait until the wedding night.*

Does that mean what I think it means?

I watch in a sort of stupor as he takes care of the rest of the business. Makes a phone call to someone, taps a few things on his phone. I stand beside him in a sort of daze, fixated on what happens next.

I'm surprised when we leave the morgue that it's still sunny out. It feels as if we've been in the dark, cold interior for so long that it shouldn't be so brilliant and beautiful out here.

I close my eyes and give myself the luxury of a deep, cleansing breath of fresh, sun-kissed air. Spring flowers in Tuscany bloom like brilliant balls of fire, red roses and Tuscan poppies. They line the pathway to the parking lot, the lingering scent more delicate than the most exquisite perfume.

Oh, Tuscany, I've missed you.

I like it even more now that I know my family isn't here anymore.

Tavi takes my hand when an elegant gunmetal gray car glides to a stop where we're standing.

"You drove here," I say in confusion.

"I don't want to drive home."

I give him a curious look as he opens the door to the waiting vehicle. It purrs like a content kitten. "After you."

Not surprisingly, Ottavio Rossi has not only the typical Italian charm but the manners to boot. He'll pay for my meals at restaurants and carry heavy things. But how far does his chivalry go? Only time will tell.

I slide into the back seat. It's warm and luxurious in here, permeated with the scent of soft, buttery Italian leather and a "new car" scent. I sink into the cushions and watch as he folds his large body into the seat beside me. A uniformed attendant shuts the door behind him. The windows are so tinted it's hard to see much behind us, but there's a shadow of a car just like this one following.

His bodyguards.

Bodyguards.

Piero.

I close my eyes to fight the rush of emotion and the pang that hits my chest.

"You alight? Carsick, Elise?"

The concern in his voice shouldn't make me want to cry. Goddammit, everything does. If I was a normal woman, I suspect I'd seek therapy. But I'm not. I was born a mafia princess, and I'm soon to be a mafia queen. So I blink back tears and hold my head high.

"I do not get carsick." I force myself to open my eyes and once more slam the lid on the memory that wants to break me. "Ever."

"Good," Tavi says with a wicked gleam in his eyes. He moves closer to me, swallowing the small distance between us. "I want to taste your mouth again."

I blink at the sudden nearness of him, the sudden irrefutable *maleness* of him, from the hard planes of his chest, to the strong fingers that weave through my hair, to the lingering, harmonious, masculine scent of citrus and fire, woodsy and heady.

My eyes flutter closed when his fingers trace along my scalp as if memorizing the feel of me. He lowers them so his grip along my neck is sure and confident, holding me in place before his mouth meets mine. I put my arms around his neck when he becomes more serious, every trace of boyhood humor gone.

He whispers, his breath hot against my ear. "I'll have your mouth any time, any place I want."

I nod. Of course he will. I know this.

My eyelashes ruffle against his cheek as one of his hands travels to the small of my back. It's almost an embrace, a reminder of ownership. And for the first time since he claimed me, since he made me his unwilling betrothed... I like it.

And I want more.

I'm vividly, keenly aware of every place his warm

flesh touches mine—fingers along my scalp, his nose to my cheek, his mouth to my ear. Every place he brushes feels hot, and yet I long for more. I move closer to him. My breathing hitches.

I move even closer to him and sigh, relishing the way he holds me, the way his lips touch mine with exploration and hope. This isn't the brutal kiss of before, where he forced himself on me to prove that he owned me. No, this one's lighter, gentler, still intense but without the hidden edge of a threat. It's consual and carnal and erotic. My heart beats wildly in my chest when he grips my hair tighter.

The pain melds to liquid heat that pools between my legs, and when I gasp from the rough pull, he massages his fingertips where it hurts. I sag against him, grateful for his warmth and strength. I'm boneless and pliable when he does this to me.

His plundering kiss flirts like a tease when his lips soften, the flutter of butterfly wings before his tongue meets mine again. The deep guttural groan he tears from me startles me. By the way his hand on my back flattens, I can tell that he likes that.

I want to please him. I want to heal him. I want to ease that anger in him until he's as yielding as I am. I know what a man like him battles, and I want to claim his victory.

The ride is too quick, as we glide to a stop outside his Tuscan home. When he pulls his mouth off mine, he groans in reluctance.

I sit, blinking, a little shell-shocked. I've never been

kissed like that before. Ever. A pang of memory burns then quickly fades.

He taps on the window that divides us from the front of the car.

"Si, signore?"

"*Tutto fuori.*" I blink in surprise as he goes on in Italian, ordering everyone out, even his gardener and housekeeper and bodyguards.

He's just directed every single member of his staff to take the day off.

My heart begins to race.

Now that I didn't expect. When I was with Piero, we found our way to each other. We founds little pockets of space and privacy where no one ever knew where we were.

What will Tavi do to me when he has me alone?

"*Si, signore.*"

"Come here." Tavi tugs me onto his lap so my ass is nestled in his crotch. His erection presses against me. I grind myself against him like a wanton whore, just to hear him groan.

Ah, yes. Just like that. Thread by thread, I pull a little control back from him.

I like the feel of his warm, rough palms on my thighs, like little brands reminding me what he can do with those hands.

"Tell me, Elise."

I squirm when he calls my name. I'm not sure why. It feels deeply intimate, maybe, like we've gone through every step of this process on hyper speed and now he's circling back to the way things should have begun.

"Tell you what?"

"Everything. I want to know what you like. What you want. What you need."

It takes me a second to register his request. I'm a little shocked. The painful grip on my leg reminds me he's expecting an answer.

"Like… in life or in bed?" I look up at him, and my heart beats madly. I sometimes forget how handsome he is.

A corner of his lips tips up. "For now, I want you in bed. So start with the bedroom. But later, when you're lying with me naked, we can talk about life stuff."

He says it like it amuses him. I suppose he's never done anything like this before. *Aw.*

"What do I like in bed?"

"Yeah, lovely," he says, while we watch one member of his staff after another exiting the house. "I know you're not a virgin."

My cheeks flush pink. "How do you know that?"

Without warning, his eyes flash at me. "Because no fucking virgin ever kisses like *that*. And I *will* punish you for that."

Another throb of my pulse. "For what?"

"You know the rules. You come to the marriage bed undefiled. Virginal."

I look away from him. It's a serious offense, and I won't pretend otherwise. If circumstances weren't what they are, he *could* refuse to marry me and demand my father pay up another way.

But my father's dead, and Tavi wants me to pay. Marriage to him is punishment, my time in purgatory, and he won't let me forget it.

I swallow, but my throat's dry. I'm not sure if he's baiting me.

When I don't answer, he slaps my thigh hard then grips where he slapped. I gasp at the sudden pain. Yanking my chin up, he makes me look into his eyes.

"You will learn to answer a question when I ask it. Do you understand me?"

I nod. He wants my obedience? He craves my compliance? I'll give it to him, all of it, so he doesn't have anything to hold against me.

It's the last thing he'd expect from me.

"Yes, sir," I say contritely. "I'm sorry, sir."

His mirthless chuckle makes the skin on the back of my neck crawl, even as my sex spasms. It seems I've got a taste for the bad boy vibes.

"What's so funny?"

A flick of his thumb under my chin makes me feel strangely chastened. My cheeks flush.

"That you think I buy that for a minute."

"Buy what?"

"Your submission." A beat passes while we lock gazes. I don't reply. It seems he isn't that easily fooled. Outside the car, I hear a door bang and a car start. All around us, his staff obeys him, scurrying like little ants to do their master's bidding. He commands a small army, but what he really wants is to command *me*.

"You think," he says almost thoughtfully, as if sifting through his thoughts, "that I expect a woman like you to bend so easily to my will?"

"A woman like me?" I ask, half stalling, half curious.

A thoughtful look flits across his features as he brushes the pad of one thumb across my cheek. My skin burns in its wake.

"Yeah, baby," he whispers. "A woman like you. Bold. Willful. Wily."

"Wily? Aw, now, Tavi, you *flatter* me."

I shiver when his hands frame my face to keep my eyes on his. "You know who you are, Elise. And so do I."

I swallow. He saw right through me, way more easily than I would've expected.

This man will not be so easily fooled.

"I'll have your submission, Elise. But it won't be handed to me." Slowly, he shakes his head from side to side. I'm fixated on the strong cut of his cheekbones, his vivid eyes, those wicked lips. He'd walk into a room of strangers and all eyes would come to him because they would know that he's a man to be followed. He'd blow his whistle and they'd come like children following the pied piper.

The low thrum of his voice drops to a seductive purr. "No, lovely. We'll make a game of it, you and I, won't we?"

I hold his gaze and refuse to back down. "Yes, sir," I say, giving him exactly what he needs. "We will."

CHAPTER 7

Tavi

Something happened back there. Something broke in me when I saw my cousin's dead body. Elise saw me at my lowest.

I would've thought she'd think me weak, or that she could take advantage of me when my guard was down. After everything we've been through and everything she's done, I sort of expected something from her that was an almost self-fulfilling prophecy.

But she didn't take advantage. She didn't kick me while I was down or try to capitalize on my weakness. No.

She did the opposite.

She welcomed me, imperfect and broken, and she understood.

It was the hottest, most erotic thing she could've done.

I've been with women who let me use and abuse them, women who spread their legs and would do anything I asked. It isn't hard for a guy like me to find a fucking harem. Money and charm go a long way in bed.

But there's more to sex than getting off. If there wasn't, I'd never need to do more than hire a hooker or hit a strip club. I could have any woman I want and have, but it's a hollow sort of pleasure.

There's no chase. It's too easy.

Everything about Elise is pure challenge.

I want to conquer her. I want to plunder her. I want to bring home the spoils of war and keep her as my bounty, a prize I'd cherish for I know she's hard-won.

So I don't buy it when she hands me her submission. She can pretend all she wants, but I see straight through her.

I'll have it, though, just not easily.

When the last of the staff leaves, including the driver in the same car we're sitting in, the sun's begun to sink lower in the sky. Between sleeping late, our meal, and our visit to the morgue, the day's nearly over.

But in some ways, I feel like the day's only just begun, like the sun has just risen.

"In the house, Elise," I tell her, giving her pert ass a little swat. She squeals and flushes pink.

I'm fully prepared to dominate this woman. Knowing that she likes it?

She's in for the ride of her life.

When she doesn't move quick enough, I give her ass another smack. "When I give you an instruction, you do it promptly. You understand me?"

"Yes, of course, right." I love the way her cheeks flush pink, and imagine her ass cheeks the same color.

Fuck. She's got a perfect ass. Her whole fucking body's goddamn perfect.

We waste no time going inside, and when I have her where I want her I slam and lock the door behind us. I press her up against the wall and cage her in with my forearm along the wall. "You know what this means, don't you?"

I love the way her eyes go wide when she bites her lip and shakes her head. "Not sure, no."

"We're supposed to wait for our wedding night."

"For sex?" she says in a voice that's so hopeful it almost makes me want to fuck her right up against this door.

"Yeah, baby. For sex."

"Oooh," she says. I don't miss the way she begins to pant. "Means if you knock me up we get a shotgun wedding with a JP, hmm?"

"Yeah. It means going to my brothers and demanding a wedding now, not in the four week time frame we planned on. It means telling my mom she doesn't get to plan her ridiculous gala she's been dying to have."

"Tavi," Elise says, sliding her hands up my body to my shoulders. Slowly, she begins removing my suit coat. "You know there are ways to prevent babies, don't you?"

"Say that again, woman, and I'll whip your ass. *No.*"

She looks like she's going to roll her eyes but thinks better of it. Good. I mean it.

"Then what do you want? You don't want to knock me up now, you don't want to wait to have sex…"

"Didn't say I have a problem knocking you up now."

I watch as her mouth drops open in shock. "You'd get me pregnant? Now?"

I shrug. "The Rossi family beliefs tells us that children are a king's crown jewels, that they complete our lives. You'll have my babies, Elise, whether now or later, whenever."

"Oh. Oh, wow," she says, biting her lip as she thinks this over. "Romeo and Vittoria don't have children, do they?"

I shake my head. "Not yet."

Romeo, the Boss, has been trying since he married Vittoria but they've been unlucky with pregnancy. As Boss, his position isn't threatened, but I know how badly he wants a child. Orlando and Angelina's having a child strengthened The Family. If either of us brothers has a child, it will only help us even more.

"Well. Okay, then, I knew that going into this and Angelina's got a baby. But here's the thing, Tavi, even if you knocked me up today, we could still get married in four weeks. I won't be unable to get married. Things go on as planned." She nods pragmatically. It's the first time I'm thankful I'm marrying a woman who was raised in the mafia. I don't have to fight the tradition and expectations.

I only have to fight *her*.

And then I'm kissing her, and our conversation fades into a whisper of silence.

I love the way she feels in my arms. I love the way she melts against me so our bodies merge as one. I can't fucking wait to strip her down so we're skin to skin, and I can feel every inch of her golden skin against mine.

I want this woman. All of her. I want to taste her pussy and feel her sex clenched around my cock. I want to run my tongue along every inch of her skin, to taste what's mine and scorch the memory of any man that's ever touched her from her mind. I want to own her. I want to dominate her body, suffuse her mind, and possess her heart. I want to be the first person she thinks of when she wakes and the last she thinks of when she goes to sleep. I want her for me. *All of her.*

I reach for her ass and hoist her up. Her legs automatically wrap around mine. I frame her face in my hands and kiss her again. I can't get enough of her mouth, her lips, her tongue. She tastes like sweet, golden sunshine and the more I taste, the more I crave.

My dick presses up against her, throbbing. She reaches down and strokes me through the fabric, grazing the head with her thumb. My hips jerk.

"Fuck, baby," I groan.

"I love it when you call me that," she whispers, grinning against my ear as she kisses me.

I have to admit, a part of me's glad she's not a goddamn virgin. She's confident and daring, and her boldness only makes me want her more. If she were a virgin, I'd have to take it easy, ease her into things. I don't want to.

"You like when I call you what? Baby?"

"Yeah," she whispers. "I like it a lot. No one's ever called me that before, and it's nice."

I lay her down on the bed. "I'll remember that. Clothes off."

She scrambles to obey, and it only makes me harder. I watch as she tosses her clothes to the head of the bed.

She's perfect, all curves and grace and soft skin, with a body that begs to be worshipped.

"You're so beautiful," I whisper, before I kiss one little shoulder where she's dotted with a freckle. I bring my mouth to her nipple and lick it until it hardens.

When she reaches for my belt buckle, I let her. My cock throbs for her touch. I hold my breath when she slowly pulls down my zipper. Her eyes look to me for approval, and I barely manage to eke out a tortured, ragged, "Yeah. Do it."

"Let me taste you," she whispers. "Please, Tavi."

She doesn't have to ask me twice. I sit on the edge of the bed, and she falls to her knees in front of me. Eagerly, she licks the tip of my cock, stifling a moan. I fist her hair and force her mouth harder down my shaft.

"Touch yourself while you suck me," I order. I thrust in her mouth with a groan. *Fuck.*

I close my eyes, basking in the feel of this. I've lost count of how many blow jobs I've gotten, but nothing, *nothing*, compares to this. She licks and sucks my shaft and weighs my balls in her hand, then she suckles the head of my cock. I'm drowning in the hot, seductive feel of her mouth on me, the way she bobs her head, eager to please me. I reach for where my belt lies on the bed.

"Don't you fucking stop," I warn her. Her eyes widen a bit when she sees the leather dangling from the buckle in my fist, but she keeps going, keeps pleasing me. I fist her hair and move her head up and down. I'll fucking relish every second of this.

"Jesus, baby," I groan, then my voice trails off in Italian when she does something magical that makes my cock spasm and jolt. I lift the belt and slap it on her naked ass. Her mouth tightens on my cock.

"Keep sucking," I order, then slap her ass again with the belt.

Sex is the ultimate domination, second only to spanking her. I'll have Elise's submission if I have to whip and fuck it out of her. Hell, I'll enjoy every damn second.

She groans, rocking her hips while her fingers work her pussy, sucking my cock as I fuck her mouth and lash the tip of the belt against her ass. We work ourselves to a frenzy until her eyes flutter closed and I can tell she's about to come.

She won't own the climax, not now. Her orgasms belong to *me*.

I stop my hips and drop the belt. "On the bed. Get on your knees."

She hastens to obey, flopping on the bed, then rushing to her knees when I slap her ass. Her eagerness is a definite turn-on. I love her pert, pink ass, kissed with the tip of my belt. I kneel behind her and reach my hand to her breast. I love the way she moans. I love the way she gives this all to me. The pretty pink petals of her pussy are slick and welcoming when I drag my cock along her heated red ass.

"Fuck baby," I groan, when I feel her wet, tight pussy. I tease it with the head, and she arches her back, silently begging for more. "Jesus, sweetheart. You're perfection."

I glide my cock through her damp folds, then slowly tease her entrance. The walls of her sex clench around me, and I have to hold myself back when she gives a genuine moan of delight.

She heaves a sigh. "This. God, you feel so *good*."

I feel good? I'm so damn primed after the blow job. I rest my torso against her, framing her body with mine, sink into her and build a slow rhythm. I savor the feel of her pussy milking my cock, the way my balls slap against her naked, hot skin.

I love the way her soft, gorgeous curves yield to me like a gentle caress. I love the way she's as eager as I am. I love the way she's giving fully into this, without a trace of holding herself back.

I thrust and savor her moans, the way she rocks her hips. I finger her heavy breasts that drag along the bed when she arches her back and weigh them in my hands.

"You've got a greedy pussy, don't you?" I whisper in her ear. "I should whip you for that."

"Think you already did," she says, rocking with me as I thrust over and over.

"That was a warm up." She gets turned on by being spanked. I'm gonna have fun with that. I slap my hand against her thigh, making her moan even harder. "They say pain heightens a climax."

"Oh?"

I slap her ass again, and again, never slowing my thrusts as her skin blooms pink. I reach for her throat and wrap my fingers around the delicate skin. I remember pushing her up against the wall, choking her. She hated it then. Now, she gasps. When I release her throat only long enough to stroke it, she bends her head back and kisses my arm.

The harsh, irregular cadence of her breathing tells me she's close to coming, just as a familiar shiver of need courses through me. We're both close.

"Oh, God," she murmurs. "Oh, God, Tavi, I'm gonna come."

"Climax with me."

I may not be the first she's ever had, but goddamn if I'll be the only one she remembers.

I thrust hard, and she moans out loud. I feel the first clench of her spasms as she begins to climax. I'm shocked at the intensity of my own need to come, like she's awakened a response deep within me.

"Come, baby. Let yourself go. Come."

"Tavi!" she screams, my name echoing in my room

at her first wave of pleasure. My cock jerks inside her. I milk every drop of pleasure from her and she rides me until we're panting and exhausted.

We lay, joined together, our bodies still coupled, for long minutes. She's naked but I'm still partially dressed. It doesn't matter. I drag my fingers along her shoulders, a gentle touch. She reaches for my hand and kisses my palm, and if that isn't the sweetest damn thing I've ever seen.

I hold her beneath me, a little stunned that I'm gonna marry her.

I'll call Romeo today. We'll move the wedding up. We'll deal with Mama and Nonna and whatever shit my family gives me.

I gave up everything for my family.

I'll take Elise.

This woman's *mine*.

CHAPTER 8

Elise.

What.

Just.

Happened.

I've had sex before.

But that wasn't... *sex.*

I completely surrendered myself to him.

He's a master in the bedroom, and I'm his *goddamn* slave.

And I liked it.

A part of me, a very small part, granted, sits stunned by the magnitude of my feelings.

My legs are numb. My breasts still tingle. My ass burns, but in the best possible way. He just eviscerated every memory of sex I ever had, and I don't have any regrets.

I should… I should.

Something happened earlier today after he identified the body, I know it did. Something between *us*. I'm not a sentimental girl and never have been, but there are moments in time that burn in your memory like a brand, and today's one of those.

It wasn't really what he said or what I said. It wasn't what we did. It was more of a mutual understanding. I saw a vulnerable side to him I didn't anticipate. And he trusted me with what I'd bet few, if any, have ever seen before.

I'll honor that.

I could feel his need to dominate me when we came in this house, and my body responded like it was made for this. That he could hurt me but didn't… it's more than an aphrodisiac. It fuels my need for more.

Silently, he undresses and pulls his T-shirt over his head.

"Could've done that before you fucked me. You owe me, Mr. Rossi," I tease, because the view of Tavi shirtless is something you'd find in a men's mag centerfold.

"Watch it, woman," he says, in that husky voice of his, but there's a softness to him brought out by our lovemaking.

If making love to this man is what mellows him, I'll make love to him night and day.

I mentally tally my cycle, when I'm due for my period. I obviously haven't had birth control since I've been his prisoner. I guess it's a crap shoot, really. Vittoria has never gotten pregnant, and I'd guess that's not for lack of trying. Meanwhile Angelina was pregnant within months of being with Orlando, maybe sooner. She's happy with that. But me... I don't know.

So much of this is inevitable. Marriage to him. Having children. Solidifying the Rossi family by extending branches on their family tree. I know all this, and a part of me really, truly *longs* for a child. One look at Nicolo's soft curls and sweet, chubby cheeks, and I could feel my need to hold a child of my own growing.

But a child with a man I barely know...

I've long since given up illusions of having a child with a man I loved. I close the door on that thought before it grows to fruition.

"C'mere," Tavi says, rolling me over to him. He takes his tee and cleans me with it lazily. It's warm and smells like him, and his touch is so gentle my throat gets a little tight.

"Thanks."

"Of course." He props pillows up in the bed and whips the dirty tee into a hamper by the door. "I'm fucking exhausted and this was one long day. Let's order food."

Ah, right, he sent his staff away. In this small, remote part of Tuscany, the selection of food to order is slim, but there are a few options, all of them very good. But it isn't necessary.

"I can cook," I offer helpfully. "I mean, as long as there's food. I'm actually not bad."

It's a massive understatement. I studied cooking from the greatest chefs my fathers hired, and I love it.

He quirks a brow up at me. It's adorable. "That's right. You can cook?"

I nod. "Yep. You picky?"

He shrugs. "No, but I watch my macros and shit. Eat high protein. Starting a lifting regimen with Orlando."

"But you own a pastry shop?"

"Eh. Cheat days. I lift enough I can burn off the cannoli." He flexes his bicep, and I reach my fingers to stroke it. His skin's taut over smooth, firm muscle. *Yum.*

"That you do. And *mmm.* Cannoli."

"You bake, too?" A breeze flutters through the window and ruffles my hair. Wordlessly, he tucks it away from my face and behind my ear.

I like this gentle side of Tavi. I wonder how I can make him stay.

"Sadly, I do not. I leave baking for those more skilled than I am."

"Doesn't matter."

I give him a sidelong glance, and my mind immediately conjures up an image of him dressed in nothing but an apron with powdered sugar on his nose. Hel-*lo*. "Do you?"

"I can and did, but usually hire people to do it for me. No time."

Of course he doesn't have time. He's the damn Underboss.

A little voice in the back of my mind wonders... will he have time for *me*?

I look at the setting sun outside his window. "Ah, but time slows in Tuscany, doesn't it?"

His gaze follows mine outside the window. I watch as he lets out a sigh and tucks his hand behind his head. "It does, Elise."

Men like him are married to their work. I've never seen any of them actually care about a wife for a purpose other than show. It's a very common theme in mob life: the wife runs the home and solidifies family bonds with children and outward support, but the mistress pleases him in bed.

God, I hate that. I hate it so much.

The Rossis, though... the Rossis seem to have defied the mob's expectation of married life. At least, to a certain extent. One could hope, I guess.

Orlando dotes on Angelina. He's exacting and borderline controlling, but she also has him wrapped around her little finger. I don't know Romeo and Vittoria as well, but one can spot a happily married couple a mile away.

I look around me. Tavi's room is nicer than the guest room, bigger, and somehow more masculine. Whereas mine is adorned in soft, white, feminine curves, his is bedecked in solid wood furniture with gorgeous hardwood floors, but it still has the Tuscan flare. I could imagine someone standing just outside this window with a canvas, painting against the stunning backdrop of rolling hills.

"Let's see what we've got for food here," he says.

After all we've been through, after all we've done, it's almost funny to me how pragmatic it is to obey the call of my appetite. I yawn and stretch my arms up over my head, which apparently is an open invitation for him to bend and kiss me.

"Next week," he says softly, before he brushes his thumb over my cheekbone.

"Next week what?" I know exactly what he's going to say, but I want to hear him say it.

"You'll marry me."

"But your mother," I say, teasing him because I know if he wants to marry me that's exactly what's going to happen. "She'll have a fit."

"I'll call her right now."

"Right now?" I gasp and bring the bedsheet up over my naked breasts.

He bends and reaches for his pants on the floor to extract his phone. "Put the sheet down. I'm not doing a goddamn video chat."

My fingers grasp the edge of the sheet. I want to disobey him. It's a lot easier to submit to him when I'm horny.

But when his eyes flick to me, narrowed in warning, before they flick to his belt that dangles on the edge of the bed, I remember that Tavi isn't just a dominant in *bed*. And I drop the sheet.

I like the way his eyes rove over my body while he makes the call. It's warm in here, and I'm so comfortable I could nap if my stomach wasn't growling with hunger.

"Mama. Did I wake you?" Oops. It's like eleven o'clock at night in Boston. "Oh, good." I watch as his brows knit in concern. "Marialena okay? Alright, I have no idea what that means, but I trust you. Listen, we need to talk."

When he reaches for my hand, I lace my fingers through his. I roll over and lay my head beside his shoulder. He rests our folded hands on top of his chest, right over a seriously kickass tattoo with an eagle and a moon entangled in roses. I circle the ink with my index finger.

"I don't want to wait four weeks to get married. There's no need to wait. The only reason we were was so you could get the big wedding you wanted, but can you make it all happen sooner?"

He flinches at Tosca's high-pitched scream and holds the phone from his ear, then gives me a thumbs-up. I feel my eyebrows rise incredulously. Ah, that didn't *sound* like a thumbs-up.

They talk over details, but he's quickly "mhming" her to death until he finally says, "Listen, we're starving and need to eat dinner. I'll follow up with the girls tomorrow, okay? And anything you need, Mama. I'm right here in Tuscany and can pick stuff up and send it home. Yeah, of course we'll do the cake. Okay. Yeah. Night."

Without a pause, he hangs up the phone and calls Romeo.

"Rome." He gives Romeo the same spiel as he did Tosca, but Romeo needs far less explanation.

"No, haven't knocked her up. Not yet, anyway," he mutters. I feel my cheeks flush pink, but it passes quickly. I should know better than to expect anything short of crass references to *sex* with the Rossi men. *God.*

I pick up my own phone and text Angelina, but she doesn't answer. She's probably asleep in between nursing sessions with Nicolo. I send her another text.

Call me tomorrow. We've got to talk.

I turn my attention back to Tavi, who's moved from the wedding to talking to Romeo about what we saw today at the morgue. All semblance of sadness or emotion have fled. He's one-hundred-percent business.

"Yeah, Boss. Of course. I'll find who did this and there'll be payback, big time. Coming home for the wedding first, though. Obviously we have our usual suspects."

I block it all out. I don't want to hear anything about his work. I had enough of it growing up that the whole damn thing gives me indigestion. I make a vow right then and there to invest in those fancy noise-canceling headphones.

I sit up and reach for his hand. I give him a little tug.

I point to the kitchen. I need to inventory what he has on hand. I saw fresh herbs outside the window by the garden, and suspect if he has a housekeeper and an on-site cook that he's got a well-stocked pantry to boot.

I pause when he shakes his head, though, and makes a little walking motion with two fingers. He's coming with me, I guess.

I clean up in the biggest bathroom I've ever seen, then find myself a pair of his boxers and a clean T-shirt. The boxers are laughably huge on me, but the T-shirt hits just below the ass, so it works. Tomorrow, we shop. I know we were supposed to today, so I'm guessing he'll have no problem with it if we shop tomorrow.

Tavi pads noiselessly behind me as I walk to the kitchen and do a quick inventory.

"Wow," I breathe to myself, since he's still talking in Italian on the phone. The pantry's stunning and fully stocked with rice, flours and breads, onion and garlic and hard root vegetables in a wooden bin, spices and herbs and non-perishables. It's beautifully organized like one might find in a home and garden cooking show. With a little squeal of delight, I fill my arms with a bottle of olive oil, a few onions, some garlic cloves, and thick carrots with the stems still on them.

I walk over to the stove and lay them beside it, then hum to myself while I take in the fridge. It's as well-stocked and beautifully organized as the pantry, boasting a variety of cheeses, cream and butter, lettuces and prepared salads, meats wrapped in fresh butcher paper, and pretty glass dishes filled with soups and casseroles that make my mouth water. I don't want to eat any of the prepared food, though. I want to cook for Tavi.

I take some thin-sliced chicken and baby spinach with the heavy cream and chicken stock, and head to the stove. I'm still humming to myself while the water boils. I cut thick slabs of fresh bread I find wrapped in paper on the counter, rub the wedges with a clove of garlic, brush fresh butter and olive oil on it, then broil. Soon, the kitchen smells like heaven.

I've blocked out Tavi's conversations, so I don't realize he's talking to me when he curses in Italian.

I turn and look over my shoulder at him. I didn't hear what he said. "You talking to me?"

"Yeah, baby," he says in his best gangster accent. "I'm talkin' ta *you*."

I have a slice of bread in one hand and a clove of garlic in the other. *"Quindi, che cosa vuoi?"* I ask him. *What do you want then?*

"I said where'd you learn to cook like *this*?" Before I answer him, I turn involuntarily and look back at the stove. Seared chicken simmers in a creamy sauce made with cream, butter, and chicken broth. Leaves of basil and spinach as well as freshly grated parmesan-reggiano cheese sits in a glass ramekin, ready to garnish. The pasta boils behind it, and I have a small dish of chopped salad with a homemade vinaigrette on the side. The kitchen smells of toasted bread and garlic.

"Oh, I learned from one of the chefs when I was alone one summer in Tuscany."

"Fuckin' glad I don't have you back in America. Jesus, baby, I might not ever take you back."

I look at him in surprise, not sure if he's joking or not. "What?"

"My brothers would smother me in my sleep to get to you."

Oh, right. I forgot the Rossi brothers come to blows over food. I smile to myself.

"Well lucky for you, we're shacking up."

He doesn't so much as crack a smile but pushes himself off the stool by the counter and stalks over to me, his eyes glowing with ferocity. I take a step backward, and my back hits the stove.

"What?"

"It's sexy watching you cook."

"There's no damn way you're hard again." I put the food down and wash my hands quickly by the sink. I close my eyes when he comes up behind me, his flank at my back, his hard cock pressed to my ass. I close my eyes.

I always dreamed about this. I'm not really sure why. But this, this right here. I fantasized about a domestic setting just like this, where my husband would catch me doing something mundane and simple like washing dishes or cooking dinner. He'd come up behind me and sweep my hair to the side so he could kiss my neck.

I love that fantasy. It's so... so normal. And after everything I've been through, I crave normal.

"Keep cooking," he says. I squeal when he grabs my

hips and yanks me so that he can grind against me. I squirm in anticipation. And keep cooking.

I stir the sauce and roll the basil before I cut it into thin, vibrant green strips. It smells like sunshine and summer. I've always loved fresh basil.

I groan when Tavi's tongue laps the back of my neck. My fingers flick open over the bubbling pan, and the basil melts into the sauce.

With him still at my back, I open the oven and take out the garlic toast, just as the timer goes off for the pasta. He backs off and gives me space to do the more dangerous kitchen tasks, but when I begin plating the food, he's back at me, his hands at my breasts and his mouth at my neck.

"We're ready to eat," I whisper.

"Yeah, baby, I'm ready to eat you," he responds. My thighs clench together and a deep spasm of need washes over me. Oh God, he's so hot it's unnerving.

"Well first, let's eat some *dinner*." I turn to face him with a plate in each hand. "Shall we?"

"We shall."

We opt to sit side-by-side on little kitchen stools by the counter.

He groans with the first bite.

By the second, his eyes are closed.

At the third, he asks me to marry him.

"We're already getting married," I say, taking a sip

of wine. It's so crisp and clean, my tastebuds sing. "And my God, where'd you get this wine from?"

"From our vineyards."

"Nooo," I breathe. "I heard of the Rossi family vineyards when I was little! I forgot all about them."

I twirl the pasta around my fork and spear a bite of chicken. He's right. It *is* good. "Okay, this is delicious but it has more to do with the quality of the ingredients than anything else."

"Uh." He shakes his head. "Don't you dare go all modest on me."

"But I'm not going to brag. My father taught me never to talk about my own accomplishments."

"And if you don't brag, I'll spank you," he says nonchalantly. "So take your pick." He takes a huge bite of chicken and groans again. "Your father was a prick."

He was. No argument there.

"Tell me about the rest of your family."

He's spearing more pasta with his fork when he asks, so I don't get to look in his eyes. I guess it doesn't much matter. I'm marrying him. I won't be a Regazza anymore, and thank God for *that*. Still, I'm curious if he's fishing for intel or genuinely curious.

"Why do you want to know?" I ask, filling my own mouth with pasta and not answering at first.

That earns me a stern look from beneath lowered lashes. "Excuse me?"

"What?" I say around a mouthful of food.

"You don't balk when I ask you a question. You answer. Thought we'd covered that."

Definitely not just a dominant in bed.

"I'm curious why you want to know."

My heart does a little somersault, half expecting that I've riled him, but he only takes another large bite of food, follows it with an entire slice of garlic toast that he eats in two large bites, and washes it down with enough wine to drown a small boat.

"When you marry me, your family becomes my family. It's only custom and logic that demands I ask about your family."

Ah. Well, that makes sense. "Not much to tell you. You know I was an only child. My mother's alive but estranged, and I haven't seen her in years."

"Why?"

He eats another slice of bread and groans before downing more wine. Wordlessly, I refill his glass. He nods his thanks.

"I don't really know, except that she hated being married to my father. He had mistresses." I pause, not wanting to give more information. It isn't that any of this is a secret so much as I want to see his reaction to *mistress*.

"Ah. Women hate that." He's bare-chested, hunched over as he shovels bite after bite into his mouth. I make a vow right then and there that I'll ask him to give his cook another job, because I think I might slap a bitch that would try to feed this man. That's *my* job. It's better than sex, and that's saying something.

"We do. I'm surprised you know that."

He snorts and twirls another bite of pasta around his fork. "I've got a mother, a grandmother, and two sisters at home. I'd have to be a total dumbass not to know that women take the oath of fidelity seriously."

Not all women, but yes.

I feign nonchalance as I take a tentative bite of bread, but the toast nearly gets caught in my throat. I quickly take another sip of wine. "But what about you? Do you take your vow of fidelity seriously?"

Slowly, Tavi puts his fork down. He folds his large hands together and sits up straighter. If he were a king, he'd make a decree to begin a war with a look like that.

"I take *all* my vows seriously."

My heart beats faster. "All of them? To your wife or to your brothers?"

Tavi leans toward me, elbow on the table. The light glints off his eyes, making him look feral. My belly begins to quiver. "*All*. The oaths I take to the brotherhood. The oaths I take to my wife. And the oaths taken to *me*."

Oh dear. A myriad of emotions washes over me— relief, excitement, but alongside them is a deep, abiding sense of fear. Relief that he'll be faithful to me. Hell, I don't even want another woman *feeding* him. Excitement at his stern nature, because I've been dominated by this man and I crave another taste. But fear… fear because I wonder if I'll uphold the vows I take to him to his liking.

It explains why he's sought to punish me. My marriage to him will be like discipline meant to teach and correct in the face of wrongdoing. My palms grow sweaty. I wipe them discreetly on the edge of my T-shirt.

"I understand," I tell him. Because I do.

I'll take a vow to love, honor, and obey this man.

A few weeks ago, that would have unnerved me. I would've walled my heart against him in the hopes of never feeling anything at all for a man I don't love.

But a thread of hope has woven through me. Tavi has a heart. Somewhere deep in the recesses of this stern, forbidding man… he has a heart. A heart that may have forgotten the warmth of love, the heat of passion, or the promise of tomorrow.

Maybe it's up to me to reawaken it.

CHAPTER 9

Tavi

"Marialena. You're literally speaking Greek to me, kiddo." I roll my eyes and gesture for Elise. "And no, doesn't matter if you're fifty, I'll always call you kiddo. Can you please talk to Elise?"

Elise gives me a curious look. I roll my eyes and hand her the phone. I cover the mouthpiece. "Marialena wants to know something about a train or bus, which makes no fucking sense since we're taking a goddamn car."

Her brows crease but she takes the phone and starts chatting. I'm finishing emails when I hear her pretty, throaty laugh.

And just like that, I'm hard. It doesn't take much when it comes to her.

Could be because we've had more sex in the past

two days than I have in the past five years. Could be because she's managed to irrevocably wrap herself around my heart, and maybe she knows it. But whatever the reason, we're landing in Boston in ten minutes and I need to get my act together.

I made absolutely zero headway in Tuscany finding more information about my cousin's death. No one knows a damn thing. I don't even have any men stationed in Tuscany, which is why it took so long for me to come identify the body.

I wonder if he was lured there. I'll have to question Uncle Leo when I get home.

"Tavi, honey," Elise says, her fingers over the mouthpiece. "She meant the *wedding dress* train, and the *bust* on it. She's trying to find me a dress, remember?"

No, of course I don't remember and seriously do not even give a shit about things like dresses and shoes and trains and busts, unless it's *her* bust and my mouth is on it. I wave my hand at her. "Whatever. Get whatever you want."

I watch as she bites her lip and twiddles with a piece of her hair. She's mulling something over.

"What?" I ask while I check on the latest email I got from Santo. He looked at the former Regazza property while I visited Tuscany, and there are a few things of note.

"I really wanted one of those custom Pronovias dresses."

136

"Get it," I say absentmindedly as I flick through the updates and pics he sent me.

"Tavi." She pauses, insistent. I glance up.

"What?"

"It costs *ten thousand* dollars." The sheepish look on her face is priceless, as if she's expecting me to say no. I know the woman likes to shop and I know she's got expensive taste. "But it's... it's literally stunning. It's completely designed with fine fabrics and the embellishments are gold, platinum and silver. The entire bodice is made up of—"

"Don't tell me," I interrupt. "I don't care. And I don't want to hear about what it looks like until I see it on you on our wedding day."

"Ten thousand dollars!"

"So?"

"*So?*" Her eyes widen. "Are you *serious* right now."

I put my phone down and meet her eyes. "Baby. I don't fucking care if you get a million dollar dress handsewn by enchanted field mice from Paris. Whatever you want, get it. The only thing I ask is that nothing you order or buy delays our wedding next week. Got it?"

Her eyes shine as she taps the mute button on the phone. "You are getting the best fucking blow job of your life for that," she hisses, before she taps the phone and goes back to her conversation with my sister.

Well now. Worth it.

Maybe we do have something special here.

Am I going soft, like I vowed I never would?

I narrow my eyes at her. "Elise." My voice is sharp like a well-aimed slap.

Her eyes come back to me, those long lashes of hers fluttering. "Yes."

"Hang up the phone and come here."

There's the briefest second of hesitation and I wonder if she's processing my request, but the next moment she speaks into the phone. "Gotta go. Call you right back. God, I know, right?" She verbally rolls her eyes, but I let that one slide.

When she hangs up her call she slides the phone onto her tray and walks over to me on wobbly legs. We're flying steadily but she doesn't walk too well when we're in the air.

"Yes, sir?" she asks in that singsong voice of hers that's totally gonna get her spanked.

I snap my fingers and point to the floor. I watch as she hastens to obey. *Fuck.*

"You said I was getting the best damn blow job for that," I say, my voice hoarse and affected.

"I did," she says, her eyes shining and cheeks a little flushed. Somehow, by some miracle, I landed a woman who likes giving the damn things. She licks her lips. "Right now?"

I stroke my thick cock through the silky fabric of my pants and groan. No. Not now. We're landing in minutes and any second, the flight attendant will come back and tell us to prepare for landing. Still, I grab her hair and fist it, dragging her mouth between my legs. "Not now, baby," I say, even though it kills me to tell her no. "But tonight. Later. When we're alone, me and you. Got it?"

"Mmm. Yes," she says, before she bends her mouth and kisses the fat bulge in my pants. "Your wish is my command."

I stifle another groan. Fucking *perfect*.

"Later," I grate out, when her eyes fall to the open email on my phone. A visible look of surprise crosses her face she quickly conceals, but not before I note it.

"You see something there?"

I expect her to lie, to pretend that she didn't see anything at all, but she doesn't. Her brows knit in concentration. She rests her forearms on my knees. "May I please see what you're looking at?"

It belonged to her father. Honestly, I'm not sure why I didn't show it to her before.

"You recognize these?"

"Of course," she says, cradling my phone in her hand. "I'm a shopper. I was the one who picked out the merchandise my father sold here." There's a note of nostalgia in her voice.

"Seriously? I'm surprised a man like your father allowed you anywhere near it."

She shrugs. "Oh, he didn't know about it. But I befriended the manager in charge of inventory, and she let me pick out whatever I thought would sell. Strange, I thought these burned down in a fire."

There was never a fire anywhere near the place. "Why'd you think that? No fire that I know of. Everything's in good shape, just abandoned."

Her frown deepens. "It's what my father told me." She shakes her head. "Huh. It's where Piero—"

She stops short and covers her mouth with her hand. What the hell? But before she can speak again, we hit a pocket of turbulence. Her face smashes into my knee and she gives a cry. *Jesus.*

I quickly pick her up and tug her onto my lap. "You alright?" But I can't answer because my voice is swallowed in her scream. The plane nosedives. I throw my arms around her to keep her from hurtling about the plane. Another dip and the plane shakes with the effort of staying upright. The pilot's voice comes over a speaker.

"Nothing to worry about, sir. We hit an unexpected pocket of turbulence. I'll have us right back on course in no time."

Back on course? How far have we drifted?

"Oh God, oh God," Elise says, tears squeezing from beneath her eyelids.

"You'll be okay," I tell her, but when we hit another rough patch, she screams and flails like she's possessed.

"Elise. *Stop.*" But It's no use, she's terrified and can't stop herself from hyperventilating. Gasping for air, she claws at her throat.

I give her a hard smack to the side of her leg. She gasps for breath, her chest heaving.

"Stop," I order. "We'll be fine. *Breathe*, baby." I grasp her cheeks hard between my fingers. She winces but looks a little more pink.

"Alright, babe. We're okay now. You okay?"

I slide her into the seat next to me. My heart breaks for her when she puts her head back, still crying. Her lower lip wobbles like a small child on the verge of a breakdown.

"Shh, baby," I whisper, gripping her knee. "We're alright. You're okay. I won't take you on another plane anytime soon, okay?"

"Maybe," she pants. Little beads of perspiration dot her forehead. "Maybe just, like, drug me or something. I do love Tuscany and would rather be there than America anyway, it's just the *to* and *fro* that kill me."

She's so damn adorable. "I can easily drug you or something. Not a problem."

"Of course," she says with a little laugh. "Probably keep a little vial of sedative on your person or something, eh?"

Not quite, but I'm glad she can make light of it. I do have methods of sedation.

"Okay, alright." She's still panting, her eyes still closed.

I take her hand in mine as the Boston skyline comes into view through the window. "I'm guessing you don't want to open your eyes, so I'll just tell you. The Boston skyline's magic tonight."

"Oh yeah?" she whispers. She takes in another shuddering breath.

"Yeah," I reply. "All twinkling lights like dots of fairy dust."

"That sounds like something *I'd* say."

"Perhaps." I smile to myself. Maybe she's affected me.

"So no budget on the dress?"

"Are you changing the subject?"

"I so fucking am."

"I seriously do not care how much you spend on the dress. It's a once-in-a-lifetime event. My mother's already spent thirty thousand dollars just on the goddamn *chairs* we sit our asses in."

"Does she have money to burn or what?"

She absolutely does, probably my father's investments she doesn't want to touch.

"Elise," I say in a bored tone, reading through the notes from Santo. I want all this bullshit behind us.

"Mmm?"

She's flipping through a bridal magazine when we hit another pocket of turbulence. Her audible gasp concerns me.

"I—I hate flying," she says, squeezing her eyes shut.

"Wish I knew that before we decided to take a few flights to Tuscany. This week, before the wedding, you'll answer anything and everything I ask. Got it?"

"Sure, but will the same apply to you?"

"It will."

She nods. "Good. Who starts?"

"Me."

"Why does that not surprise me?"

I flip through the pictures and make a mental note to have Santo talk with Elise under my supervision. It's not that I don't trust her. He's the one I don't trust.

"Do you like to read?"

"Lots, mhm. I do. You?"

"I do, but I read more when I was younger. Work and all that. My family always called me the little bookworm. Nonna approved, said a well-read man was a benefit to society. But my father…" It's hard to keep the bitterness out of my tone when I talk about him.

"Let me guess," she says. "Thought there were better uses of your time than in the pages of a book, right?"

"Yep."

Her voice lowers. "Did he… get angry at you for it?"

I huff out a cold laugh. "My father got angry if you peed too loud in the toilet on the third floor of The Castle when he was in Tuscany."

"Oh, ugh," she says with a grimace. "Sounds familiar, though. My father once said I *chewed* too loud, and from then on I was banished to eat my meals in my bedroom with my nanny or tutor."

"Jesus."

She fiddles with a little silver ring on her finger, spinning it from side to side. It glints in the overhead light.

"For the record, you don't chew loudly."

"Well. Give me time," she says with a wink.

"Your turn."

"Oooh, I get a turn." She wriggles in her chair when the flight attendant gives us a five minute warning. "What's the best movie you ever watched?"

"Saving Private Ryan."

"Yikes, Tavi, you don't play around, do you?"

I shake my head. "Nope. Yours?"

"You have to promise me you won't laugh "

"I will make no such promises."

She's adorable when she frowns. "Alright, fine. My all-time, number one favorite movie was the live-action Beauty and the Beast."

I don't laugh at all. "That was an excellent movie."

"Wait, what? You *watched* it?"

"I did. Marialena begged me to go on opening day. I mean, it wasn't up there with my favorite top ten or even top fifty, but might be the top hundred."

"No way!"

"Way."

"Wow. You're just full of surprises, Ottavio." I like that she calls me Ottavio sometimes.

Jesus. She has no fucking idea. *None.* But I have a few weeks to ease her into this.

"Earliest happy childhood memory," I ask.

"I remember waking up on Christmas morning. We were in America that year, and my father had bought me a pony. An actual, real, bona fide pony."

"Seriously?"

"Yep."

"You still have it?"

"No, God, no. We sold it. Poor thing was kept in a small paddock but I was never allowed to actually *ride* her. I barely petted her. She was happy as a clam when I went to go see her, but my father was afraid that I'd fall off."

"What's the purpose of a pony if you don't get to actually do anything but pet her?" Why would someone do that to a kid?

"Good question," she says, unable to hide the note of bitterness in her voice. "I found out the answer when we had our next party and he bragged about giving his daughter everything, including the pony she wanted."

"Good thing your father's dead," I mutter.

She snorts. "Why do you say that?"

"Because I'd have to beat the shit out of him."

"It shouldn't make me happy to hear that, but I have to admit it does." Another dip in the plane and she squeals and squeezes her eyes shut, but this one's only a brief one. It isn't until we're steady again I realize my hand's atop hers, steadying her.

I like the warm feel of her fingers beneath mine.

"Thanks," she whispers. I nod. "Your turn. Favorite Christmas present."

"First Ka-Bar."

She whistles. "Wow, isn't that like the most dangerous knife you can own?"

I nod. "Well, I wouldn't say the most, but it's up there. Damn good fighting knife but useful as a utility knife too. I whittled with it until..." Nah. I won't tell her that.

"Until what?"

"You don't need to know."

"Nothing I haven't heard or seen before, Tavi. Why start hiding things now?"

She's right. The plane dips a bit. I'll distract her until we land.

"Until I had to question a guy who betrayed us." I'll never forget the look of terror in his eyes or the way he begged me to leave his wife and kids alone.

"Ahh. So you had to torture him with the knife?" She winces a little but otherwise seems unaffected.

"Yeah."

I cut his fingers, one by one, and watched him bleed. I woke for months after that, imagining my own fingers were scarred and bloody. I'd flex them in the darkened room, until Romeo caught me doing it one night when we were traveling. He made me tell him what tortured me in my sleep. Just telling him somehow made it better. I hadn't thought about that first incident—hazing, I guess you could even call it—until now.

"So if you didn't like what he made you do with it, why'd you like having it so much?"

"Why do I like having it? Never got rid of it," I tell her. I run my thumb along the top of her hand. I shrug. "I guess every one of us has a rite of passage, don't we? For a woman or a man. Something that brings us over the threshold of childhood to adulthood, don't we?"

"Yeah," she says with a nod, but doesn't offer me hers.

"For me, that was crossing over. And I was ready to be rid of my childhood."

She doesn't ask me why. She likely doesn't have to. We both know why.

Children like us don't get an actual childhood with friends and family and carefree times. Yeah, we play like anyone, but the overhanging expectations, the loss of childhood innocence, the knowledge that we're born into mafia life and we'll never escape, impact all of us in one way or another. Some guys remember their first date, some remember when they got their first car, their first job, or lost their virginity. It isn't like that for us.

"I want something better for our children, Tavi," she says softly, almost meditatively. That she's really thinking about having children with me means something. I wasn't sure she really accepted that.

"Better?" I laugh bitterly. "What's better than knowing you can walk in a room and have whatever you want? That people fear you? That you'll have whatever house you want, whatever car you want?"

"Autonomy?" she says softly. "Freedom? Peace?"

We begin our descent.

"Yeah."

I don't offer much more than that. I don't know what else to say.

Our kids will be born into mafia life, just like we were. If I have a son, he'll inherit the keys to the kingdom one day. And if I have a daughter… I look at Elise and close the door on that train of thought.

"Did you go to college?" I ask, changing the subject.

"A little, but it was boring so I dropped out," she says with a shrug. "You?"

"Got an offer from Harvard but didn't accept."

She tips her head to the side curiously. "Wait. *Wait.* You could've gone to *Harvard?* So you're smarter than I thought."

"Watch it, girl."

I reach over and tickle her ribs. She squeals with laughter. "Did you… like, do special science experiments? Join the robotics team in high school?" I tickle her harder but she doesn't stop. "Were you *in a band,* Tavi?"

"That's for me to know and you to find out."

Maybe all of those things.

God, it feels so good to relax, to really let loose with her.

We're touching down, and she breathes a bit more freely. The sun sets outside our windows. Now's the time to ask her, to get to the dual purpose of my questions.

I clear my throat and sober. "Next question."

"Yeah?"

"What'd you see in the warehouse?"

She looks out the window and doesn't hesitate. She likely knows there's no point in hiding anything from me.

"There was a broken pair of sunglasses in the corner of the room. They looked like ones that belonged to someone I once knew, but they couldn't have been. He's been dead for months."

"Could've been there for months, no?"

"No," she says hollowly. "He was with me during my escape. They belonged to my bodyguard, Piero, but he hasn't been to America in years."

Piero.

The man I ordered killed.

I drop the subject.

CHAPTER 10

Elise

The next week passes in a sort of blur, and I have to admit, this is the best time I've ever had since I came to America as the Rossi family prisoner.

Technically, I still *am* a prisoner. He still has that godforsaken thing implanted in my arm like a psychopath. But I know now he really isn't one. Santo, on the other hand... now he may be. But I have very little to do with him if I can help it.

At least that's the plan.

The day before the wedding, I'm getting my final fitting for my dress. Something smells delicious in the downstairs kitchen, but I'm too nervous to eat. The door bursts open and Marialena comes in, carrying a few grocery bags.

"Tonight, we party, loves!"

"Party," as if we won't have half a dozen bodyguards on us at any given time. Tavi's given his consent for all of us to go into the North End, though. We'll start at Orlando's restaurant.

"Ta-da!" the seamstress says proudly. She spins me around so I can get a look in the full-length mirror.

"Oh. Oh, wow," I breathe.

Marialena whistles, coming up beside me. "Oh, honey," she says with a wicked gleam in her eye. "My brother is gonna lose. His. Mind."

Tavi was able to score the dress I really wanted. He paid a small fortune to have it overnighted from Italy, and the seamstress got started the first day it arrived. I think he liked that I had a pretty crazy request, though. It was one thing he could do, one thing he could control in all this.

Thankfully, the alterations were minor, but it needed the hem brought up and a good tuck. The brocade fabric has a shimmery, pearly finish, and the entire upper part of the dress is made of small flower petals handsewn into a strapless bodice. Fitted tulle gathers at the waist then flows like a waterfall in a glittering skirt that makes me feel like a princess.

The back looks almost bare, but it's a sheer fabric with a swirl of rhinestone-studded pearls, as whimsical as wispy clouds on a summer day.

"It's... it's perfect," I breathe. I spin and twirl and glance over my shoulder, and every damn angle's as magical as the first.

We're in the guest room on the second floor with the door closed but we can hear the men chatting and laughing in the reception room below. Tavi's down there, likely toasting his wedding before his bachelor party tonight.

I wish he could see me. I feel suddenly nervous and agitated, but I don't know why. I crave his stern, immovable presence. If there's anything Tavi's got going for him it's that he's solid and dependable.

I hear heavy steps outside the door, but they're too slow to be Tavi's. The door opens without a knock, and Nonna comes in bearing a tray of golden butter cookies piled high, the edges fringed with delicate pink sprinkles.

"*Mangia*, Elise!" She goes on to scold me in Italian, telling me I'll keel over at the alter if I don't put some food in my belly.

I shake my head, still anxious. "Save me some, please," I tell her. Her biscotti are the best I've ever had, and my mouth waters to taste some. "I can't eat them, not now." Not when I'm wearing this dress.

"Here," Marialena says, twisting the top off a protein shake. She plops a straw in it. "Sip this. Don't need you withering away."

Nonna rolls her eyes and mutters something about skinny girls and thick thighs.

"What is she talking about?" I ask Marialena.

"I have no damn clue," she responds. "I think she thinks you need fattening up. Thinks you're sick or something."

"I've actually gained six pounds since moving into The Castle!" I inform her. The food's just too damn good. Maybe I need Tavi to train me with his gym regimen.

Maybe.

"She lives to feed people, relax. It's just her way. Geez, it's like you've never been around an old-school Italian nonna."

"I haven't," I remind her. I had cooks and nannies and tutors and bodyguards, but never the presence of real family.

"Ah, right. Lucky you." Mario, dressed in designer jeans and a tight-fitting tee, walks in next. When he sees me in my wedding dress, he covers his eyes with his hand.

"Jesus, is this bad luck?" he asks me.

"Not unless we're the ones getting married, so you're good. Can't say the groom won't beat the shit out of you, though, for seeing me before he does." He very well might.

"Good point. You girls should warn a guy." Mario turns right around and heads for the exit. "Marialena, Santo said you and Rosa don't have the tracking on your phones activated and neither of you leave here until you do."

The door shuts with a bang. Marialena rolls her eyes. "And no overbearing, bossy brothers either?"

"Nope." Nothing. Just Angelina and Piero.

The memory of Piero fades with each passing day. I both hate and am grateful that it does.

On the one hand, I wrestle with guilt over marrying another man. I wanted to be Piero's for the rest of my life. On the other hand, I'm glad to have a new chance of life with Tavi. I know that if Piero couldn't have me, he'd at least want me to settle down with a man that would take care of me.

Or is that just what I tell myself?

I feel as if I've shared so much with Tavi, but I don't know if I'll ever be able to tell him the whole truth about Piero. He knows that I escaped, and he knows that Piero aided me in that, but he can't know everything. If he did... As always, I shove the thoughts away.

"Girls, before we go to dinner, can we head to the new store?" Tavi's put me in touch with Santo, who's had me ordering new inventory for the retail store they plan to open after the wedding. My email tells me the handbags I ordered arrived today, and I'd love to look at the stock with my own eyes. We'll be in the same general area, so it makes sense to stop by.

"Santo would definitely prefer if we did," Rosa says. "He's completely obsessed with the new store, isn't he?"

I nod in agreement. The man has a focus that even an atomic bomb couldn't rattle.

It's a little astounding to me how quickly Santo and his men have prepared these buildings for retail. Tavi looked into it, and apparently this is part of my inheritance. The Regazza family didn't advertise the fact that we owned retail property in Boston. Santo found it through a series of investigations. Tavi's given this to me, and Santo will help manage it.

It didn't need as much work as we thought it would, and after a deep cleaning job, a new coat of paint, and some new fixtures Santo had brought in, the shop is looking beautiful.

Something plagues me at the back of my mind though. I remember when Tavi showed it to me. I saw those sunglasses... They looked like Piero's. I bought a pair just like them. He had them when we were in Tuscany, but I was confident that he no longer had them when he was taken from me.

I didn't see Piero killed. I saw his body, though.

How could his sunglasses end up in Boston? It isn't possible.

I was the one that found Piero. I felt his lifeless wrist under my fingers. I put my head on his chest, so still, *too* still, and wept for him, moments before I realized my own safety was compromised and ran to call Angelina.

Rosa unzips a small garment bag. The jarring sound of the zipper drags me back to the present. I focus on the soft unfolding of the bag, revealing Natalia's little flower girl dress. It's a soft, petal green, adorned with hand-sewn flowers. It was once traditional for a bride to wear green the night before her wedding, so we gave a little nod to old Italian tradition with my flower girl.

"Oh, it's gorgeous," Rosa says. "You did good, Elise. She can't wait to toss rose petals at you."

Roses, the Rossi family signature flower, are inked on the forearm of every made man in The Family.

They remind me of Tuscany.

"Glad you like it. I'm just happy we found things in stock."

We've put this entire wedding together in a week. It helps that Tavi didn't give me a budget. Tavi's been busy at work, and I know he's spent a great deal of time trying to get answers about his cousin's death. Santo isn't convinced there was foul play, but Romeo trusts Tavi's intuition. They've been hard at work asking questions but don't have all the answers yet.

So I've been planning the wedding of my dreams.

I sat down with Tosca, Rosa, and Marialena and got everything done in record time. Thankfully, most of the guests were willing to accommodate our quick change in dates, so Tosca's on cloud nine because she still gets the big wedding she's longed for.

"Has your mother seen it yet?" I ask.

"Seen what?" Tosca walks in. The seamstress's eyes widen a bit, maybe because it seems the entire Rossi family wants to congregate in my changing room.

"The flower girl dress for Natalia." Rosa holds it out against her body, and Tosca gasps.

"Gorgeous," she murmurs. And then she looks at me for the first time, and covers her mouth with her hands. "And you, Elise! *Oh, mamma mia. La sposa è bellissima.*"

I flush. "Why thank you."

Marialena stands behind me and stabs her fingers into my hair. "Just wait until I get my hands on her hair and makeup."

"Which you will soon, very soon," I promise her. We decided to forgo the traditional rehearsal dinner in favor of allowing me a night with the girls and Tavi a night with the men, but we are having a small appetizer and cocktail gathering before we go out. Guests have flown in from all over the country and elsewhere. We had a family of ten arrive just this morning from Tuscany. Nonna and Tosca are in their glory.

"You are now my favorite," Tosca says with a teasing wink. She waves her hand and rolls her eyes. "The other girls didn't indulge me like you are."

"Oh, so I missed the memo?" Angelina sits on a stool with the baby and gives her a look of feigned hurt.

"It isn't your fault, of course," Tosca says. "You, I forgive. But my sons…"

Angelina grins. The two of them get along well.

Tosca waves her hand. "None of us knew you were going to marry him like that."

Orlando married Angelina in an arranged marriage ceremony the very day he was released from prison, and Tosca was not privy to that. He came home married, with a wife she'd never met.

That rankles in Italian tradition. It's partly why we've given her free rein with this wedding. This isn't a wedding either of us has chosen. So while we'll make the best of it and enjoy what we can, we aren't hung up on any details.

In the distance, I hear the strings of a violin playing. "What's that sound?" I ask.

"Ah." Tosca smiles. "My cousin Alexandria arrived. Wanted to practice for tomorrow."

"Oh, she's the one that plays the violin?"

"Yes, you'll meet her soon."

The song wails and cries, then changes course and lilts like magic. My heart aches and swells.

"Now, wait until you see," Vittoria says. She's standing by the window, excitedly rocking on the balls of her feet. "Oh, Elise, we are all excited about this. You know I kinda had a slapdash wedding, too."

So I've heard. "Yes."

"So it's fun that I got to play around a bit, too. Romeo told me to spare no expense, so…" She steps away from the window. *"Voilá."*

Still wearing the dress, I sashay my way to the window and look out. I gasp.

"Oh my God. What did you do? Vittoria!"

I feel a little emotional about all of this. I put a hand to my mouth and swallow hard. I've gone from hating being here and being Tavi's prisoner to feeling almost as if… as if I could belong. I don't yet. I don't know anyone, really, but Angelina, but they've welcomed me with such open arms I can't help but hope.

Behind The Castle lies a beach, typically cold in the winter on the North Shore of Boston but warmer now that we're heading further into a light and airy New England spring.

Along the beach, in a half-moon semi-circle, white chairs are arranged so prettily they look as if they were set with the cast of a magic wand. Stunning white flower arrangements with elegant petal green accents sit at the end of every row, and at the very head sits an elevated platform. An arched trellis beckons us, adorned with red roses.

Large vases filled with delicate, lacy flowers give the whole ensemble a whimsical look.

Tomorrow. There. Tomorrow, I'll walk down that aisle and say *I do.*

 Sudden panic swoops in my belly, and I don't know how to process all of this. It looks so gorgeous, even though this isn't the marriage of two people who've fallen in love.

Nothing is ever as it should be here.

I don't feel like a bride about to be married. I feel like we're having a party and I'm wearing a fancy dress. That tomorrow, I'll take the next step and do what I must, because it's the only choice I have.

A part of me longs to see Tavi. I want to feel his solid, immovable presence beside me. I want to feel his hot, warm skin next to mine. I want to hear his rock-solid voice and look into the depths of those strong eyes of his that give me the assurance of his safety and protection.

It was the very thing I wanted when Piero was ripped from me.

I press my forehead against the windowpane and allow the cool glass to still my pounding heart.

"Hey, guys," Angelina says softly behind me. "Give us a minute?"

I've never been so grateful for my best friend.

When the door closes behind them, I feel Angelina's hand on my shoulder.

"Hey," she says in a soft voice. "You okay?"

I nod, and swallow the lump in my throat. "Just pre-wedding jitters. I'd say cold feet, but that's so cliché."

"And implies you made a choice in this," Angelina says quietly.

It's funny sometimes how a bestie can put into words exactly what's bothering you.

"Yeah," I whisper.

She sits on a little stool beside me. The baby sleeps peacefully over her shoulder.

"Look at you," I whisper. "I'm so proud of you."

"Proud? Of me?" She tips her head to the side curiously. "Why? And don't you dare change this subject."

"I'm not," I insist. "I promise, I'm not. It's just that you did this for me. And you didn't make lemonade from lemons, Angelina. You built a goddamn lemonade *franchise*."

She grins at me, rocking side to side with Nicolo, and shrugs. "Honey, it wasn't like that. Yeah, I didn't plan this, and Orlando knows it." She shrugs. "But sometimes, two people find each other. Like two grains of sand on a beach. It's impossible, right? The odds. But they find in the end that it isn't impossible at all because somehow, some way... maybe they were cut from the same rock. Right?"

I shrug. "I think I'd need a better understanding of geology to answer that accurately."

I laugh when she sticks her tongue out at me. "It's just that... we make things so complicated, I think. Sometimes, we overthink the most obvious things, don't we?"

I sit on a stool beside her. Or, more accurately, *flounce*, as a billow of fabric poofs then settles all around me like a cloud.

"Like how?"

"Like we think marriage is this perfect *match,* and that if we don't find the perfect match, we should scratch it all and start again."

I'm thinking of her father and his many wives and affairs. Vittoria and Romeo, brought together despite all odds, Angelina and Orlando, thrown together in the wildest of circumstances.

"But I don't think that's how it is, no..." her voice trails off. "I mean, I believe in soul mates and all that. But sometimes you just start with... well, a spark, right?" She shrugs. "And it's up to you to kindle the flame. To keep it going. To make it work."

I think this over. "I don't know," I say softly. "I've never known a happily married couple. Until... well, until the Rossi family."

"Well, that's just it, babe. Isn't it? I mean, you met Orlando. And did he check off those boxes on my list in the journal we wrote together?"

I laugh, remembering the romantic notions we had and silly lists we wrote to each other in journals we shared as teens.

"Some, yes, but definitely not all."

"And yet here we are," she says softly. "Orlando loves me, Elise. He truly does. Just like... well, in a sense, just like you did. You saved my life once, and I'll never forget it."

Her eyes fill with tears. The baby stirs, and she holds him closer, either to soothe him or herself, I don't know.

"I did," I whisper. "And I'd do it again." It was my proudest moment.

I remember that night so vividly. We were only teens, two girls who were forced into circumstances neither of us had ever imagined. Whereas my life was a carefully-orchestrated drama complete with acts, stages, and a script to follow, hers was a reckless chasm with no boundaries or rules. Complete opposites, really.

And one night we ventured out alone. Her, under the premise of spending the night with me and me, having bribed Piero to give me one little taste of freedom. We drank stolen nips of peach schnapps and thought a little swim in the quarry, a known teen hideout in Quincy, would do us a little good.

Honestly, it did. A night apart from the controlling oppression of my family and total apathy of hers. We were talking about our plans for the future, our hopes and dreams and fears. We swam way too deep, in over our heads, but craved the exhilaration and danger and freedom.

"You turned too quickly," I whisper, reliving that night like I have, over and over and over again. Both of us could've endangered our lives in so many ways —between the friends her father's kept and the dangers that lurked at my door—but no, we were two stupid teens who made a reckless choice. "I can still see the way you hit your head on the steel beam."

I didn't know humans could sink like lead, under the right circumstances. I remember pulling her up to breathe, swimming with her tucked under my arm, dragging her onto the pine-needled ground and performing CPR.

"Was the first time I ever kissed a girl, and don't even remember it," Angelina says with a smile.

I jokingly smack her arm.

She sobers. "I would've died that night if not for you."

I sigh. "You gave up everything for me because I saved your life. And it was my fault that you almost lost it. I hardly think we're playing quid pro quo here."

"Babe," she says softly. "Don't look at what I gave up. Look at what I *gained*."

She kisses the fuzzy top of her baby's head and twirls the diamond wedding band on her finger. "I have a family now. A real *family*. A husband who adores me. And you, my best friend, will become my sister." Her eyes shine.

"I know," I whisper. "And all because I saved your life, because you were a dumb teen who didn't know better than to swim out by the quarry drunk and alone?"

"Did you, now? Both of you? Went to the quarry and got drunk?"

I hear Tavi's deep voice and immediately throw my hands over my gown to block him from seeing me.
  The door to the room creaks open, but I'm still hidden behind it on the other side.

"Ottavio Rossi, don't you *dare*! I'm in my wedding dress!"

Angelina leaps to her feet and holds the baby with one hand and tries to shove me behind her with the other.

Tavi sighs heavily but doesn't walk in any further. "I bought the dress. Can't I see it?" Oh that voice. I'm ready to hand over my panties and he's only teasing me from the doorway.

"Not *now*. Tomorrow! Oh my God, don't you make me call Nonna and your Mama on you!"

"Oof. Playing hardball, baby. Don't tell me you believe those stupid superstitions?"

"Of course I do!"

I could write a book about Italian wedding traditions. We've got enough going against us, the last thing we need to do is test the anger of the gods.

Rain on the day of the wedding means good luck. He's not supposed to see me *or* the dress before the ceremony, we're not supposed to buy our wedding rings at the same time, and we cannot arrive in the same manner or time to the wedding.

"Oh for the love of–"

Angelina comes to my aid. "I'm her matron of honor, Mr. Rossi, and I will make sure you do not break those traditions if it kills me!"

"Fine," Tavi says in a tight voice through the door. "I'll leave, under one condition."

"Yes?" I say.

"You don't *ever* call me Mr. Rossi again, Angelina!"

She grins at me and winks. She isn't his, so she gets a little bit more freedom than I do. I wink back.

"Elise?"

"Yes?" I walk to the door and stand on the other side of it, my head pressed against the wall. I like the sound of his voice.

"Be careful tonight, baby. I'll be checking on you. And if anything threatens or scares you at all, fuck traditions, I'm coming. You get me?"

From the corner of my eye, I see Angelina give me a smug smile.

"Yes," I say softly. "I get you." Not just in this, but I

like to think in more ways than one. At least I've begun to understand this man. Whereas others might feel they know their partner when they're about to walk down the aisle, I feel like it's something he and I have just begun.

So we do things a little backwards here.

"I hear you're going to the store?" Tavi asks. "Before dinner?"

"Mhm. Are you just making small talk at this point?"

He sighs. "Maybe." Another pause. "I miss you."

I reach my hand to the door and place it palm down. "Put your hand on the door. My hand's palm-down on the other side."

"Done."

I close my eyes and imagine I can feel his hand through the door. Tomorrow, when we see each other, we'll be joined together. It feels symbolic.

"Be good." His parting words.

Angelina's making gagging motions when I turn to see her. I roll my eyes and grin.

Tomorrow, I won't marry the man I love.

I'll marry the man I will learn *how* to love.

It's a distinction, but one that fills me with hope.

I love you, I whisper to myself, as I get ready to go into town. Fake it 'til you make it, right?

I love you, I think as I do my makeup and step into the killer heels Rosa got me. *I love you,* I think, as I take the limo into town and laugh with the girls while we share flutes of sparkling champagne. I don't love him yet. I need time. But there's a little spark of something there, a little bud that's been planted deep in the earth, and with enough time and attention, water and sun... it could grow into something more.

CHAPTER 11

Tavi

Goddamn tradition.

Can't see her. Can't touch her. Gotta keep my hands off her.

I don't put as much stock into these damn traditions as my family does, but I go along with it for the hell of it.

Italians.

No one says I can't fucking *call* her, though. "Hello, beautiful."

"Ohhh. Hello. *Tavi,* are you supposed to be calling me?"

"There is literally nothing in any of the rule books about *talking* before the wedding."

"It feels wrong, though."

My heart jumps. I keep my voice calm. "What does?"

"Talking to you before the wedding."

I release an audible sigh. "Oh, right."

"Tavi, what did you think I meant?"

I shrug, even though she can't see me, and lean back in the plush leather seat of the chair in my private room. "I thought you meant... well, all of it."

"No," she says softly. "No, not at all. Honestly... well, if there's anything that feels *right,* it's... it's us." I don't miss the way her voice cracks at the end.

I agree.

"Good. You ready, babe?"

I put the call on speaker. She sighs and doesn't answer at first. I stand in front of the mirror and adjust my tie.

"Elise."

"Yes?" she says, and her voice is a little wobbly.

"Fuck tradition, babe. I can come to you right now. I don't like being apart from you, and I–"

"Want to keep me under your thumb. I get it."

I blink in surprise at the tone of her voice. She isn't sad, but resigned.

"I want to keep you *safe*," I amend. I glance down at my phone on a stand in front of me, with the little flashing *dot*. She's so close to me.

"Right," she says softly. "I once—that's all any of them ever wanted, or so they said. My father." Her voice trembles. "My—well, everyone. Wanted to keep me safe."

I sink into an armchair and check the time. Romeo will be here in an hour. We're heading into town. She's more important, though. *This* is more important.

"Because you matter, baby." I close my eyes against the rush of heat that floods me. I open my mouth but can't speak the thoughts and words that want to choke me.

"See, Tavi? That's just it, isn't it?" Her voice rises, strengthening, and I can see her. Standing tall, with her shoulders back. Those beautiful amber eyes of hers alight with fire, her slender, lovely hands fisted by her sides. "I matter because I'm a commodity. *I* never mattered, did I? Do I?"

I watch the little dot on my phone move.

I open my mouth and start to speak, but she cuts me off. "No. No, please. Let me talk."

I wish she was next to me. I nod. "Go on." I can give her this at least.

"I mattered as collateral to my family, Ottavio. I got perfect grades. I kept my body in perfect shape. I fear... I fear being anything less than exceptional. I wore perfect clothing and perfect shoes. I did everything right, and I... I'm drawn to you because of all of this, this... baggage."

I feel my brows pucker. "What do you mean?"

"You're successful and powerful and handsome. You could've gone to *Harvard*. You're the whole package, you know?"

I shrug. Whatever. I don't want to detract from what she needs to say, though, so I only encourage her to go on. "Okay, I see what you mean, yeah."

"And I'm afraid that... that our relationship will be just... perfect, but that you'll always be... well, emotionally distant."

I pinch the bridge of my nose. Goddamn if she hasn't nailed my very own fears with striking precision.

"Touché, baby. Touché," I whisper. "Give me a minute."

I send Romeo a quick text. *I won't be going tonight. Wine and dine 'em, bro. I'm needed elsewhere*

His text comes back immediately.

Romeo: Where?

I take in a deep breath and let it out slowly.

My bride.

Romeo: Go. I've got this.

"Elise?"

"Yes?" I walk to my door and open it.

"Get in here."

She's sitting right outside my door and gives me a sheepish smile. I don't wait for her to come to me. I go to her.

I bend, lift her in my arms, and carry her into my room. I kick the door closed behind me.

"This is bad luck," she whispers. "We don't need bad luck, Tavi."

"Fuck bad luck. I don't believe in good luck or bad luck, baby. I believe we dig our own graves or make our own fortunes."

I hold her to me.

"Do you?" she whispers.

"Yeah, Elise." I kiss her soft pink cheek. "So let's make ours. Me and you. It doesn't matter who we were. It doesn't matter where we've been. It's just the two of us, together now."

She closes her eyes and I kiss each eyelid. Her lashes flutter on my lips. I slide my hand down the small of her back and hold her to me.

"Now what the fuck are you wearing?"

"What, this thing?" she says with a fetching giggle. When she sticks her tongue out at me, I give her a playful smack.

"Yeah, this thing." My voice is a low growl. The dress looks like it's fashioned with gauze, all filmy

174

and lacy and feminine. The soft pink neckline dances low across her breasts, and the high waist's cinched tight with small, white daisies. The back's cut so low I can see the little dimple above her ass, and the hem hits high mid-thigh.

"Ottavio Rossi," she says warningly as I nibble her earlobe.

"What?" My hand ghosts across her back, and she shivers adorably.

"You should wait until the wedding." She doesn't put much emphasis behind her words. I'm not convinced she really wants me to stop.

I lay her back on my arm and kiss my way along her neck. "Now why would I do that?"

Her heart's beating faster. I can see it when she swallows, the delicate skin on her neck fluctuating with emotion.

"Because it's… it's more special that way."

I exhale a belabored sigh. "Fine," I tell her with a sigh. "*Fine.*"

Laughter rings out downstairs.

"Those your girls?"

She nods and reaches for my hand, as she nestles in the crook of my arm. I look curiously at her, but she doesn't meet my eyes. "I don't want to go with them. I told them to go without me."

My own heart quickens. My voice is a little dry and husky when I respond, "Yeah?"

"Yeah," she breathes.

I don't know if it's the actual wedding she's afraid of, or if she fears what she's already voiced, a deeper, more abiding loss, fear about what comes next.

Will we exorcise each other's demons that we wrestle or will they destroy us?

"No sex until we take our vows, Tavi?" I can tell she wants to phrase it as a command, but she knows better than to do that.

I nod reluctantly and shift her on my lap. "Fine. No sex until we take our vows." I lift her to her feet. "No more putting your ass in my crotch then."

I love the way she smiles.

"I told Romeo, too," I say, shoving my hands in my pockets. I have no regrets.

"Told him what?"

"To go on without me."

Her eyes go soft and she hooks one little pinkie finger in mine. "Ah. Thank you. Did he give you shit about it?"

"Nah."

The door downstairs opens and closes, and for one moment, the laughter's even louder and voices rise. Our cousins have come to join us. Then all voices hush, and Romeo's deep, low register commands everyone's attention. He says something that makes everyone laugh, then the door opens again and the voices recede.

"Romeo's a good guy, isn't he?"

"Eh," I say with a grimace. "He's good to The Family, no doubt. Anyone in The Family knows he'll stop at nothing to protect them. He's loyal."

She nods. "Yes, of course. And I've seen the way he looks at Vittoria." Her eyes have grown a little wistful. I watch as she bites her lip and twirls a delicate thread of gold at her neck, as if she's polishing silver.

I nod. He adores her. He wants a baby, I know it, but until then, their nuclear family of two delights in each other.

"But I wouldn't call any of us good, Elise. I'm surprised lightning doesn't strike the goddamn church when we're in it."

When she waves her hand, her engagement ring glitters along with her eyes. "Well, don't flatter yourself, sir. I'm not so sure your sins are any worse than any of the others that darken the doors of that church."

I feel my lips turn upward in a smile. I love how she takes everything in stride.

I thread my hand along her back and open the door. Doors slam, wheels crunch on gravel, and voices fade. I hear her breathe in relief.

"You okay?" I ask. A little wisp of hair curls on her forehead. I bend and kiss it. "You remind me of an old movie star."

"Old?" she asks, her head tipped to the side. "Whatever do you mean?"

"That," I say, kissing the opposite side of her forehead. I tap the little freckles on her nose with my index finger. "The way you talk. The way you hold yourself, all graceful and coquettish. It's charming. You'd grace a pin-up with perfection."

I can see her now, her hair wrapped in a winsome little bandana, tied in a bow at the nape of her neck.

"I have a secret to tell you," she whispers, before biting her lip.

Right. As if she could have any secrets from me. Still, I play along.

"Yeah? You hiding something from me, baby?"

I love her little laugh. It's adorable. I lean in so she can whisper in my ear.

"I wear glasses sometimes."

I shake my head from side to side in mock sternness. "That's it. Wedding off."

"Ha! You used to wear glasses!"

"I did. And I hate to break it to you, but I know everything about you. So I've known for a while you wear glasses."

"Can I see yours?" she asks shyly. "I want to see you wearing them."

That makes me smile. "Sure. And I'll fuck you wearing nothing but those glasses, Elise."

I love making her blush.

We walk downstairs to find the front part of the house uncharacteristically vacant. Despite the two of us not attending our events tonight, my family will not turn down the chance at a party, so all have left

Staff still remains in small groups, some on the lawn tending to the landscaping to prepare, and I imagine we've got many in the kitchen preparing for tomorrow. For the first time since my entire family went to Tuscany several years ago, there will be no dinner in the dining room tonight.

"Wow," Elise says.

"Weird, isn't it?"

"So weird."

And then I get an idea. We've had many formal dinners and gatherings, and tomorrow, we'll have white-glove waitstaff, bubbling champagne, and a five-course meal. Tonight, I want something more casual. Something to emphasize that it's just the two of us.

It's an unusually warm day here. Even though a New England spring is predictable, it's still a crap shoot. We've had both blizzards and heat waves.

Today, however, the sun beams down like a summer day. Even the waves on the beach are tamer than usual.

"Tavi," Elise says in a voice tinged with amusement. "You've got something up your sleeve."

I shrug. "And what if I do?"

I lead her past the reception room, past the coat room where we had our most recent stand-off. Past all the other formal rooms that take us to the back of the house to the more secret rooms—the library, war room, offices, the secret wine room.

At the entrance to the dungeon, she shivers. She spent time down there, once.

A lifetime ago.

I take her all the way to the walk-in pantry beside the kitchen. I find one of the reusable zipper freezer bags hanging on a hook inside the pantry door.

"Oh, wow," she breathes. "I haven't been this far along the tour yet. This is one *epic* pantry!" She runs her fingers along boxes of pasta and strings of garlic, then lovingly touches large, bulbous bottles of golden-green olive oil.

"You haven't cooked for me since we were in Tuscany," I admonish. "We'll have to fix that. For now, help me pack." I unzip the bag and slide a small bag of rustic crackers inside.

"A picnic?" she asks, her eyes as bright as a child's on Christmas Day. "Oh, I *love* a picnic."

"You love so many things," I say. "And I love that about *you*."

Love, love, love, a word we throw around so casually sometimes. A word I'll take with me tomorrow, and the day after that, and the day after that…

I once told myself that it didn't matter what I've done. Our past is in the past. If I can forgive what she's done to my family, maybe she can forgive what I've done.

I'll spend the rest of my life making it up to her.

"I've got it," she says excitedly. "Let me play around in the fridge a bit?" She glances around the doorway and peeks in. "Looks like they're using the stove but the center island's vacant. I won't be in anybody's way."

"Baby, you belong here as much as anyone else does. You're not in anybody's way."

I don't expect the way her eyes brighten, or the way her lips turn upward in a smile. "Thank you for that." She draws in a breath then cracks her knuckles. "They'll be gone for hours, won't they?"

I nod. "Hours, babe."

I take a seat on one of the stools and watch my future bride work her magic.

CHAPTER 12

Elise

We sit by the stone wall of The Castle that overlooks the ocean and feast on *everything*.

I found a loaf of French bread and made little sandwiches with thick slices of turkey breast, gouda, and avocado. I wrapped them in foil and made a small salad with greens and bottled dressing I nestled into a little mason jar, then sliced ripe strawberries for dessert. I squeal with delight when Tavi pulls out foil-wrapped chocolates he brought home from Italy. We eat them together while looking out over the sunset.

When our bellies are full, we sit back and look out over the water. The sun is lower in the sky, and the balmy weather's grown only a little colder. Still, I shiver when a wind kicks up over the water.

The waves crash on the shore in front of us, then drag right back out to sea again. The salt air tingles my nose.

"Tavi."

"Yeah, baby?"

"Why don't we move to Tuscany?" I ask, imagining my favorite place on the other side of that water. "Have you ever thought of that?"

Tavi looks out over the water. Thoughtful. Meditative. "Not sure that would work. I'm needed here. Doesn't mean it can't hurt to ask, though. See what Romeo thinks. You know I love Tuscany, too."

I'm not so sure I want to be apart from Angelina, either. And I have to reluctantly admit, I like his family, too. "I know what you mean. But maybe for part of the year? Like snowbirds going to Florida, you and I could spread our wings and fly to Tuscany." I close my eyes and imagine the warm kiss of wind on my cheeks, and the vibrant green of the Tuscan landscape around us. Though Tavi's well-loved in his family, he came alive in Tuscany.

"And you've got the business here, too," he reminds me with a serious nod.

"Eh." I shrug. "I could make inventory purchases remotely."

He nods. "You could."

We sit silently for long minutes, and the tide begins to go out to sea.

"Elise, I've made a decision."

"Yeah? You'll let me name our children Gwendolyn or Lancelot after all?"

"Uh, *no.*"

"Dammit. Then what?"

"It's time to take out that tracker."

"Oh. *Oh.*"

The decision feels monumental. I tell myself that it was insane of him to even put this in, but Ottavio Rossi doesn't play by the nice guy rules. "Uh. So. How does that get done?"

"I brought what we need."

I blink in surprise. I want this out, but the prospect of having it removed scares me.

Still, I don't want to go to the altar tomorrow with this in me. It feels like a chain.

"I can take it out, baby," he says softly. "I can take it out right now."

My heart beats a little faster. "Will it hurt?"

He shrugs. "Little bit. Could use a little something to numb the area…"

Then I remember, this pretty little dress is functional. It has pockets, and I just happen to have contraband tucked into one of them.

I take out the joint Marialena gave me and show it to him.

"Would this help?"

"Where'd you get that?"

"Do I have to tell you?" I wince. I don't wanna rat his sister out.

He growls, but doesn't make me tell him. He knows Santo and Rosa smoke, and probably figures Marialena does, too.

"I don't like messing with my head," he protests.

"I know," I respond, twirling it in my fingers. "It's the control thing, isn't it?"

"Mmm."

"Maybe sometimes it's good to let go of a little control. Gets tiring, doesn't it, Tavi?"

It's exactly what he'll be doing when he takes this out of my arm.

He doesn't respond for a minute. The waves crashing below us have an almost lulling effect. I sigh.

"Give it to me, Elise."

I half expect him to toss it out to the waves below, but he doesn't. Instead, he reaches into his pocket and pulls out a lighter. The flame flares in the darkness and soon, the sweet, acrid smell fills the air around us.

"Just a little," he says, handing it to me. "When I tell you to stop, stop."

He holds the end of the lit joint out to me but keeps it still between his fingers. I take a slow drag, the smoke filling my lungs, then release it, letting it dissipate around me. I nestle back against him and he takes it back. Behind me, a little flare of light tells me he took a drag of his own.

We go on like that for silent minutes.

"Letting go?" I ask. The lines of the world around me fade a little, as if painted by watercolor, and the tension I felt in my chest begins to soften. I'm feeling oddly sentimental. I smile to myself.

"Yeah, baby," he says. His voice sounds softer than it was before. "Sometimes maybe it is good to let go of a little control. A little, anyway." I look over at him, surprised to find the joint to his lips is hot as fuck. "So to take that tracker out, I have to cut you. But it's a tiny incision. And where it is, no one will even see the mark when you wear the wedding dress."

I sit up straighter and hold my arm out to him. "Do it. Please?"

Frowning, he holds my gaze, then puts the lit end of the joint out on the ground. "I trust you, baby. I'll keep you safe without that damn thing in you. You get me?"

"I do." I nod.

"But you will never go out without my permission."

186

"Of course," I agree. I'll agree to anything to get this out. I will not leave him, no way. After all I've been through, running again wouldn't make sense at all.

"You'll always have a man on you *at all times*. Am I clear?"

I give him what he wants. I nod. "Yes, sir. Of course."

"And if you ever leave without my permission, if anyone ever hurt you—"

"You'd punish me and kill them. Got it," I finish matter-of-factly.

He grunts, draws in a breath, then jerks his chin to the little package of hand sanitizing wipes I packed for our picnic. I hand him one.

I shake when he washes the spot on my arm with the tracker, a tiny spot on my underarm that will be hidden when I put my arm back down.

"Lay back, baby," he whispers.

I do. I close my eyes.

"Relax."

I'm as relaxed as I've been in ages. My heartbeat slows, my breathing's regulated. I sync my breaths with the waves on shore.

I feel him pinch where it is and open one eye to see him with something that looks like a scalpel. I squeeze my eyes tight again.

There's only a brief pinch of pain, then the cool of

the wipe a second time, and when I open my eyes again he's gently placing a bandage on my skin.

"That's it?"

He nods. "That's it, baby."

"Jesus. If I knew it was that easy—"

"Do not finish that sentence."

I smile at him. "Thank you." I feel freer somehow. Unencumbered. Ready to take this next step with him. The area he cut feels numb and stings a little, but everything's muted right now.

I nestle into him, my back to his front, his arms around me. I love it here. So safe, and warm, and protected.

We weren't meant to be comfortable, though. If I want to take this next step with him, I know what I have to do.

Now.

Now's the time.

Tomorrow, I'm taking vows with him, and I don't want to taint those vows with anything that could come between us.

"Tavi?"

"Mmm?"

"I want to talk to you about something, but I... I don't want to. I'm afraid that you'll think less of me."

Gently, he strokes the top of my hand with the pad of his thumb. "Elise, do you have any idea the things that I've done?"

Actually, I do. I know them well. "Of course."

"Then you should know there's nothing you could tell me that would surprise me."

I nod, still fixated on the darkening waves out at sea. The sun sinks even lower, and bright lights on the beach spring on, illuminating a boardwalk far below us.

I draw in a breath and let it out slowly. I'm not exactly sure why it's so important for him to know. Or maybe it's important for me to say it?

"I was in love once," I whisper. And for some unknown reason that I can't quite explain, I follow this up with, "I'm sorry."

I'm sorry?

Am I?

He's grown still. I'm distinctly aware of the hard planes of muscle behind me.

"What's in the past can stay in the past, Elise. Can we make a pact? Right now. Between the two of us. We'll forgive what happened in the past and put it behind us. Tomorrow, we start over."

I swallow, trying to gather courage, but surprised at the well of emotions that threaten to choke me. I expected him to be surprised, or maybe angry, but sympathetic... there's so much I don't know about my soon-to-be husband. Every day brings something new. I'm eager to know more.

"I… I loved Piero, Tavi." I close my eyes and steady my breath. That was harder to say than I thought.

"Piero?"

His tone sounds a bit… colder.

"He was my bodyguard."

Behind me, Tavi sits up straighter. Gently but firmly, he turns me to face him. All traces of humor have fled when he reaches for my chin.

Did I make a mistake?

"The man who's dead?" he asks. But he doesn't seem surprised.

Dead.

The word echoes in my mind like the bang of a gavel.

I can only nod.

There's no surprise in his eyes, and it strikes me as a little odd. Did he suspect this?

Whatever compassion I once imagined in Tavi's eyes is gone. Before me now sits Ottavio Rossi, Underboss to the notorious Rossi family. The man who kept me prisoner and demanded my obedience.

"Did he ever hurt you?" Tavi asks.

I shake my head. "Never. He protected me."

"You were only a child, Elise…"

Is he angry at my dead lover? It makes sense, though, when I think about it. Tavi's so jealous of me I wore a chip in my arm so he didn't lose sight of me. Of course he's hung up on the concept of an ex-lover.

"You and I both know we gave up childhood long before we ever should have, Tavi. It's been a while since I've been a child."

He nods, still brooding, then pulls me to him. "I knew you suffered something terrible. I could tell that you'd been hurt, too. Like me."

I'm so grateful he's understanding. He turns me to face outward again, nestled back up against him.

"I'm sorry, Elise. I'm sorry." I'm not sure what he's apologizing for. Maybe all of it. "I need you to forgive me for the shit *I've* done."

I nod, feeling oddly sentimental, like all my emotions have magnified but I can take it somehow. I feel relieved, too, to have that out in the open.

"And how about you?" I ask. "Have you ever been in love?"

His arms tighten around me even more. "Not until… well, not until now."

I turn to face him. Is he saying what I think he is? When my eyes meet his, he cups my face between his hands, bends, and kisses me. It's a gentle, almost chaste kiss.

"I was never in love, but I was engaged to be married before you."

I blink in surprise. "Were you?"

I suppose it's good that we're purging this before our wedding. It had to be said. But I don't like the thought of him with another woman, not at all.

Is that how he feels, knowing I was in love with another man?

I shiver when a brisk breeze chills me. He slides off his jacket and nestles it over my shoulders.

"I never met her," he says, his voice almost cold.

"What happened to her?"

He releases a breath before he answers. He plays with my fingers, gently stroking them, almost thoughtfully.

"She killed herself."

A slash of pain hits my chest and my throat gets tight. Suicide is one of life's greatest tragedies.

"Tavi, *no*."

Oh, how awful. I can't even imagine.

"I didn't know her," he says, but you don't walk away unscathed from even a peripheral*- knowledge of such a thing. "But it got in my head, you know?"

I nod. I do know. Oh, God, do I know.

"Made me think I had to *be* someone unbearable. If the thought of marrying me was something that drove someone to kill themselves... well it was almost like a self-fulfilling prophecy."

How sad. How achingly sad. I nod, encouraging him to continue.

"For a long time, seeing Orlando with Angelina made me jealous. So jealous. I have to admit, I was pretty mean to her when I first met her."

I laugh a little. "Yeah, she wasn't a big fan of any of you guys at first."

"We have that effect on people."

I smile sadly. "I'm sorry, Tavi. That's terrible, though."

"Yeah. I really got down for a while. Thought, you know, fuck this. I'll never really have anything close with a woman. And what's the point? Even if I did, they'd just leave me, you know?"

"Wow," I say, shaking my head. "I really need to get you high more often."

"Oh yeah?" he asks, tickling me a little. I squeal and writhe to get away.

"*Oh* yeah. I like this Ottavio."

"Which one?" he asks. We're sitting on a blanket with soft moss beneath us. A warm breeze ruffles my hair when he lays me on my back and pins me down. His dark blue eyes dance at me, challenging.

"The one who speaks about real things," I whisper. "The one who makes himself vulnerable enough to trust me."

Slowly, he shakes his head. His thumb presses against my wrist, as if checking the speed of my pulse. It's such an Ottavio Rossi gesture—possessive and physical, but nothing sweet about it.

"I told you," he whispers. "Don't ever say I didn't tell you, Elise."

My heart beats rapidly. "Tell me what?"

He bends and brushes his lips to my cheek. "That we aren't good men."

If he knew what I've seen, what I've grown up with, he'd understand we have very different definitions of what it means to be good.

He arranges me so that I'm lying on the blanket and he's up on an elbow beside me.

"I vow to love you, Elise." And I don't know if it's because I'm high, or relieved from telling him the truth, or excited about the wedding, but the fears I had seem to evaporate.

We could have this, all of this. Devotion. Commitment. Family. *Love.*

"And I vow to love you," I say back.

With a tenderness I didn't know he was capable of, he traces a fingertip over my face, my eyebrows, my eyelids, the curve of my nose and my lips, as if memorizing me.

"There," he whispers. "We said our vows."

I don't protest when he shimmies my dress up my thighs, or when he threads his fingers in my panties and drags them down my legs. "*Now* I get to make love to you."

CHAPTER 13

Tavi

IT SHOULD BE A BEAUTIFUL DAY. And by all accounts and reason, it is. The sun shines. My family surrounds us with love and support, everything a guy could want.

And my bride... God, my bride looks as if she stepped out of a bridal magazine, so beautiful it makes my heart ache.

The wait, the struggle, all of it... worth it. And that dress was worth every damn penny.

We take our vows under a flower-strung archway overlooking the ocean, Orlando and Angelina by our sides.

I mean every word of the vows I say to her, and I can see the sincerity in her eyes when she takes her vows as well.

"You may kiss the bride." Father Richard pronounces us husband and wife amidst cheers, confetti, and sobs from Mama and Nonna. Cameras flash, my brothers slap my back and kiss my bride, and we line up for pictures Mama will have framed to within an inch of their lives.

Last night, we shared something between us, something that I won't ever forget. Truth that had to be let out.

But she doesn't know the whole truth. And it's up to me to tell her.

I feel like a cheat. Like I've conned her into marrying only a shadow of me, and when she sees me in full light...

I couldn't do it last night. I couldn't bring myself to tell her that the man she once loved is dead because of me. And part of the reason I can't tell her is because I don't regret what I did. I can't apologize for what I did, because I know that if I had it to do over again, I wouldn't do anything differently.

He loved a woman that didn't belong to him. He touched a woman that wasn't his. In the laws of our world, that merits swift and severe punishment. Some might argue his death was a mercy.

I'd expect the same if I'd ever crossed a line—no, *lines*—like that.

But would Elise see it that way?

I bring myself back to the reason for our marriage, the conviction that's driven me from the beginning, and I know... she'll never forgive me when I tell her the truth.

I tell myself we didn't marry for love. We married out of duty, and I'm determined to keep my vows.

I promised her an oath of fidelity, and I *always* keep my promises.

Our day is perfect, and by God, I'll give her this day.

"Oh my *God*," Marialena says, when they wheel out the wedding cake. "Elise!" She smacks Elise's arm. "Did you pick out that cake?"

Elise turns to see the cake I had made for the occasion, and she gets that look that makes me melt, almost childlike in wonder. "Ooooh. Tavi!" She grabs my arm, pulling me closer to her. "Is that a cream cake I spy?"

I nod. "Of course."

I had my bakers fashion an Italian cream wedding cake, laced with vanilla, coconut and pecans, frosted with generous mounds of whipped cream frosting, and decorated with delicate, petal-green spun sugar in the shape of flower petals with sugared raspberries for contrast.

"It's too pretty to eat," Rosa says, snapping a picture.

Natalia, adorable in her little flower girl dress, shakes her head. "Ah ah, Mama. There's no such thing as a cake too pretty to eat."

Orlando elbows his way up to the front. "Dude, I got scammed out of having a wedding cake like that. Hook a brother up, will you?"

"Already done." I signal to the waitstaff. The double doors to the outdoor pavilion where our guests are gathered open, and the staff brings in trays and trays of pastries and cakes.

"I don't want any Rossi brother beatdowns on my goddamn wedding day," I tell Orlando. "I'm prepared."

I've ordered chocolate mousse cake for the "groom's cake," a flower girl vanilla Chantilly cream, and platters of every pastry we sell.

"*Mamma mia,*" Elise says with a grin. "I need a nice, tall glass of milk for my after-school snack."

Five minutes later, we're sitting down to feast, and Nonna brings Elise a glass of milk, bends, and kisses her cheek. Elise squeals and claps her hands.

God, I might love this woman. She's tough as nails and simply beautiful, but the way she delights in the ordinary makes her exquisite.

"You're fuckin' adorable," I whisper in her ear. "But did you eat your dinner? No dessert without dinner first, young lady."

I wag my finger at her. She flushes a little pink. "And what if I didn't, Daddy?"

Aw, fuck. I like *that*.

I whisper in her ear what happens to little girls who don't do as they're told, and she squirms adorably beside me. The music plays on.

A few yards in front of us I see Santo take a call. He turns quickly toward the house and marches away. A second later, I see Romeo reach for his phone, and he signals for Orlando and Mario.

Goddammit.

"Something's going on," Elise says to me quietly, while Mama laughs to my right, and waitstaff refill coffee cups.

I love that we're on the same wavelength. It makes things… simpler.

Still. I can't help but sigh.

"Yeah. Never a dull motherfuckin' moment, is there?"

She laces her fingers through mine and squeezes. My heart squeezes in unison.

Elise gets me. She gets our life.

"Any idea what it is?" she asks quietly. "Any little thread or inkling of what travesty or beatdown or lucrative deal or *whatever* it is now?"

She makes me smile even as I shake my head. "Nope. You?"

"Well, it was kind of weird. I saw Mario arguing with Natalia's nanny. Do they know each other?"

I don't know if they know each other but I'm going to find out. "No idea. Arguing about what?"

She shakes her head. "I don't know, because Maria-alena was arguing with *her* bodyguard, and then Santo and Rosa got in on the mix."

Jesus. What the hell is going on? "Everyone seems fine now." She takes a sip of wine and nestles it back on the table.

"Maybe they're playing nice because it's our wedding day. We're Italian. We argue for sport."

Her lips twitch. "Didn't stop Mario and Santo from practically knocking each other out for the last crostini."

"Well, that's nothing unusual, though. How'd they solve it?"

"Romeo literally cracked their heads together then ate it himself."

I chuckle to myself, reach over, and drink the rest of her wine.

"Hey!"

But before I can respond, Romeo enters the back. He motions for security. They walk to him rapidly as the party goes on.

I get to my feet. I look to Elise. "I'm sorry, baby."

"Don't be," she says, shaking her head. "Please, go find out. I want to know as much as you do." I give her a parting kiss and head to Romeo.

"Rome."

Romeo looks at me and sighs.

"It's your wedding day, Tav."

I shrug. We all know that all good things come to an end. And in our lives, that's often sooner than later.

"Yeah, I know, but I don't want you guys pussy-footin' around me. What's going on? Don't keep me in the dark, brother."

"You won't believe this," he says, running a hand through his hair. He looks away, as if he doesn't want to tell me what's bothering him. It's unnerving.

"Romeo."

His gaze swings back to me. He's not usually one to skirt an issue but dives straight in. "Elise's mother's here."

I blink in surprise. I expected him to say pretty much anything but that.

"Her… mother?" That's the last thing I expected. "Just showed up," I say, feeling my anger rise. "No contact, no phone call, no goddamn email?"

Romeo nods with a scowl. "Exactly. And she's… well, let's just say she's no Elise."

"Fuck. Where is she?"

"Orlando and Mario have her in the Great Hall. She's insisting on coming in here to see you and her daughter, but we didn't want her just barging in here and ruining everything. Plus, you know, we haven't run a damn background check on her, *nothing*. I have no idea who she's with, if she has any alliances or enemies. Nothing."

I frown. It isn't nothing. I'm skilled in connecting the dots. Even in sleep, my mind puzzles pieces together, and this one feels as if it's finally taking form, like I've formed the outline and the small, irregular pieces are starting to make a picture.

A dead body in Tuscany. A vacated building. Her family in Lombardo, and an estranged mother. Somehow... somehow it all fits.

But first, we have to deal with her mother.

"So we have two choices, then."

"Yep."

"Escort her off this property, or keep her in check and bring Elise to her."

"Exactly."

I shove my hands in my pockets and think this over. I glance back at my gorgeous, beautiful bride, who sits in the pavilion with the beach behind her. She smiles at me and raises her glass. I smile back.

"I'll go talk to her mother first." Then I remember who I'm talking to. "Sorry, man. You know sometimes I get carried away. Can I go talk to her mother?"

"She's your family now, man. Go. This is your call."

I hate this. Our one perfect day, marred by her family that will *not* leave us the fuck alone.

As we walk from the pavilion to the Great Hall, I ask Romeo to give me the rundown.

"What do we know about her?"

"Just that she was estranged from Elise's father. He gave her an ample trust, per their pre-nup. They never divorced, so she wasn't entitled to all of it, but she's been living pretty well on his dime."

"And when he died?"

"Well that's just it, Tavi." He shakes his head. "The woman's going on and on about being owed money, how half of what Elise owns is hers, blah blah fucking *blah*."

Jesus. I'm glad Elise isn't here for this, not yet.

Since the pavilion sits at the back of the house, we have to walk past the kitchen, meeting rooms, dungeon, and library before we get to the main meeting rooms in the house. When I pass the kitchen pantry, I hear her voice.

She's screaming her goddamn head off.

"What the fuck?" I mutter to Romeo.

If this were literally anyone else but Anna Regazza, she'd be on thin, thin ice. As it is, we're not going to roll out the red carpet.

I can hear her voice clear as day when we draw closer.

"You will let me see my daughter!" I enter the room to see two guards holding a woman dressed in a formal black gown that's form-fitting and tight, more suitable for Vegas than her daughter's wedding. Her dark brown hair's in a loose bun at the nape of her neck. She has her daughter's same amber-colored eyes, but they're colder and wild with thick, black lashes underscored with vivid eye makeup. She was beautiful once.

"Ah," she says in a haughty tone. "And here comes the groom. How nice to meet you, Ottavio." She yanks at her arms, but the guards don't budge. "Please tell these behemoths to release your mother-in-law."

"Wow," Orlando mutters under his breath. "That's one fuckin' wedding present, bro, eh?"

Mario snickers. I ignore him.

Oddly, Santo's not here.

"Anna," I say as politely as I can. I bow my head to her. "So pleased to meet you." She is, after all, my wife's mother. "Please understand, we didn't expect you here. We run a full background check on any guest who visits our property, and you weren't on the list, so we have to take precautions."

She simmers down a bit, a cold, calculating look in her eyes. Goddamn it, why can't my wife have one good parent? I saw her father lose his life in this very room. But Anna won't, not today anyway. Not here. Not on my watch.

"Please," I say, gesturing to a chair. "Let her sit down."

The guards look to Romeo, who nods his consent. They release her as she yanks her arms from their grip and sits angrily on the edge of a chair.

"I demand to see my daughter."

I sit across from her, and tally the weapons I have on my person. Gun in a holster at my waist, knife in my pocket, two hands that will do anything to anyone who tries to threaten my wife.

You can't trust these people.

"I'm afraid I can't allow that. Not yet, anyway."

I'm not surprised when she bares her teeth at me. "Is that right?"

I nod and sit forward, my forearms resting on my legs. "That's right. Tell me, Anna. Your daughter's been here now for a little while, and you chose today as the day you show up on our doorstep? Why haven't you tried to contact us before now?"

"My husband," she says tearfully, wringing her hands. I don't buy it for a second. Elise has been clear about her parents' marriage, and I know Anna didn't care about her husband in the least.

"He forbade me from coming to see her. But it was kept quiet that he died, and I didn't know." She wipes at her eyes, but I see no tears. "Not until I heard about Piero."

My blood runs cold. *Piero.* If she was estranged from Elise, how did she know him? And why do I hate that she did?

"Ah. I see. And what can we help you with?"

"What can you help me with?" Her face grows serious again, and her eyes flash at me. "I want to see my daughter."

This is nothing about her daughter and everything to do with her claiming something that may or may not belong to her. I'll get to the bottom of this. I always do. I get to the bottom of everything.

"I want to know why, Anna. This is a happy day for Elise. I'd rather not make things any harder than they need to be."

In a flash, she drops any semblance of playing nice. "Sure you would. Right. As if I believe that for a minute."

Romeo clears his throat and signals to one of our guards. "You got a car ready to escort her off this property?"

She looks wildly to him. He shrugs. "Elise is my sister-in-law now. And I take care of my own, too."

"I'm not going," she says, shaking her head wildly from side to side. "No. I came here for a reason, and I'm not leaving until I see my daughter."

"I don't think so." I've had enough of this bullshit.

"What you're gonna do is give us your contact information, and I'll talk to Elise by myself. Privately. Alone. I'll see what *she* has to say, for her wishes are the only ones that matter to me. And then if she feels up to seeing you, we'll be in touch."

I expect her to scream or rail against me, but she only laughs. "Oh, that's cute." She rolls her eyes. "I love how you think you've got all the answers. High and mighty, are you?"

"Careful, Anna," Orlando warns, his eyes snapping.

"Oh, I should be scared," she says with mock fear. "Such a big, strong man like you threatening me?"

Orlando uncrosses his arms. He's beaten the shit out of men for less than this.

"Tavi," Romeo says, warning me. She's overstayed her welcome.

"Go," I order, pointing to the guards. "Car's ready." I turn my back to her. I need to get back to Elise. I do not want word getting to her before I have a chance to tell her anything. "We'll talk after you've followed our protocol."

"Wait!" Anna screams, her voice shaking with anger. "Go get Santo. Get Santo! You all think he's one of you, don't you?" She laughs. "You don't know a thing. Go get him and see what *he* tells you."

Wait.

What?

I look to Romeo and Romeo looks back to me. We

208

suspected Elise's father had an insider here at The Castle, but we never found them. Romeo got rid of all our staff and started from scratch. But Santo? No way. I don't believe for a minute Santo's capable of betraying any of us. He's cold and some might even say heartless, but he's loyal to the core.

Still…

"Where is Santo?" I ask.

Romeo scowls, his eyes still on Anna Regazza. "Stepped outside with Leo."

I call Leo, who answers on the first ring.

"Yeah, Tavi?"

"Leo, we've got a situation here in the Great Hall."

"So I've heard." Leo's voice is slurred. He's been partying hearty today after all he's been through. "What can I do for you?"

"I need Santo."

"Santo?"

"Yeah, *Santo*." I'm running out of patience. Rome's gone very, very still.

"He ain't here, Tav. I think he left. And where's Elise? I don't see her either…"

My blood runs cold.

CHAPTER 14

Elise

"ELISE? Elise, it's time to cut the cake." Marialena, who fancies herself my personal wedding coordinator, waves from where she stands. "Where's Tavi?"

I glance back to the door he left through. He didn't tell me I couldn't follow him, though it was implied.

I'm a Rossi now. The concept both thrills and terrifies me.

Rossis get shit done.

I want to see my husband.

"I'll find him," I tell her with a smile. "Distract the crowd with your stunning good looks, will you?"

When Marialena grins, her whole face lights up. She looks like a model, and something tells me she's very aware of the effect she has. "You got it, baby."

With a wink, she tugs the little sleeves of her dress down her arms, baring her shoulders, then shakes her mane of long, *long* hair and gestures to the DJ.

"Time for a game!"

I enter The Castle amidst groans and cheers and Marialena's charismatic laugh.

A member of staff greets me in the kitchen, an older man with a balding head. "Need something, miss?"

"No, I'm just looking for my husband." *Husband.* It feels funny calling him that, like I'm trying on a new pair of shoes that fit well but haven't been broken in yet. I need to use his name, though. I need some clout. "Have you seen him?"

"I saw him a moment ago. Not sure where he went, though?" He frowns. "He headed toward the office, I think. Or thereabouts anyway." He gestures in the general direction of the secretive rooms at the back of The Castle.

The office… I've been in every room in this house and can't recall a room they referred to as the office. Upstairs, maybe?

"Ottavio!" I shout, but this place is *huge*. Though everyone but staff seems to be outside right now, quieting the usually bustling home, my voice is still swallowed by the sheer size of the place. "*Tavi!*"

Of course today of all days I don't have my phone on me. Normally, I'd call or text him.

I walk past the pantry and head to the war room. He did say this was once a place for business. Someone did, anyway. But the war room is empty, and when I glance toward the entrance to the hidden dungeon, I turn quickly away. That was not a happy time in my life. I was riddled with grief and terrified, and don't want to remember that.

But when I turn, I hear a voice. I pause. I hear several, actually, muffled. Do the voices sound strained or pained?

I lean against the door and listen.

No. This isn't my business. I don't care if they have a prisoner. I don't care if they're questioning someone or punishing them, *I don't care.*

I turn quickly away and march back toward the library.

No one's there, either.

I sigh, trepidation growing with every step that I take.

Where is he?

When I come to the courtyard, adjacent to the Great Hall, I recognize Romeo's voice. "Secure her," he snaps. "I do not want any more surprises until Tavi speaks to Elise."

Secure her? Does he mean me? I just took vows to Ottavio. That means I'm free now, not...

I come to a sudden stop. I wish I could push a button and make myself invisible. I have a terrible feeling I shouldn't be here.

No. No they're talking about someone else.

"Elise? Elise, where are you!"

I nearly cry in relief at the sharp but familiar sound of Tavi's voice somewhere behind me. I look and don't see him. He's trying to find me, then.

The courtyard stands quiet, the indoor pool inside the majestic columns as still as water. The Castle holds no number of surprises.

"Tavi?" I walk quickly past the courtyard, and come to a sudden stop.

He stands in the dining room, the one room that links the library and kitchen together. When I see him, still dressed in his tux as if nothing's changed from when we took our vows, my heart squeezes.

I found him.

Has anything changed? Or is it only that I'm reminded that nothing has?

Over time, during my lengthy imprisonment and the past few weeks up close and personal with him, I've observed that Ottavio Rossi has perfected the man glare, the resting angry face, and the stern glare that would intimidate anyone.

But at the moment he just looks...lost.

"There you are," he says when he sees me, unable to mask the flood of relief he feels. "I've been looking all over for you." He clears his throat. I can tell he has something to tell me. "It's... time to cut the cake."

I blink in surprise. Right. There's a wedding reception out there, and we're supposed to perform.

"The cake?" I repeat stupidly, as he makes his way over to me.

I just heard Romeo tell his men to secure someone. I heard someone in the dungeon. But no, none of that matters because... we have to cut the cake.

I want to trust him, but I feel as if there's a yawning chasm we have to cross before I can get to that point.

"Yes, baby," he says, but the term of endearment doesn't soften his harsh tone, or the way his eyes flash at me. *"The cake."*

When he reaches me, he grips my upper arm so hard it almost hurts, as if he's afraid I'll evaporate and he needs to anchor me here on earth. His fingers graze the nearly invisible bandage under my arm, just tucked under the sleeve of my dress. A stark reminder that only hours ago, he removed my *tracking device.*

"Alright," I say, my voice hollow in the enormous room. "Did you..." My voice trails off. No, I'm not going to pry. If I'm going to learn to trust him, I'll give him space to tell me whatever he needs to in his own time. There will be secrets in this new life of ours. That much I know.

He's my husband now.

And yet a small thread of fear weaves its way through me. Is he hiding something from me?

"Did I what?" he asks, and his grip loosens a bit and seems to soften.

He's so handsome in his tux. He shaved for the occasion, but he already sports a five o'clock shadow, so ruggedly handsome it makes me ache for him to touch me.

I yearn to be swallowed whole by him. Utterly, irrevocably *consumed*. My gaze is fixated on the full lips of his now pressed in a thin line, and the frigid blue of his eyes.

I once thought him cruel, like an angry god. And while I know now he is capable of cruelty, the absence of pride makes him so much more... *human*.

I reach my hand to his face and cup his chin. "You're angry. Why are you angry?"

Why can't this be simple? It never is. Everything in our lives is so damn complicated.

His hands span my waist. I step closer to him.

"I couldn't find you." His voice cracks a little, again reminding me of a lost young boy. I want to hold him to me. I want to assure him that I'm not leaving.

"I'm right here, Ottavio. I came looking for you."

The tension in his shoulders eases, and he leans his forehead to mine. My throat tightens.

"You're right here," he repeats. When he pulls away, a worry line still creases his forehead.

Some people, after experiencing what he has, fear they'll never be capable of true intimacy.

Is that his fear, too?

I saw the pain in his eyes when he told me about the woman who killed herself rather than be married to him.

Does he wonder if he makes life unbearable for others?

Every one of us believes lies that we tell ourselves, lies that fester and plague and sometimes choke us. Lies that keep us from being who we're truly meant to be.

I wonder at times if the key to true happiness is seeking raw, vibrant, vivid *truth*. Of finding a way to silence the lies that steal our peace of mind and our hope for the future. For what is anxiety, if not worry of the future? And what is peace, if not content for the present?

"Maybe you should've kept that tracker in me," I say with a teasing smile. "Would that have made you feel better?"

His low growl sends a little jolt of awareness through me.

"Maybe," he says with a small smile of his own. "And I changed my mind, Elise Rossi."

Elise Rossi.

Now that's something different.

"Oh? About what?"

My hand still rests on his face. His warm skin and prickly, scruffy beard make me want him even more. I reach my face to his to kiss him.

Before he grants me my wish, he tells me what he's changed his mind about.

"You and I are taking a honeymoon."

"Oooh," I breathe. "*Yes.* Where to?"

"Italy. I've got staff packing for us right now. I've got business in Tuscany first, but then we'll shop and eat and do all the things *normal* people do."

Italy. I feel as if my whole body exhales.

"Perfect," I say with a smile. The "business" he has in Tuscany involves finding who killed his cousin, but I don't dwell on that right now.

This is who I married.

This is who I am.

"I'd like that," I tell him. "But first, let's cut that cake before your sister sends a search party out for the both of us, or your brothers get into a fistfight over who gets the largest piece."

He kisses me, still smiling.

I love his smile.

We walk through The Castle hand in hand, heading to the pavilion outside. "Tavi?"

"Mmm?"

"I… overheard Romeo. I didn't mean to. I was looking for you."

Our footsteps click on the hardwood floors as we make our way back to the reception outside.

"Still, you shouldn't have been eavesdropping. You know better than that."

"What am I supposed to do, walk through The Castle with my fingers stuck in my ears?"

He growls in response. I barely refrain from rolling my eyes.

"What did you hear him say?"

I can't remember exactly. "Something about… waiting until you told me. What's he talking about?"

"And that's exactly why you shouldn't listen in on conversations you're not involved in."

"Hey. *You're* avoiding answering the question."

He blows out a breath, and the stern, implacable look on his face is back. I wonder if I imagined any softness. "Let's cut the cake. Let's wrap up this reception. And later, when we're alone again, I'll tell you everything."

"Everything?" I ask.

His eyes quickly dart away, then back again. "Yeah, babe."

"Fair enough."

It feels good to be walking hand in hand with him. It feels even better when we step outside and Marialena shouts out a greeting in a microphone, and the entire reception bursts into applause and hoots and hollers.

We head back to our family and friends and do everything we're supposed to. Cake cutting, bouquet tossing, greeting and smiling and laughing. We eat pastry and drink champagne, and when the sun sets low behind us, and our guests begin to leave, we head inside where our bags are waiting for us.

"Tavi." Tosca looks like she's going to pout. "Why so soon? You just got here, my son."

"I came to get married, Mama. You know that."

She stares forlornly at the luggage by the door, as Mario enters.

"Got rid of her," he says to Tavi.

Tavi looks sharply at me, then back to Mario. "I'm talking to her on the plane, man. *Jesus.*"

"You should stay," Tosca says, reaching for my hand. "You can talk him into it. You're the only one who's ever had any sway with that pigheaded son of mine."

I can't help but smirk at that. Tavi narrows his eyes at me, but he shares a smirk with me, too.

"I may be his wife, but I'm not a miracle worker. I'm sorry. When Tavi makes up his mind…"

She waves her hand at me. "Oh, yeah. I know all about that. Still, come home soon you two, will you?"

Nonna presses a large plastic bag with something wrapped in foil inside. "For you," she says. *"Mangia."* Then she pats my belly, and tells me in Italian I need to feed my body to prepare for the baby. If she wasn't so adorable and sweet, I'd roll my eyes. Instead, I kiss her cheeks and thank her.

"Hey! Don't give her all the food!" Mario protests.

Orlando smacks his arm, hard. "Don't be a dumb-ass. She'll make more. Let her take it." He shakes his head. *"Jesus,"* he mutters, as if he didn't nearly get into an all-out brawl with Mario over a platter of canapés earlier today. The Rossi men and their food…

But I'm still hung up on what she said.

"Nonna," I say on a groan. "I don't look pregnant!"

"No look. *Be,"* she says, shaking her head. "Soon. We need many, many small Rossis. Fatten you up *now."* She walks by Romeo and makes the sign of the cross. He only rolls his eyes.

Tavi shakes his head. "You trying to fatten up my new bride?"

"Of course," Nonna says sternly.

Tavi grins. "Alright by me."

"Hey!" I make a vow to do a few crunches before I go to bed tonight. Fatten me up indeed.

Tires crunch on the gravel outside the door. "That's our ride," Tavi says. "Let's go, Elise."

"Wait!" Angelina's on the stairs, the baby over her shoulder. "Let me tell you goodbye." She trots down the rest of the stairs, but on the last step, she catches her foot. Nonna and Mama gasp, but Orlando moves swiftly and catches her just before she falls, the baby clutched to her chest.

"Oh my God, that was scary," she says before she exhales.

With a scowl, he nods. "I told you to be careful walking down those stairs."

"Hey, I didn't want to miss Elise!"

"She's only going to Tuscany!"

"Alright, alright," I interrupt. "I am going to go Tuscany and she didn't fall, so let's say goodbye?"

Yikes. I guess the Rossi men *are* all the same.

Angelina kisses my cheek. She's got an odd look in her eyes I can't quite place. I'm not sure what's going on.

"You okay?" I ask.

She looks quickly over to Tavi and then back to me. "Yeah," she whispers. "And here we are. Both of us, married into the Rossi fam." But it feels as if she's changing the subject. There's something she isn't sharing with me.

I smile at her. "Here we are."

She kisses my cheek. "You were a beautiful bride, and your ceremony was the stuff of dreams, babe. Enjoy Tuscany. Call me every day, will you?"

I give her a huge hug. "I will. Promise."

When I turn away, I find Tavi staring at us. I can't quite read his expression. Wordlessly, he reaches his hand to me. I take it, and they break out in *applause.* They cheer and shout and clap their hands. I look in surprise at Tavi, who only shrugs.

"We like family," he says. "And you're one of us now. Be ready to duck." He opens the heavy front door. I follow behind him. "Duck?"

At the very second the words leave my mouth, a shower of confetti unlike anything I've ever seen before explodes in the air around us. A myriad of multi-colored paper flutters to the ground and nearly blinds me. Natalia squeals with laughter, before she shoots something that looks like a squirt gun filled confetti right at me again.

"Oh my God!" Tavi and I run to the car, nearly blinded by the swath of multi-colored paper and streamers. Out of the corner of my eye, I see Orlando pop a bottle of champagne. It shoots into the air like a geyser, as Tavi opens the door to the car. Rice pours from the car like a waterfall.

Oh my God.

"I'm gonna fuckin' beat the *shit* out of you guys," Tavi says with a growl, turning on them. Mario snickers and Tavi points his finger at him. "You first, kid."

Mario flips him the bird, but at the look on Tavi's face, runs.

"Go, bro, I'll kick his ass for you," Orlando says affectionately, as a limo pulls up. There's no way we're driving the rice-filled car to get our plane.

"Thanks," Tavi mutters. "Make it a good one."

They're joking about beatdowns like they talk about handshakes, and… well, actually, I'm not *entirely* sure they're joking. I don't know if I'll ever get used to the Rossi brothers.

"Get in," Tavi says, half smiling, half growling. "Before I have to shake your goddamn bra down for confetti."

"Too late for that," I say with a laugh as I slide into the car and collapse against the plush leather seats. "And I'm not wearing a bra."

He slides in beside me. "All day long and I didn't know you weren't wearing a bra?" It takes him seconds to slide his rough palm down the front of my dress.

"Hey!"

"Don't try to stop me, wife," he says with a warning shake of his head. "You're mine now."

I've been his since my feet touched American soil ten months ago, but I'm not sure it's a very good time to remind him of that. When his fingers touch bare skin, he groans. The evidence of his arousal tents in the rich cut of his tux. Ha.

"How long 'til we get to the plane?" I ask.

"Long enough," he responds. "C'mere."

To my surprise, he slides onto his knees in front of me before he smacks a black button on the door. A privacy screen noiselessly rises behind him.

"Lift it up, Mrs. Rossi," he says, his eyes trained on me. "The train, the bust, whatever the fuck you call that thing."

I bite my lip and hike the skirt up. I'm wearing a thin, satin thong I bought just for this occasion. He groans at the sight before him, bends, and presses his mouth to the vee of satin between my thighs. My head falls back on the seat behind me as he positions himself in front of me and drapes my legs over his shoulders.

"God*damn*," he curses, when he kisses me again and inhales deeply. "Fuckin' exotic."

"My..." I giggle. "My pussy's *exotic*?"

"Mmm," he says, without a trace of amusement. I gasp when he presses the tip of his tongue on the satin. My clit pulses and I feel myself go slick. I want more.

"I want to taste you. I want to hear you call me husband when you come."

"Hel-*lo*."

"Shh, baby. I want to eat my wife out. Don't interrupt me again unless you want to be punished on your wedding day."

I love it when he talks dirty to me. And then my mind's wiped clean, a blank slate, as he pulls the tiny scrap of fabric down my thighs. He moves one leg so he can pull it down to my ankle, then positions me right over his strong, sturdy shoulders again.

"There," he says with a low groan. "Fuckin' gorgeous. Later, we make love, baby. I want a taste before we do."

I close my eyes and lose myself to everything. The way his mouth works its magic, licking his way up my seam to where I'm pulsing with need. The way he grips my ass like he owns it, so hard it's nearly painful. The way he alternates suckling and fucking me with his tongue, savage thrusts in and out. I can't think of anything but the new stroke of his tongue, the pulse of heat between my legs, my racing pulse and yearning sense of need.

This. God, this. This is what I need. This is what I crave.

The limo glides effortlessly over every bump, and he never loses his position, works me perfectly to the edge of climax with the tip of his tongue. When he takes his mouth off me to whisper dirty, seductive things, I want the feel of him again. I whimper with need and claw at his hair. I stab my fingers in the dark, silky, tousled locks.

"Do you trust me?" he asks. I nod crazily, eager for him to finish what he started. "I love you, Elise. And we're starting over now, the two of us. We chose this. We're here. And every day forward, we'll learn how to do this." He laps lazily at me, and my hips jerk. "Won't we, baby?"

I nod. "Yes. Yes, we will. Oh God, Tavi, that feels good."

"We'll learn together," he says, as if trying to convince himself, too. "We start over. Right here. Right now."

I like that. I don't want to remember who I was or where I've been. I'm Elise Rossi. Wife to Ottavio Rossi.

He grins against me and licks me again. "There. That's my girl. Come on my tongue, baby. Come for me."

I do exactly what he tells me just as we cruise to a stop. He slams his palm to lock the door, giving me space to fully relish every spasm of perfection as I come so hard I feel as if I'll shatter.

CHAPTER 15

Tavi

IT'S A GODDAMN COPOUT, and I know it, but I don't want even the glimmer of dissension or sadness on our wedding day.

I managed to get her out of there without seeing her bitch of a mom.

Now I need to get her to Tuscany.

We told each other we forgave the past and moved forward into the present.

We'll forgive and forget *everything*.

But I know it's an excuse that I haven't told her about Piero.

I was afraid doing it on our wedding day would ruin everything. I will tell her.

I start with her mother.

When we're secured on the plane, she digs her fingers into my palm.

Oh, right. Damn near forgot she's terrified of flying.

"How'd you make it back and forth from America to Tuscany? How'd you handle the to and fro?"

"Honey," she says, digging her fingernails into my palm until they look like they're ready to bleed. "There was not a lot of *fro*. I mostly lived in Tuscany. I didn't come home very often. Before my last trip to America, when I came to the Rossi house when Angelina was still your prisoner?"

I nod and swallow. I don't like to talk about this time. "Yeah?"

"I hadn't come here in *years* before then."

I nod. Interesting.

"Alright, well, you asked me to drug you up on the way back, so I got something that will help."

"Why Mr. Rossi, have you gone back on your standards? First we share a joint, and now you're handing me prescription sedatives?"

"Operative word *prescription*," I grunt. "This one will take twenty minutes to kick in. But listen, before you take it—"

Too late. She's already reached her trembling hand to mine and shoved the pill in her mouth. I shake my head when she sips from a small glass of water.

"Oops." She gives me a sheepish grin.

"I'll talk fast, then." I draw in a breath. "During the wedding today, we had a visitor." There is no easy way to say this.

I love the way she tips her head to the side. "Who?"

I swallow hard. "Your mother."

The only reaction she has is her eyes widening for a fraction of a second before she schools her features again.

"Think you might have the wrong person?" she says with a self-deprecating laugh. "Surely not Anna Regazza." She makes a sound of disgust and looks out the window. "Figures, though."

I lace my fingers through hers. "Why?"

"Probably wants money. Believe me, when there was anything of any materialistic value to be had, she was *on it*. But Tavi, why didn't you come and get me? I would've liked to talk with her."

Why? It's a good question. One I'd ask myself if I were in her position. "Because she was volatile, Elise. And we weren't prepared for her. Hadn't run a check, nothing."

She sits up suddenly, spilling the water all over herself. "Did you bring her to the dungeon?" The tone of her voice suggests that'd be unthinkable.

I shake my head. "No. Why would we?"

"I don't know," she says coolly, looking away. "You put me there."

"And for good damn reason, Elise. You know why we did."

Her eyes meet mine in bold challenge. "And if you had it to do again, would you?"

"Absolutely."

Shock flits across her features. Her jaw drops open, and her eyes are wide and frightened. "Why, Tavi?" I don't miss the reproach in her voice. I expected as much, but it still stabs my heart.

"Because I did then what I thought I had to. And with the knowledge I had then, I'd do the same. But you have to understand, Elise." I hold her to me. "My loyalty to my family is more important than anything."

"Even to me?" she asks in a little voice.

"Baby," I say warmly, holding her to me. "Why do you think we marry? Why do you think I wanted to take vows with you now instead of waiting four weeks?"

"Well," she says thoughtfully. "It wasn't because you wanted to have sex, because nothing came in the way of *that*."

I kiss her temple. "Right. You're my family now, Elise. It's why I wanted to take vows early. Why it mattered to me. Because we have oaths that we take, all of us, and I couldn't make you as important to me as I can now, before I took those oaths."

"Ah," she says softly. "I understand."

I'm not sure if she really does. I'm not sure anyone outside my circle of brothers ever does.

"What are the oaths you take?"

"We take many," I tell her. "And we seal them in blood. We don't ever go back on the oaths we take. I can tell you some but not all of them. You know all of us take vows of silence, obedience, fidelity."

It's late at night, and we'll arrive in Tuscany well past midnight. Her eyes are heavy and drooping. It will be better for her if she sleeps now, before we touch down. Her medicine's kicking in.

I want to tell her everything. I need to tell her about Piero. It's my hope and prayer that preparing her for the truth by telling her about my loyalty to the Rossi brotherhood, the truth about having no regrets with her imprisonment, and the promise that we've forgiven the past as we embrace the present, will prepare her for what I'll tell her myself.

"Tavi?"

"Mmm?"

"How exactly did you leave things with my mother?"

"I told her I'd talk with you, and that after I did, I'd get back in touch with her."

"Oh."

She plays with the wedding band on my finger. "It's a nice ring," she says with a soft smile. She spins the gold back and forth. "So it wasn't my mother in the dungeon, then."

"No."

I can't tell if that pleases or disappoints her. There's a pause, and she swallows hard before she asks, "Who was it, then?"

"I don't know, baby. No idea."

"And if you did know…" she begins.

"I wouldn't tell you unless it involved you. But I wouldn't lie." I really don't know the answer to the question.

Slowly, she nods. I hope she's starting to understand where I'm coming from.

"Isn't failing to tell someone the truth the same as actually lying, though?"

My guilty conscience plagues me. If that were the case, I've been lying to her from the beginning. I frown. "Sometimes, yes. Sometimes, no."

"I get it, Tavi. I do," she says. "I mean, I *think* I do." But growing up in the mob doesn't mean we lived parallel lives. Her family was very different from mine, and even though we have many similarities, they aren't the same. "Still… What does my mother want from me?" She makes a sound of disgust and looks out the small window, as the plane's wings dip to the side. I hold her tighter.

"I don't know, but she said something about the inheritance and you getting a share."

"Inheritance? Like I fucking *care* about any of that." She wrinkles up her nose. "She can keep it."

"Even the shop in Copley?"

Her eyes widen a bit and she shakes her head. "Bitch better leave my shop alone."

That makes me smile.

"We'll look into why she came, while we finish our business here," I tell her, threading my arm over her shoulders. I've told myself from the beginning that she couldn't know everything that happened, that our marriage was a marriage of convenience and nothing more.

I also told myself I couldn't ever really love someone. I couldn't become vulnerable, and open myself to the prospect of being hurt.

How many more lies will I believe?

"I bought you something." Maybe if I ignore this long enough, it'll go away.

Maybe if she really learns to love me, she'll forgive me.

"You're just trying to distract me from the fact that we're dropping in altitude, aren't you?" She bites her lip and looks out the window. "Tavi."

She plays absentmindedly with her wedding band,

twirling it on and off her finger. I watch as she tugs it off and spins it, then slides it on again.

I don't like her taking it off.

"Didn't even notice the drop in altitude. Hey, we're almost here. Focus on me, now."

Ah, she's focused on me alright. Her fingers are digging into my palms again as if to anchor herself. I reach into my pocket and pull out a small, wrapped box. Orlando and Romeo both pulled me aside on two separate occasions, and both told me to prioritize getting her a gift. Elise likes beautiful things. It was easier finding the perfect gift than I thought.

"Oh, Tavi, I didn't know you knew how to wrap gifts," she says with a teasing lilt in her voice.

I shrug, and she laughs out loud. "Someone else wrapped it for you, then?"

"Maybe." I shrug. "Just open it."

"Alright, alright, Mr. Impatient," she says, but I can tell by the way her eyes shine she's excited about this. "I do feel badly I didn't get you anything, though."

"I told you not to," I remind her. "And I meant it. If you dared, you would've been in big trouble."

"Oh, that's fair." She snorts.

"One hundred percent." I reach my hand out to her. I feel like I'm betraying her, like I'm buttering her up so she forgives me when the truth outs. I stroke her back. "You're my gift."

But I mean everything I say.

I watch the way she bites her lip before she slips her finger under the foil-wrapped paper. I thought long and hard before I bought this for her, and when I saw it I knew it was exactly what I needed.

"Did you have someone buy it for you?" she asks, not meeting my eyes.

"No, babe. Picked this out myself."

"Well done," she says with a soft smile. Her eyes have grown tired. It's been a long day. But she can't hide the way she lights up at the prospect of a gift.

A champagne-colored velvet box sits in the palm of her hand. "No one's ever bought something for me like this before," she whispers.

"How do you know? What if it's nothing?"

She doesn't know, though, that the little box in her hand is only a distraction. It isn't the only gift I've gotten for her, nor the most important one.

"Oh. My. *God,*" she gasps when she opens the box to reveal the delicate diamond tennis bracelet. It glitters like diamonds. "Tavi. This looks just like the one that... no, wait." Her eyes widen and she pales when she looks at me. Yup. Orlando's advice to buy *this* one, suggested by Angelina of course, was spot on. "Tavi, it isn't."

It is, the very same that was displayed in Boston at the Museum of Fine Arts. The one-of-a-kind bracelet's handmade, a work of art, pink pearls studded with glittering diamonds, all set in a delicate gold chain.

"There, now you won't have to get jealous of Angelina's necklace."

I saw her gawking at then fawning over Angelina's necklace Orlando bought, which prompted Angelina telling Orlando to tell *me* to buy something that would wow her.

She reaches into the box gingerly and extracts it. "This is a lot nicer than that thick gold band you used to make me wear," she says with mock reproach.

"Mhm. My sentiments exactly. Here, let me."

She offers me her bare, slender wrist. I clip the bracelet on with a swell of pride. It's gorgeous, twinkling in the overhead light.

"Thank you," she whispers.

"There's more. Wait."

I pull out my phone to show her the video feed of her store in Boston.

"What is it?" Her brows draw together. "You're showing me footage of the store? Ugh. I'll have to have Angelina look in on it when I'm gone."

"Santo will, too. But look. Do you remember the vacant lot *behind* the main location?"

"Yes, of course."

I swipe my phone to the left, revealing a panorama of the expanse behind it. "Voilà. It's all yours."

She stares for long moments, as if she can't truly comprehend this. "The... the what? What do you mean?"

"You had this area here," I explain patiently, smoothing my finger over the rough patches. "And now you have this. You said you wanted to do more than you had, expand to include more than what we have the room for here. So I bought that area as well. It's yours."

"Tavi." Her eyes well with tears. "I... I can't believe you did this."

She likes it. My heart swells with the knowledge that I pleased her. Maybe we can make this new chapter of our lives mean something.

Maybe we can make this new chapter of our lives... mean *everything*.

This time when we land, she closes her eyes and leans into me. I lay my arm over her shoulders and hold her tight.

I wish I could hold her like this forever. I wish I could protect her just like this.

CHAPTER 16

Elise

WE'RE SO tired when we arrive in Tuscany, we practically collapse onto his big, massive bed. I barely remember removing my makeup and brushing my teeth before I climb under the sheets and he climbs in behind me.

But I wake to him nuzzling my neck and whispering sweet nothings in my ear. I roll over, already turned on and ready. He cups my breasts and kisses the underside of each one before he licks and suckles them. I can't stifle my whimpers or moans as I turn to him.

I decided to fake it until I made it. I might love this man.

Sometimes, self-giving love is bound in lovemaking just as anything else. Sometimes, physical intimacy bridges a rift.

And sometimes it doesn't.

He lays me on my back. I crave his weight on top of me, his hands on my wrists, his mouth imprisoning mine. I sigh as my body begins to mold to his. As I fully let go and yield to him.

He nudges my knees apart and grinds himself between my legs.

"Who owns you?" he whispers in my ear as I spread my legs for him.

"You do," I breathe. My wedding band and bracelet feel almost heavy, stark reminders of my marriage to him.

"Whose babies will you have?"

"Yours," I moan, when he strokes between my legs.

I'm eager and ready when he slides into me, making slow, sweet love. So close, it feels like heaven, so intimate, it feels like the best-kept secret. My body rises with his and falls with his. My need to climax pools into a bundle of nerves as he thrusts and groans with his own pleasure.

"Come, baby," he whispers in my ear when he can tell I'm close. "I want to watch you."

When I'm lying on his chest, I hear the sound of gulls flying outside our window and know that we haven't just come here to honeymoon. We lay like that, after lovemaking, holding each other.

Finally, he breaks the silence.

"I'm meeting with my cousins today. You're coming with me."

I nod. "Of course."

"I have some suspicions and need to work them out."

I nod quietly. There will be no real escape from this side of things. "And?"

He doesn't answer.

I don't ask again.

As I shower and he takes phone calls outside the bathroom, I wonder what else he hides from me. Do we call it hiding when he doesn't even pretend? He didn't tell me my own mother came to our wedding. He didn't tell me who he suspects in his cousin's murder. Is there anything else he hides from me? No doubt.

The better question is, when I find what he hides from me, will I be able to bear it?

We eat a simple breakfast prepared by his staff—scrambled eggs, rustic slices of thick, buttered bread, and a delicate fruit salad. He fills me in.

"We're heading to my family's home first," he says. "Leo has a home here in Tuscany. I'll introduce you to the guards you'll be with here, and go over your rules."

I nod, even as my feminine ire rises at the sound of "rules." I know this is Tavi. This is my life. He may dote on me and have claimed me as his own, his "family" now, but he hasn't softened at all.

"Alright," I say, even as I grit my teeth.

"Elise," he says warningly.

"What?"

"You have that look on your face."

"What look?"

He purses his lips. "You know. The one that says, *fuck off.*"

"I didn't say that."

Frowning, he pushes away from the table, spreads his legs, and points between his knees. "Come here."

I swallow my pride and stand, dragging my feet as I walk over to him. "Okay. Here I am."

Wordlessly, he threads his fingers through my hair. I can't help the feeling that he's walking on eggshells. He isn't afraid of offending me. Then what is it he's hiding?

My phone buzzes with a text, then another. He gives one short shake of his head. A part of me wonders if this is a test. "I have to do shit I don't want to do today." I bend and kiss his cheek.

"Thank you, baby," he says softly. "Thanks for that. Remember to do what I say today. Got it?"

I nod. "Got it."

We're halfway there when I look at my phone. It's a number I don't recognize.

Unknown: Nice of you to get married and not even tell your mother.

I glance at Tavi, who's deeply invested in a phone call. He catches my eye and smiles. I'll wait until he's done.

Unknown: Do not tell your husband I sent this.

Yeah, what's she gonna do about that?

Pursing my lips, I reply.

Me: And who is this?

As if he doesn't have my phone tapped and won't see this.

Unknown: Don't play dumb with me. You know who this is. Ask your husband why he didn't let me see you yesterday. Ask him what Santo's doing in Tuscany. Ask him to tell you everything.

My blood runs cold. What?

Me: What do you want from me?

Unknown: I will not have your new family rob me of what's rightfully mine. You'll meet my demands or suffer the consequences.

Oh no she does not.

I go to type a reply when my phone's swiped right out of my hands. I blink in surprise to see Tavi holding it. I watch his eyes go from the typical angry look to downright furious.

"Who the fuck does she think she is?" he mutters.

"Hey, I was reading that."

He ignores my protests.

"She's just popped her head out of nowhere, like a stubborn weed," I mutter. "And what the hell is she talking about, about yesterday? I don't understand. What does she think is hers?"

"Something about your inheritance."

"My inheritance?" I thought all that belonged to me was the shops, and like I said, she gets nothing. She took my father's money and ran with it.

"We need to talk with her. Let me check with Romeo to see if he found anything before we do." He hands my phone back. "Tell her we're in Tuscany and we can meet with her on a video chat tonight around dinnertime. Should give me enough time to check on things before we do."

I nod and type out a text, then slide the *off* button on my phone.

We're on our honeymoon, and I'm gonna enjoy this.

Tavi isn't supposed to meet with anyone until lunchtime, so we head to the shops. I buy fine alabaster vases in Scarperia, a small kitchen rug made of *panno casentinese*, hand-woven orange wool, in Casetino.

"I'd love to shop food next," I tell him, but we have to meet with his associate first. I'm craving the handmade biscuits from Siena and pecorino cheese from Peinza, as well as some of Tuscany's signature Chianti.

"I was going to tell you, but we have to visit my family's vineyard. There, you can take any of the wines you'd like, and we also stock local handmade cheeses and some cold-pressed olive oil."

"Mmm," I say, already planning what I'm going to make my new husband for dinner. "Please tell the staff we won't be needing them to cook dinner tonight."

"You have plans, baby?"

I smile. "I do."

As we drive to the vineyards, I can't shake the strange feeling that we're being watched. I look over my shoulder a few times, but see nothing.

"Tavi," I say, as we drive down the long, winding road uphill that takes us to the vineyard entrance.

"Yeah?"

"I feel like I'm being watched."

"You are, though," he says, unbothered. "None of the Rossi brothers have brought a new wife to Italy for some time. They've been waiting for this."

"For what?"

He smiles as he takes a sharp turn and continues his drive. "For you."

But no. I don't think it's just the locals or his staff whispering to each other behind their hands, or casting furtive looks in my direction. No… something else is off.

Tavi's on a phone call, and I don't want to interrupt him. Something is amiss. I know my mother's causing drama, but that's nothing new. Something else is at play. I wish I knew what.

His phone's ringing off the hook, one call after another, until finally he grabs it and slams the *off* button; when it powers off, he throws it on the dash and exhales.

I wait a minute before I talk. Give him another minute to take deep breaths. I reason that it'll help calm him.

"Tavi," I say gently, reaching for his hand. I won't fear the man I'm married to. But I also won't stick my head in a hungry lion's mouth.

"Yes?" he says, before he lets out a breath.

"What's going on? Can you tell me now?"

I watch as the crease between his brows deepens. He's a few years older than I am, but right now, he looks as if he's a decade or more older.

"Santo's gone missing."

I feel as if ice pumps through my veins. Santo, the cold, calculating one, my business partner, the one who follows every move Rosa makes under her brothers' watchful eyes, the one I would call first if ever I needed to hide a body—he's gone missing.

"Do you think he's been taken prisoner?"

He pinches the bridge of his nose with his free hand. "We don't know. We have hardly any clues. He went missing yesterday at the wedding. He was supposed to be with Leo, told Leo he had to take a call, then he just left. Your mother said something about asking Santo, but Santo's loyal. We were going to ask him what the hell she was talking about, but then he was gone."

"Wait," I say slowly, as I mull this over. "You mean to tell me that Santo went missing at the very same time my mother showed up?"

"Exactly."

"Well, Tavi," I say slowly, shaking my head as I think this over. "Is it possible my mother was only a diversion? All of you, and many of your soldiers and guards, were distracted by her tantrum, right?"

He sits up straighter. "Yes."

"And then he went missing?"

"Right."

I shake my head from side to side. "Tavi... Tavi, why is Santo the one who works with me in town? Why him, and not one of the lesser-ranking members of The Family?"

"Because he's the one—*Jesus*." He shakes his head. He grits his teeth, and shakes his head again before he continues. "Because he's the one that told us about your father's business."

I look out the window and tap my fingers on the dash. "Yeah, babe. You've got to find Santo."

He powers his phone on and hands me mine, as mine buzzes with a text.

I grit my teeth when I see another text from the unknown number. My goddamn mother. Tavi would likely intercede, but he's on the phone with Romeo as we head back to the house.

Unknown: Ask Tavi what happened to Piero.

CHAPTER 17

Tavi

I CAN HARDLY UNDERSTAND the concept of one of my brothers betraying us. No. No, it isn't possible. It can't be. I won't believe it.

Santo was raised as one of us. He isn't a blood relative but adopted into the family by my father when he was a child. He was the only one my mother ever let my father have free rein with, and as a result, he's more ruthless, more conniving even, than any of us.

But like any of us, he'd lay his life down for us. I know he would. I'd swear my own life on it.

It's the only reason I ever let him work with my wife to begin with.

My family's vineyard in Tuscany serves a dual purpose—first, we actually grow grapes here and make our own wine. Our Chianti's won awards year after year, and we've gotten some pretty tempting offers to sell it in a retail location. We won't, though. It was one of the few things I ever agreed with my father about.

Instead, we bottle and ship our wine to our family and friends. An entire wall in our dining room consists of nothing but bottles of our homegrown wine. It's some of Italy's finest.

We grow olives here, as well, at a much smaller volume, and make our own olive oil. But here at our vineyard we hold the Rossi family headquarters.

The vineyard in Tuscany is what The Castle is in America: a central meeting point for us to conduct business… among other things.

Leo was the last to see Santo but was so damn plastered he doesn't remember a thing. I could kick his ass. Orlando says he hasn't seen him, and Mario says only that he knew he spent the morning of the wedding at Copley, tending to business.

"They wanted Elise to come the night before to look over inventory, but she was busy with you," Mario says. "So Santo said he wanted to go instead."

Something's off. Something's wrong.

Maybe she came as a diversion.

I call Romeo next. "Rome."

"Yeah, brother?" I can tell without him saying a word that Romeo hasn't slept since I left.

"We need to take a closer look at all security footage around the time of Anna Regazza showing up at my wedding."

"Consider it done," Romeo says. "Why, though, Tav?"

I tell him what Elise said.

"You sure *she* isn't the one involved in any of this?"

I look at my beautiful bride, standing atop a hill that overlooks the valley of vines, the green behind her like a painted scene. I sigh.

"I'm not," I tell him. "But I'd bet money she's innocent."

"Money's expendable, Tavi," Romeo says. "Don't let love or whatever the fuck cloud your judgment."

It's then that I realize... that I've fallen victim to the exact weakness my brothers have.

"I'll ask her again," I say. A sort of cold decision sweeps over me as I look at my beautiful wife. I have to interrogate her in a way that gets the truth out but doesn't break her. I need her to tell me everything she knows.

She can't lie to me when she's being dominated. She gives me nothing but the bold, honest truth.

Romeo's gone brooding and quiet. Not a good sign. He's demanded anyone with word about Santo report back to him immediately.

"Elise," I say quietly.

She turns to me, and the wind rustles her hair. She's so lovely it makes my heart ache. She brings light to my darkness. Warmth to my cold.

I punished her once for her act of betrayal and told myself never again, that she'd paid the price and we'd start afresh.

But I can't let even one stone go unturned.

"Yes?"

"Come here, please."

I point to the ground beside me, slightly damp with morning dew.

She doesn't come at first. She looks back over the vineyards with a look of sadness on her face. My hands clench by my sides. What's she playing at?

But before she's made the decision to disobey me, she turns and walks to me. I take her hand and drag her right up next to my body, so her chest brushes mine.

I need to question her. I need to make sure there isn't a thing she's hiding from me. But when she reaches me, the scent of roses and lilacs wafts through the air and I'm caught in the spell of her amber eyes.

"I love you," I tell her, the words springing up without my consent, as if they've grown out of my very soul and won't be hindered any longer.

"Do you?" she whispers.

I don't know what I expected her to say, but this isn't it. I don't care.

I kiss her. I lace my fingers through her hair and pull her to me, my mouth on hers so insistent she gives a little startled cry. I let her go with reluctance and take her by the hand.

"Where are we going?" When I don't respond, she fidgets anxiously. "Tavi?"

We go around the back of the house to where a greenhouse sits. I open the door and tug her in, grab a stool and sit her on my knee.

"We need to talk."

I don't miss the way her eyes grow wary. So it surprises me when she nods. "We do."

"And this is how we'll talk."

I spread my knees and pull her belly down. She kicks her legs and squirms.

"Hey! Wait. Hey, what do you think you're doing?"

"You can't lie to me when I've got you in this position, baby." I lift up the little skirt she wears and pat her ass. "Can you?"

I rest my palm on the swells of her cheeks.

"Well... Well, no, but I don't lie to you." When she turns to me, her cheeks have reddened. She's obviously angry. Without hesitation, I give her a sharp smack.

"Did you have anything to do with Santo missing?"

"What? Are you out of your mind? Tavi! *No*. No, of course not."

I give her another sharp slap. "Did you know about his disappearance?"

"*No*. Tavi, no, of course not. Let me go! Let me up. This isn't fair. My God, who do you think—"

"I am? Your husband. And I'm not punishing you. You're not in trouble. I'm getting the truth out of you in a way that I know works. You can't hide from me like this."

Her mouth drops open as I spank her again, and again, until she bucks on my lap. I press my fingers between her legs to where the fabric's gone damp.

She always likes it when I dominate her.

"Did you know your mother was coming to our house the day of our wedding?"

"*No*. No, I have literally nothing to do with any of this. Why would I be so upset you didn't tell me? Now let me *up*."

Unable to stop myself, I stroke between her legs, but she pushes off of me until her knees hit the soft outdoor carpet we keep in here. She's damp with sweat, small curls of hair curled around her forehead. Predictably, it's warm in the greenhouse.

Furiously, she scrambles to her knees and comes to me, resting her arms on my legs. It's an odd position for her to try to take control. She's literally kneeling between my legs. But there's a look in her eyes I haven't seen since I imprisoned her in The Castle dungeon.

"Now *you* have questions to answer," she says.

"Watch that tone of voice, woman."

But she ignores my warning and plows ahead. "You married me. You said for better or for worse. You said all of that. And in the plane after our wedding, you said we were starting fresh. Only *I* was the one that came fresh, Tavi. Not you."

Her chest heaves. Goddamn it. I had to get the truth out of her, but now she needs to get the truth out of *me*.

"Go on," I say, my voice husky. It's time she knows. It's time I told her. But I don't want to take this away from her. She has the right to ask me anything she wants, and I don't want to assume anything.

"Why did you marry me?" she whispers.

"You know why I married you." I hold her chin in my hand, my eyes fixed on her. "Your marriage to me was to be your punishment for your betrayal, wasn't it?"

"Ottavio," she says reproachfully. It always gets my heart when she calls me by my full name.

"Yeah?"

"What did you have to do with Piero?"

I close my eyes as the heat of emotion chokes me. I'm a coward for not telling her sooner. I fucking hate cowardice. I force my eyes to open and shake my head.

"Elise…" I reach for her face, but she jerks away.

"Tell me. Please," she whispers.

I draw in a deep breath. "We found out that he'd taken you, and Angelina was in your place. You were supposed to be married that night, Elise, and you know it."

"Of course. We've been over this." Her voice is choked. "It's why I've been punished. Why I was forced to marry you."

Somehow the *forced to marry you* stings far worse than I ever anticipated. My heart aches.

"I knew he was the one that betrayed the Regazzas, and because he left with you, he was the one that betrayed *us*. He stole from us. And you and I both know that theft from The Family warrants death."

"Say it," she whispers. "Just fucking *say* it."

I release a shaky breath. "I didn't kill him myself, but I was the one that ordered his death." I exhale angrily. "So it's the same damn thing."

"Tavi," she whispers, her voice breaking as she shakes her head. "And Santo was the one who did it. Wasn't he?"

I nod.

My phone rings. I let it go to voicemail, but then it rings again insistently. We have so much to say, so much to uncover. But the call's from Romeo. I'm not allowed to ignore a call from Romeo.

"I have to take this."

Elise gets to her feet and waves vaguely at the phone, a look of resignation on her face. "Get it," she whispers. "Of course. What the family needs always comes first, doesn't it?" The hollow, painful ring of her voice twists my heart. "Go on. Get the phone, Tavi."

I answer the call. "He's in Tuscany. Find him."

Elise has gone out of the greenhouse. She stands, her back to me, as she wipes at her eyes.

"I'll do it." I hang up the phone.

"Elise," I call, but she only shakes her head at me. She needs a moment. Maybe ten. Maybe days. Or weeks.

Maybe forever. *God.*

"Santo's in Tuscany, baby."

When she turns and faces me, her face is contorted with rage. "Don't you call me that."

"Elise—"

"I'm not your baby. I'm not your... your anything. I'm your wife by law, and we knew going into this that we'd have a business arrangement." She shakes her head and a tear splashes on her cheek. She swipes it furiously away. "Just like everyone else."

Not everyone else.

I stare at her, not sure of how to respond. I want to tell her that I was within my right to order the hit on Piero, but I don't think logical reasoning will help now.

"Elise." I gentle my voice. "I'm sorry."

She turns away and doesn't respond. And worse than any of the pain I've been through, this one stab to the heart aches so deeply my throat gets tight and my nose tingles. I believed there could be something between us. No, not *something*.

I believed for a little while we could have it all.

"Find who?" Elise says, swiping at her eyes again.

"Santo."

She laughs mirthlessly and shakes her head. "Oh, yes. Let's find him. When we do, I have questions for him, too."

"Elise."

"What?" she snaps. And this is how it begins, I think to myself. The slow descent into a joined union where we hate each other. Like my father and mother, who sought comfort in the arms of their lovers. Like Elise's parents, who made a business deal and moved on with life. Like goddamn nearly everyone in The Family.

They all started off with hope. Just like I did.

"How did you know he was here?" she asks. I hate the cold, detached tone of her voice. It would have been easier for me to accept that she was cold and detached before I saw the real Elise—the beautiful, brilliant woman who makes magic in the kitchen, who transforms an empty building into a business worthy of the centerfold in a magazine. The woman who hugs my Nonna thank you and eats my Mama's pasta and revels in the taste of fresh herbs, good wine, and homemade food. The woman who makes a homecooked meal an orgasmic experience. The woman who put up with all the bullshit my family put her through and still stood at the altar with grace and dignity and took our vows.

I got to know the real Elise. The one who loves. The one who lives.

The woman before me now is only a shell of the woman I brought back to America and kept hostage.

I don't have time to make this right. Not now, when her safety and the safety of my family is on the line. Romeo called to tell me Santo was in Tuscany, but I need more than that.

And I need to keep tabs on my wife. An angry woman's like a ticking time bomb, and I won't let her detonate on my watch. We can't fix this now. The first step in fixing anything, or at the very least preventing anything else getting fucked up, is finding Santo.

"Get in the car," I order her. I unlock it and signal for her to go over. She stomps over with a haughty expression. I'm not sure if she's hiding her need to cry or her need to hit me, and I don't care. Before we can fix this, we have to find Santo.

I make a few phone calls before I join her, my mind as always working things through, like twisting a Rubik's cube. If I turn things around the right way, the colors will line up.

Santo.

Anna.

Piero.

Jenoah.

They're not random pieces of the puzzle. They all fit together.

How?

I could start at the morgue. My cousin's body's been claimed and we've sent him to be cremated. My family's due to arrive in a few weeks for the funeral.

No. The morgue won't give me the answers we need.

I pull up footage of The Castle and frown as I scroll back to the date of my wedding.

There she is. My beautiful bride, waiting at the foot of the stairs near the reception room. Her bouquet's held up to her chest as she scans the crowd, her eyes a bit apprehensive. Then Angelina comes down the stairs, and Elise's face lights up.

She won't like that Angelina kept the truth about Piero to herself. She'll feel betrayed, I'd imagine. I don't blame her. I'd feel the same.

And even though I denied that I regret what I've done... I hate that I've caused her pain.

I was loyal to my family. I did what had to be done, and I told myself it was the *right* thing to do. But do I feel as if it were the right choice?

Do we ever have clear-cut right choices?

Sometimes, I suppose.

Sometimes, the answer's clear. Other times, the answer's neutral and still others, our choices are tangled like a rat's nest.

And sometimes we make our choices and have to deal with the consequences.

I open the car door. Elise looks out the window, sitting as far away from me as possible in the small interior of the car.

I flip through the footage on my phone.

"So that's what you used," she says in a cold, detached tone.

"For what?"

"To watch me. When I was your prisoner."

I don't look up when I respond. "Exactly."

She makes a sort of huffing noise, but I ignore her and continue looking through the footage.

I see the two of us, standing at the altar. Taking our vows. I bent and kissed her amidst applause, and all the while, Santo was where my brothers were— standing behind us. At one point he communicated with someone at the door, but then came back. Could've been damn near anything, and it doesn't mean he's guilty.

"Why are you looking through the wedding footage?" I hate the cold tone of her voice. I look up, startled.

"I need to find when Santo left. I'm combing through footage now."

She swallows and looks forlornly out the window. "Oh. Sorry I interrupted."

Normally, I'd make her look at me, but I'll give her this reprieve. I owe this to her, this distance.

For now.

"How did you know to ask me about Piero?"

She flinches when I say his name. I hate that she does.

I remember Angelina screaming at me, furiously sobbing when she knew I called the hit on Piero.

You killed the only man she ever loved.

At the time, it was only confirmation to me that I'd done the right thing. They had no right to love each other.

But now I know.

261

Love doesn't always know the rulebook.

"My mother texted me," she says, a hollow tone in her voice that breaks my heart. "She said to ask you." She glances at me then looks away again, pinching the bridge of her nose and squeezing her eyes shut as if to block it all from her memory. "But I knew you were hiding something from me, Ottavio."

Jesus. Not my full name. It's too intimate between the two of us.

"What do you mean?"

"You…" she begins. "I could tell you were hiding something from me because sometimes you had this distant look in your eyes like you were holding yourself back from me." She sighs and opens her eyes. "Were you ever planning on telling me?"

I nod. "Yeah. Of course I was."

"When?"

When I was confident that you loved me? When I knew that the truth wouldn't cause a rift between us that wouldn't heal? When I knew the power of our love was strong enough to overcome the past?

I don't answer. "Your mother told you to ask me. And you were the one that pointed out her coming may have been a diversion." Anna Regazza has a hand in this.

One piece of the puzzle slips into place.

I speed the footage up.

We sit and drink champagne. Orlando gives us a toast. We smile for the camera.

It seems so long ago.

Then I see myself sit up straighter and head to Romeo. It's when I realized Anna Regazza had come.

"Slow," she whispers. "Right there. Look."

At the very corner of the screen, Santo paces.

Santo.

On the footage, I go inside, but I look at the outside footage where Santo is. He strolls along the perimeter of the garden. Rosa signals to him from her seat. He waves at her, and…

I pause and rewind.

He waves at her and gives a signal. Rosa stands, gestures to Natalia, and leaves Natalia in the care of her nanny. She meets Santo in the garden.

"Why the hell is he talking to Rosa?"

Elise rolls her eyes. I choose to ignore it.

A second later, Rosa walks back to the dance floor, but she wrings her hands. She paces back and forth, and when staff brings flutes of champagne, she takes one and drinks it in two large gulps. She's clearly agitated, but I can't tell why.

I shake my head. "I don't get it."

"Maybe Rosa's the one to call."

"Yeah," I mutter to myself.

Santo's back from the garden. He glances at his watch and takes a call. He paces. Then he does something strange. I watch him walk to Natalia and crouch in front of her. He smiles, says something to her, then gives her a huge hug. I watch Orlando, Mario, and our guards head into the house where I know Anna Regazza's inside having a fit.

A shadow passes the garden. Santo rises, straightens his shoulders, then takes a phone call. He looks over his shoulder, and I don't miss the way his face contorts. Anger? Rage? He's conflicted.

Quickly, I scroll to the footage of our driveway. One of our own cars waits, idling. No one noticed since we were all at the wedding reception. Santo knocks on the driver's window. The driver exits the car, heads back to the garage, and Santo takes his seat.

I pause and rewind the footage.

I've never seen the driver before in my life.

Motherfucker.

The first call I make is to Rosa. It goes straight to voicemail. I curse under my breath and call Romeo.

I tell him everything. "Rosa's in town," he says. "She didn't take your call?"

"No. Where's Natalia?"

"Natalia's with her."

I call her bodyguard, who answers on the first ring. "Yes, sir, Mr. Rossi?"

"I need to talk to Rosa."

"She's indisposed at the moment, can't talk sir."

"What the fuck is she doing that leaves her indisposed?"

"Uh… uh, I think she's getting a Brazilian wax," he says sheepishly.

I cringe. "Ah. Right." I squeeze my eyes shut. I did not need to know *that*.

"You asked," Elise mutters. I don't reply.

I text Romeo to question Rosa, then look through everything else I have recorded. Our footage goes as far as Santo heading to the highway, likely to the airport.

"What do you have here in Tuscany, and why would he come here? How does Romeo know he's here?"

"We have tracking software on our phones. It shows Santo leaving and then arriving here shortly after we do."

She blows out an exasperated breath. "And where does it show him now?"

I frown. "At the airport. Since we got here."

"So you think he disabled his phone or left it, yet he didn't leave it in America?"

"Right. Doesn't make sense that he's still in the airport, does it?"

She shakes her head "Unless… well, unless he *is* still there."

I look at her sharply. "Still at the airport?"

"Well, yes. People do business there all the time, don't they? It's the perfect meeting place for people to go incognito. Do whatever shady shit you're doing, then hop on a plane and go anywhere in the damn world."

"Let's go."

Our vineyard's closer to the Florence Amerigo Vespucci Airport than our home, so it's only a fifteen minute ride. Though there are two main airports that serve Tuscany, we always use the Florence airport because it accommodates our private flights more easily.

"I don't know why he'd be at the airport. It's all so convoluted." I give her a sidelong glance. "He might've left his phone there. You don't know anything about leaving things places so you can cause a diversion, now, do you?"

She doesn't respond, only picks at the cuticles on her fingers with a haughty look.

We drive the entire way there in silence. The drive is beautiful, but I hardly pay attention to the rolling green hills, the sun above us, or the blooming spring flowers as far as the eye can see. I'm piecing things together.

Maybe he *is* still at the airport.

Why?

"Elise, call Rome again, please."

"Whatever you say, sir," she says in a voice so dripping with sarcasm I want to pull this car over and spank the sass right out of her. I won't, though. I'll give her this space.

Later, we'll talk.

Later, we'll make amends.

I don't know how, and I don't know when, but we will.

I caught a glimpse of what life looked like with the woman that I love, and *I want that life*. I won't let this happen. I won't let anything drive a wedge between us.

I fucked up. I'll have to grovel, something I would literally *only* do for the woman I love.

The woman I love.

I want to see the light in her eyes again. I want to hear her voice go all soft and melty when she talks to me. I want to see the color on her cheeks when I kiss her. I want to hear her moan when I make her come.

She takes my phone, pulls up Romeo's number, and hits it to call him. She puts it on speakerphone.

"Tavi? You find him?"

"No, Rome, but I think I might be close. Do me a favor, brother?"

"Yeah?"

"Take the tracking off my phone."

He's silent for a minute. "Can't do that, Tav. What if something happens to you? Can't find you if I don't have your tracking on your phone. It's for your own safety."

I grit my teeth. "Romeo, you need to take it off since I'm heading in to find Santo. He left, brother. Elise called it, said Anna Regazza was at our house as a diversion. I looked through the footage. He left right when she came."

He curses under his breath.

"And I don't want him knowing I'm coming. I need to get to the airport without him knowing."

Romeo curses under his breath. "If he betrayed us, Tavi…"

I know. I fucking know. We'll bring him before us and burn the rose that marks him as one of us right off his skin. He'll be beaten before he's questioned and killed.

"I'll kill the motherfucker, Tav."

"And I'll help you."

He curses up a blue streak, then finally concedes. "Fine. *Fine.* I'll let you go dark, but you let me know the second you're back, you got me?"

"Yeah." I sigh. "Yeah, I will."

Elise looks thoughtful but doesn't say anything. I watch the screen as the small bright dot in the upper right corner that indicates tracking disappears.

It feels odd, going it alone like this. No brothers to back me up. No bodyguards. No one to call for footage or tracking. I haven't gone solo in years.

I look to Elise, who's only staring out the window. I've never felt so lonely in my life.

CHAPTER 18

Elise

I MAKE myself focus on what we need to do.

When I get my hands on Santo...

Well. When I get my hands on him, I have no idea *what* I'll do. Like Tavi, he's strong and ruthless, and it won't be like I can hurt him.

I have questions for him, though.

He's the most merciless of all of them. I remember Piero telling me that he believed Santo to be a psychopath, back when I first found out I was going to be married to one of the Rossi brothers.

And for the first time since this all went down... over a year ago now, though it feels like it might've been a decade or more... I wonder.

Why did Piero have such a strong opinion of Santo?

I bring myself back to the conversation. I was in my family home in Tuscany, my mind spiraling out of control with the very idea of being married to someone I'd never met.

I feel the grief choke me when I conjure up the image of Piero, standing in the doorway. I'd practically pried the news out of him, and him revealing my family secrets led to his demise. It's my fault. At least partly, anyway.

I served time with Santo, one of their main core. The man is a fucking psychopath. I don't want you in that family. What if they marry you to Santo? I swear he has no conscience…

Does serving time with someone really give you a glimpse into who they are? Or was there another reason why he feared my being married to Santo?

How did he know him so well?

Did they become friends?

I can hardly bear the thought of Piero being disloyal to me. *No.*

"Elise?" I focus on Tavi, whose eyes are on the road. He looks perplexed.

"What?"

"What's on your mind? I was trying to talk to you, and I don't think you ever heard me. Did you?"

I shake my head. No. No, I was a million miles away.

"I didn't, sorry," I say without a trace of actual

regret. "What did you say?"

"I wondered if you knew anything about this airport. But before you answer that, tell me what you were thinking about just now."

I feel my heart harden toward him. "No, Tavi. You've lost the privilege of knowing what I'm thinking."

Before I can stop him, his hand comes to rest on my thigh, but it isn't a possessive or tender grip. It's a reminder of his power over me. It almost hurts.

"And that's where you're wrong, Elise. You may be angry at me. You may even hate me."

I do, I do feel all those things.

"But you can't hide from me. If you don't tell me readily, I have methods of finding out."

I laugh mirthlessly. "As if you have the magical ability to get into my *mind*. What are you, a magician?"

A muscle tics in his jaw before he responds. "We have ways of accessing the mind, Elise. Don't make me go there."

I shove his hand off of me. "So you'd torture me, would you?"

A beat passes before he responds. "Only if I have to."

"Ah, what a nice way of starting a marriage." My voice catches at the end. I stare out through the passenger window so he doesn't see the tears fill my eyes.

"Elise," he says, softer now. "If you think of anything at all that can help us find Santo, it helps *both* of us. How can I protect you from danger if I don't know everything that threatens you?"

I think about this. *Protect me.* It sounds like it should be something nice, something I'd even crave. But I don't want his protection. I don't want anything from him.

Still, there's no use in hiding anything that could help us solve this mystery, and I have to reluctantly admit that he's right. It's in both of our best interests if we work together, not apart from one another.

"Before I left Tuscany, when I escaped with Piero." He nods, even as his lips thin and his nostrils flare. I don't know if he'll ever be able to discuss that time without getting furious. I don't care, either. "I made him tell me why I was being sent back to America. He reluctantly told me. But when he did, he warned me about Santo."

Tavi takes a left turn. A large sign that tells us we're nearing the Vespucci Airport looms ahead of us. We fly by it.

"Did he? What did he say?"

I tell him.

"Piero and Santo served time together? I should know that. Goddammit."

I sigh. The sky thunders with the noise of an airplane taking off. I stare at the red stripe along the side.

"When did they serve time together?"

I shake my head. "I don't know. But it's… well, it's unsettling because Piero was very determined to keep me away from Santo. He said he didn't know all of you, but that Santo was a psychopath. He seemed… like he really knew him."

"I see." Tavi frowns and flips on his directional. We fly down the ramp as a plane flies right over us. This airport isn't quite as busy as the airport in Pisa, but it's a close second. "That's good intel. Thank you."

I nod. "I don't like the thought of Piero being involved in any way with Santo," I admit, then wish I hadn't spoken. I don't want to betray the memory of the only man I ever loved. It feels like the worst form of infidelity. And then it hits me, so hard it hurts.

Piero wasn't the man I took an oath of fidelity to.

Ottavio Rossi is my husband. He's the man I've vowed to be faithful to.

It's possible to be faithful to someone you don't love.

Do I love Tavi?

Did I even know Piero?

It feels like the worst form of betrayal.

I shove the thought away, as fiercely as I've pushed aside any painful memory of him. I want to hold onto what I had with Piero. He was my first love. The first one who ever paid attention to me, who cared for me. He risked everything to get me away from the Rossis and in the end, gave up his own life.

"I don't believe for a minute that Piero was involved with Santo," I say stubbornly, even as my reason tries to win in the mental battle of logic. "No. He knew him because they served time together. Makes sense to me."

"Elise," Tavi says with surprising gentleness. I'd expect that any conversation with Tavi about Piero would make him angry, but he seems to have some thread of sympathy in him anyway.

"What?"

He pulls into a lot I've never seen before that he accesses with his keycard.

"Look at me."

I promised to obey him. I hate that I did, but the Rossi family takes their old-fashioned vows seriously. And I won't be a person that goes back on her vows.

You vowed to love him.

How can I do such a thing? My heart aches.

"Yes?" My voice sounds aloof, but it's only masking the raw emotions that threaten to choke me.

"It's possible for someone to do terrible, even

wicked things, and not let it define you. It's possible to commit terrible crimes, and still love someone."

I know without him telling me that he isn't just talking about Piero. He's talking about himself. Hell, maybe he's talking about *all* of them.

"I know," I say stubbornly. I turn away from him.

"Now listen." Maybe I imagined any trace of kindness in his voice, because now he's all business. "We're heading in there to look for Santo. It's absolutely crucial that you do what I tell you."

Of course, all-powerful master. I manage to keep my internal thoughts to myself. I'm smart enough to know it makes sense to do what he says right now. I'm no wallflower, but I've never fought anyone. I've never beaten anyone up. I've never... killed someone. And Tavi may be someone I'll never forgive, but I'd bet my life he'd protect me.

"Right. I know."

"Elise." He grips my elbow. I swivel my gaze to look at him.

"Yes?"

"I mean it." I hear the steel in his voice, feel it in his touch. "You can hate me, but you're still my wife. And I'll still protect you no matter what. Do you understand me?"

I nod. I wish his promise to protect me didn't melt a sliver of ice around my heart, but it does. *It does.*

I swallow hard.

Piero died because of this man.

"Where does tracking put him?"

"In the conference room near the private runway we use."

I nod. Even during the stress of it all, I feel a *little* like a badass detective chick, and I kinda like that. "Got it. And who do we suspect will be there?"

He scowls. "No fucking idea." He lifts his jacket and slips his gun out of a harness. Checks the **ammuni**tion. Reaches in the glove compartment and takes another, smaller handgun out. "Do you know how to shoot?"

I swallow hard. "I do." My father would've killed me if he knew I practiced, but it was one skill I wanted to have. "And to be honest, I'm a damn good shot. I've only ever shot at... at target ranges, though." Paper. Wood. I've never shot through human flesh. My stomach rolls.

He leans over to me, closer, so he can inspect the weapon. He smells so damn good it should be illegal. The heat of his body makes my own skin warm all through.

Why? Why did I let myself fall in love with him?

"You shouldn't need to shoot at all, and you only shoot in self-protection. Got it? Shooting at the wrong place or time's like shooting a rabid animal. It will only make them angry and increase the danger you're in."

I nod and swallow. "Understood."

"We find Santo. We neutralize anyone he's with that could threaten us. Then, we question him."

"Will we bring him back to America?"

Tavi sighs. "You'll leave that part to me."

I'm happy to. I want nothing to do with a psychopathic traitor, and everything's pointing in that direction.

"We'll keep the exits in our line of vision at all times. We're just two people coming to catch a flight, nothing out of the ordinary. Santo likely won't suspect we're coming, but if we're identified by anyone at all, the gig is up." He blows out a breath. "And I don't have backup or protection with me."

For the first time, I realize he's hunting one of his brotherhood, someone he's known since childhood. Might as well be his own flesh and blood. That can't be a nice feeling.

I won't feel sympathy for him. I won't.

He reaches in the back of the small car and retrieves a duffel bag. "Here. Put these on." I look in surprise at a short blonde wig, a soft pink scarf, and a pair of sunglasses. I look inside the bag and see a stack of passports, a thick wad of cash, a variety of wigs, glasses, and even a haircutting kit and some hair dye. It shouldn't surprise me he's got an entire bag of tricks to help him go incognito whenever he needs to. And this isn't even his primary residence.

I duck my head and quickly don the wig, scarf, and glasses, when he hands me a small cosmetic bag. I don't need instructions for this.

I stare at myself in the rearview mirror. My cheeks are pale, my lips pressed together in a thin line. I look as furious and confused as I feel.

I scowl at the makeup bag, take out a tube of nude-colored lipstick, and slide it on my lips. Seconds later, I look like a totally different person. I look over at Tavi and blink in surprise. His hair's slicked back, he's wearing a scali cap, and he's got glasses now.

"I like you blonde," he says with a frown. Does he have to say everything with a frown?

I shrug. "You look like a professor."

I don't tell him whether or not I like *his* look.

"Show me how you hold your weapon."

It's cramped in the little car, but we're isolated here. I can't imagine he'd have us change our identities and check our weapons if there was any security footage here.

Piero was the one who showed me how to shoot. I swallow hard and position the gun in front of me, holding it the way I was taught. Finger on the guard, not the trigger.

"Not so tightly," he says softly, leaning over to adjust my hands. The heat of his body warms me, his voice so close I can feel a shiver go down my spine. I hate that I still react this way to him. "Loosen your grip, ba—Elise. Like that."

He almost called me baby. I try to swallow the knot in my throat, but it feels like an immovable boulder.

"Okay," I say, my voice husky. "Like that?"

"Yeah, baby," he says, as he moves his hands over mine and leans closer. This time I don't protest. "Like that."

Our breaths mingle. I can almost hear my heart beating.

"I'm ready," I tell him, my voice harsh and angry. "Let's go."

I pull away.

I can't let myself fall for him. Not again. He'll only break my heart.

He nods. "Yeah. Let's go. We're going into the main entrance where we'll scope our surroundings. I'll see if there's anything amiss, and you tell me if you see anything. We'll find Santo." His voice goes hard. "Then we'll question him."

I nod, though I don't think there's any "we" in the second part of that plan.

"We're two people who like each other," Tavi says as we head into the airport. "Remember that."

"Of course, sweetheart," I say as coldly as I can. It doesn't feel as nice as I thought it would, dammit. Turns out, I don't like being angry with him.

If only he'd say he was sorry.

If only he'd show even an ounce of remorse for what he did.

If only…

But I can't focus on that now. We're here on a mission, and finding Santo has to happen *now*.

The airport's busy today, busier than I ever remember it being before. A tour bus pulls up at the curb for drop-off, and we have to stand by and wait as an entire soccer team gets off. Tavi curses under his breath at the delay, but I use this time to observe everything I can.

To our right, a gray-haired woman with glasses holds a baby, and a much younger woman beside her kneels to help a toddler tie his shoelaces.

Behind them, two well-dressed businessmen in suits carry briefcases. They're dressed impeccably, but they don't look like anyone who might be involved with Santo. Looks can be deceiving, though. I watch them until they hit the security gate.

Regular passengers enter to the left, but to the right is the entrance to the private terminal where private flights take off. That area's far less crowded. Still, I watch one couple walk up to security, and as their bags are checked, a second couple goes by. I blink in surprise when the entire soccer team heads that way, too.

"Quickly, Tavi," I whisper to him. "Now's our chance."

He gives me a short nod, grabs my hand, and holds it tightly.

I hate that I still like holding his hand.

I hate that it still feels like we're a couple.

The tight squeeze of his hand on mine makes my wedding ring dig slightly into my finger. *My wedding band.* It felt so nice when he slipped it on yesterday.

The team exits to the left where a small group of security guards wait to check and escort them. They seem a little starstruck as they ask for autographs. Tavi and I sidle up to the same security gate, when Tavi's phone rings.

He slips a comm device into his ear casually and taps it.

"Mmm?"

Whatever he hears makes him dart his gaze to the far right, where small cameras swivel to face us, then pan back to the crowd.

"Got it. Thank you." He smiles at me. "Give me your bag, baby."

I feel as if we're in slow motion, like even the beating of my heart has a slower, steady tempo. I turn to hand him my bag, as security comes our way. My pulse spikes when I remember we're both carrying weapons.

Tavi, however, is unbothered.

Tavi smiles and casually lifts his sleeve before he turns his arm upright. I watch the security guard's eyes widen when he sees the Rossi family rose. His trump card.

"Welcome, sir," he says quietly, while Tavi takes out the stack of bills I saw earlier and peels off several hundred euros.

"Thank you," he says, still smiling. "You'll let us through, won't you?"

The guard eyes the money, but I think it's the knowledge he's dealing with a Rossi that he finds even more convincing.

"Of course, sir," he says in a low voice. "Follow my lead, please." When we draw nearer, he says in a whisper, "Please tell me we won't have trouble here today."

"If you let me go through, I'll do my best to make sure that's the case," Tavi says, still smiling, then louder, "Rodriguez killed it with his last goal, didn't he?"

The guard smiles and nods, and both of them start talking in Italian about all things soccer. When a second guard heads over to us, the first waves him off and tells him he's got us.

He pulls out the metal detector, waves it over us, and when it beeps, he shakes his head like it's malfunctioned. "Stupid thing," he mutters in Italian. "Happens all the time." Pushing a button, he gestures for us to go through.

"Thank you," Tavi says. When he goes to take our bags, he turns his back to me.

The soccer team comes through security at the same time we do, loud and boisterous, jostling each other. The security guard gestures for Tavi, and Tavi looks at me in a panic as the team sweeps past us so quickly, we're separated.

I trip and nearly fall, when strong arms go around me and pull me to the side behind a large column. "Keep walking, Elise."

It isn't Tavi. The voice isn't Tavi's, and Tavi might hold me tightly, but he doesn't feel like this.

In a panic, I turn my head to see who it is, but the arms around me are steel. I shove back.

Someone shouts, and a gunshot rings out. Immediately, chaos ensues. I fight against the person holding me, but I'm dragged along like a rag doll amidst the commotion. People scream and run, and another gunshot rings out. I look around wildly for Tavi, just before I'm shoved through a dark doorway. It clangs shut with finality behind us.

CHAPTER 19

Tavi

MY HEARTBEAT CRASHES in my chest. I can't yell for her without giving us away, so instead I sweep the place and grab the security guard I paid off.

"Find her," I grit out, shoving a few more hundred euro into his palm.

He nods in a panic before he runs.

The goddamn soccer team got in my way. They're being escorted away by security as the entire place has fallen into a panic, but I doubt they were to blame anyway. They were only in the wrong place at the wrong time.

Someone else knows we're here.

I had her. I had her hand in mine, before she was yanked away. When I finally extricated myself from the melee, Elise was *gone*.

Gone. *Fuck.* Someone knew we were coming.

Just when I realized she was gone, a gunshot rang out. Chaos ensued.

I can't tell who the shooter was, but no one's been hurt. Plaster from the roof crashed around us, so I knew immediately the shot was only a diversion, meant to distract. Still, people are running, screaming.

I survey everything with a cold, calculating eye. I will not panic. I will not be taken off guard again.

I sweep the area with my gun holstered at my side— it's distracting enough here I don't feel the need to hide it completely, but I also don't need anyone thinking I'm a danger.

Who would take her? How did they know who she was?

I make a quick scan of the place, but I'm familiar enough with it by now since I've been here hundreds of times. Bright overhead lighting beams on the private entry gate below. Against the wall there's a built-in shelf, almost like an eat-in kitchen, designed for people to work or eat while they await their flights. Spindly blue and black seats line every wall. This floor is where people board, but private flights leave from the private runway connected to this one.

There are any number of places they could've taken her, and the worst of it all is, someone could've dragged her onto a plane. If they did, there are any number of places they could've gone, and my hunt just got way more problematic. If they're still here, I'll find her.

I came here to find Santo.

But now I need to find Elise.

Something tells me, if I find one of them, I'll find both.

I push the comm device in my ear. Orlando answers immediately.

"She's gone. She was right fucking *next* to me, and she's gone."

"On it." I hear a series of clicks. I know he's accessing every camera he can to try to find her. It's the only thing he can do.

I hate that I'm helpless waiting. I'm usually the one that sits where he is, the strategist who knows every in and out of every place we go.

It's hard to let go of control and let someone else do it, especially when it's my *wife* we're looking for.

"When?"

"One minute ago."

"*Fuck.*"

"What?" I grit my teeth.

"Goddamn feed's jammed."

"I'll fucking kill him." I pace, my mind racing. "Try the backup grid. It's on another server, might still be up."

I can hear the keys of his keyboard clicking as he types. He says something in a muffled voice to someone in the room with him.

"Got it. Thank fuck. Got it back. Lemme see…"

I don't think about the betrayal. I don't think about the vows Santo broke. All I think about is the woman that bears my name who was ripped from my fucking grasp.

She may think she hates me, but Elise belongs to *me*.

I take advantage of the chaos all around me and draw my weapon. A lady to my right screams and points, but there are so many others screaming and running, no one takes notice.

I want to be ready to shoot.

I mentally go through every exit and door we have here, when something catches my eye to the left. While everyone else is running, someone's walking away from me at a slower speed. Unhurried. Damn near strolling.

It's a red flag if ever there was one.

I follow, darting behind every artificial tree and decorative column to hide me as I pursue them. Is that… no. It can't be.

Piero's dead.

I shove past a small group of women heading my way and duck again, just in time to hear footsteps leading to another exit.

I follow Piero at a safe distance.

Anna, Santo… Piero. They're all connected.

"Tavi, you see what I see?"

I nod, even though he can't see me. "Caught a glimpse before it crashed again. Can't be, brother," I whisper. "Unless Santo didn't kill him…"

I shake my head. How deep does the betrayal run? How long? How many people have been involved?

"Follow him," Orlando says, but I'm already two steps ahead of him. I don't need to be told twice.

He takes a quick flight of stairs down and heads to the escalator.

When my foot hits the top step, a gunshot rings out. I duck on instinct. It hits the ceiling above. Plaster and dust rain down on me. I look around sharply for the shooter when another shot follows, then another. Ducking, I trot down the escalator and brandish my weapon.

It's quieter down here, but a small crowd getting their luggage hears the noise and flies into a panic. *Motherfucker,* the goddamn airport is the absolute *worst* place to get caught in a shoot-out. Someone in a security uniform heads my way.

He yells at me in Italian to drop my weapon.

Ha. Not on your life, motherfucker. I feign surrender, wait until he's close enough to me. I yank him to me, knee him, and knock him out with an elbow to the side of the head. A door to my far right opens and closes. I take off at a run.

Another security guard on my left tries to stop me but I turn, see my chance, and shoot. I don't know who's with the enemy or who's just a security guard here, but I'm taking no chances. I hit his wrist. I don't wait to see what happens, but his scream of pain tells me my bullet was on target.

Ten paces in front of me's the door I saw them use. There's no telling what's on the other side of that door. A smart move would be to find another entrance, another door, come in a way they don't suspect… but I don't know the layout of the airport enough to do that.

"Orlando?"

"Can't see anything on the footage, brother. Be careful, Tavi."

If someone's on the other side of this door, I'll have to use it as a weapon. I open the door as hard and fast as I can and hit someone on the other side. I hear a grunt, come around the door, and duck, just in time to miss the blow. I act on sheer instinct and muscle memory. Swivel and hit him with the barrel of my gun. He falls on his back, still conscious.

I don't know who he is and won't leave unnecessary casualties. Injuries, yes. Casualties, no.

I grab him by the front of the shirt. "Who the hell are you?"

"Not fucking telling you," he grits. "Kill me, for all I care."

Tempting. *Jesus*. I don't have time for this but know I'm on the right path if he isn't talking. I cock my pistol and put it to his temple, ready to shoot.

"You with Regazza?" He grits his teeth and goes still. I curse. "Santo?"

Recognition flares in his eyes.

"Where is he?"

He shakes his head from side to side. *Motherfucker*.

I knock him out and push his body in front of the door as a blockade. When I turn, I find no one's come for me. I expected someone, anyone, to come and stop me, to be ready for my entrance.

I look back at the guy I've knocked out cold.

He was on watch.

For me?

"Tavi?" Orlando says in my ear.

"I'm here," I whisper.

"I don't see anything over here. It's all blank again. Jesus, they did this on purpose, didn't they?"

I don't respond. I have to stay as quiet as I can. He can't see me, but I take out my phone and send a quick text.

I hear voices ahead of me. They did this on purpose. They're here for a reason. I'll find them.

I'll find them and I'll kill them, every last mother-fucking one of them.

I close my eyes and listen. My father was an asshole, but he taught us many things, and one was how to block off one of the senses to amplify the others.

In the distance, I can hear a plane taking off. The hum of a heating vent. Someone being paged, and sirens. Police? There was a shooting, so flights will be delayed. It isn't a plane taking off, but landing, then.

I hear a voice, then another. They're speaking in Italian, but the responding voice is English. I crane my neck and listen. It's coming from my left.

I crouch, my gun gripped tightly in my hand.

If they had cameras on that guard, they'll know I'm coming.

"Tavi, you alright?"

I shoot Orlando a text. *Fine. Trying to locate the voices*

Orlando: Wish I was there

Me: Me, too

I'd give anything for one of my brothers right now.

A few feet away from me, I hear a voice. I go absolutely still.

"He's here. Let's bring him in." He speaks in English.

Santo.

A door creaks open beside me, and bright yellow light nearly blinds me.

"Ottavio. How nice to see you." I don't recognize this voice. This one isn't Santo. "Put the gun down and come here."

I put a hand up to block the light and see three men in suits sitting around a small, circular table. A quick glance around the room shows they're not the only ones here. Santo's with an older guy with graying hair, and a guy that looks a *lot* like the deceased Piero, but isn't him.

I'm guessing it's his brother, since it's not uncommon for brothers to join the mob. If Elise saw him...

"Where's Elise?"

"Elise?" the older man says with a scowl. "She isn't here. Don't tell me you brought her?"

I don't respond. It won't help me now.

"I said weapon down, Rossi." It's the gray-haired guy calling orders now.

I glare at Santo, but his face is impassive. He shows no guilt at all but doesn't meet my eyes. He acts as if I'm not even there.

I put my gun down, acutely conscious of the knife at the back of my harness and the second gun I have tucked in my boot. I'm hardly without weapons, and fast on a draw.

"Kneel, Tavi." The man chuckles. "Never thought I'd reach the day where I could tell a Rossi what to do."

He knows us, then. I glance quickly around and note the exit in bright orange at the door. *Uscita.*

"You got any more weapons there, Tavi?" Santo asks. I glare at him. Of course he knows I don't go fucking anywhere with one goddamn weapon.

"He's carrying more?" gray hair asks.

"Drop them, Tav."

I hate that he's using my nickname. I hate that he's betrayed us. I will find a way out of this, and I'll beat the ever-living shit out of him. I'll happily drag him back to America and restrain him in the dungeon where he'll await the verdict. Give my brothers a chance to pay him back for this, too.

"I don't have any other weapons," I tell Santo. I stare him straight in the eyes.

He shakes his head from side to side, then talks to gray hair. "He does. I know he does. I'll take them from him if you let me."

Oh, bring it, motherfucker.

Gray hair nods.

Santo rises and stands in front of the other two, facing me.

Then he does something strange. With his back to them, he slightly lifts his shirt sleeve to reveal the rose tattoo on his forearm. Holding my eyes, he traces the rose.

It's a signal. A reminder of his oath to the Rossi Family brotherhood.

I take a breath and wait. He holds his gun in his right hand and his left hand up to his belly. Slowly, so slowly the other two don't see, he holds up one finger.

Two.

On three, he pivots and shoots. He's so fast, they don't react. I don't wait to see him hit his target but grab my second gun and pull the trigger. I hit Piero's look-alike straight in the chest.

"Fuck!" he shouts, but I pull the trigger a second time as Santo stands over the old man and pulls the trigger again, and again, and again.

"Dead or alive?" I ask him."

Piero's look-alike stares at me, wide-eyed.

"Dead," Santo says. "He tried to kill your wife."

I pull the trigger again. His body flails beneath the onslaught of bullets.

Santo turns to me. "I'll explain everything."

A door flings open. I look up to see Elise, wide-eyed and fearful.

Elise.

I exhale a breath I didn't know I was holding before I realize she's brandishing her weapon.

She sees Santo holding a gun beside me and bodies strewn on the floor. I know exactly what she thinks, half a second too late.

"No! Elise! Don't shoot!" I yell. I need answers. But she's already pulled the trigger.

She hits Santo's left shoulder. He screams and grabs at it, then falls to his knees. Elise screams and drops the gun on the floor. It clatters and spins away from her.

"I didn't kidnap her," Santo grates through gritted teeth. "I knew they were coming for you, Tavi. I grabbed her so you'd get away. Kept her safe. I swear to fucking God, I hid her in the holding spot. They didn't even know she was there. I took her to save you."

Jesus.

I kneel over Santo and see he's injured but not badly.

"Gun away, Elise. Please."

She's kneeling beside the Piero look-alike with a look of confusion on her face. Then she closes her eyes and shakes her head. "I thought—I thought I saw him. I thought it was him." A tear rolls down her cheek. "His brother was due to be inducted into our family. Looks like they did that after his death."

She looks to Santo. He's gone white as a sheet, and his lips are pressed together. His hand is pressed to his shoulder which is leaking crimson blood onto his fingers.

"I'll tell you everything," Santo says. "I promise, just get me the fuck out of here."

"Anyone else here?" I ask. "Are there any other shooters we need to look for?"

He shakes his head. "They took a flight out ten minutes ago."

"Who?"

"Anna Regazza." He sighs. "Leo too, Tavi."

Leo.

My Uncle Leo.

I remember the day I came to claim the body. I called Leo, because it was his brother's son I went to identify.

How'd he know they were ready early for me? I thought nothing of it at the time, but if he set it up…

It all fits. It all fucking fits. Leo didn't remember seeing Santo at the wedding, said he was too piss drunk. He wasn't. He had a hand in this.

Leo, with his mistress in Tuscany.

Romeo never found our mole after Elise's father was killed on our property. He fired every member of staff and hired new people.

We never questioned Leo. We didn't know we had to.

"Don't trust him," Elise says, her voice shaking as she glares at Santo. "I don't trust him."

"You'll see everything," Santo says. "I promise, you will."

"Stand up, Santo." My voice is hard. I still don't trust him. I still don't know why he's here. "Where's Leo?"

Santo grimaces, in such obvious pain I cringe. "On his way to Bali with his mistress. Set up a team at the airport. Catch him when he lands. Trust me, Tavi. You'll see everything soon."

We have to bring him out of here bleeding.

Elise cringes when I kneel to help him and nearly slip on the blood that's spilled on the floor, but she doesn't apologize or make any excuses. She only walks to his other side while he tells us where we'll need to go through gritted teeth. Apparently there are lots of exits if you know where you're going.

"We'll need to go left," Santo says. My comm device crackles in my ear.

"Yeah?"

"You got him?" Romeo asks. *"Is he alive?"*

"So far."

Once, years ago, I was on the other side of Romeo's wrath. I don't ever want to be in that position again.

"Bring him home," he says. "I've got a private jet at the airport on standby."

I scowl down at the bodies and shake my head. "Can't do that, brother. I've got carnage here and need to figure out who's behind what." I stare down at Santo. "And I... I think he needs medical attention."

Romeo curses. "I don't fucking care. You were ambushed by our enemies. You have no backup. You're harboring a traitor with you. If he dies, he fucking dies."

There is no other reason Santo took Elise and hid her. The others didn't even know she was there.

He said he'd explain everything. And honest to God, it's not in his character to betray The Family. He's cunning and ruthless, but his loyalty to The Family can't be questioned.

"And Rome?"

"Yeah."

"You'll wanna lock down Leo, as soon as possible."

He curses under his breath again. "Motherfucking *motherfucker!*"

"Yeah."

Romeo blows out a breath. "Fine. I've got a car coming around to get you. Take him to your place in Tuscany. I'll call in extra bodyguards to protect you. You're a goddamn marked man until we sort this shit out. The second Santo's ready to fly, bring 'im home. And in the meantime, you question the shit out of him."

I stare at Santo, who meets my eyes. He nods, and winces when he tries to sit up. "I'll tell you everything brother but get her the fuck out of here. Fuck, leave me. They'll come and get me and finish me off."

"Why does this guy look like Piero?" Elise asks coldly. She stares down at his lifeless body with its vacant eyes. "Brother?"

Santo nods. "Yeah."

"Let's ask questions later," I tell her. "We want to be out of here as soon as possible."

Between the two of us, we heave Santo up. He isn't as big as I am, but he isn't small either. Elise is fierce, though, and Santo bears as much of his own weight as he can.

"Take a right, Tav," Romeo says in my ear. "Black car waiting for you. *Go.* Orlando's got the police locked down in the lobby. You've got exactly thirty seconds before anybody sees you."

My hands are hot and sweaty as I grip Santo's arm. He curses under his breath. "We have thirty seconds before the police come." We've got cops on our payroll, but it's a lot trickier in Tuscany than Boston. "Go, *go.*"

Santo curses, nearly crying, but Elise holds onto him tightly with not an ounce of sympathy. "Get in the car," she says, half dragging him. It's then that I remember Santo killed Piero. She'll have questions for him.

Santo drips blood onto the leather back seat, leans back, and closes his eyes.

"I'm not sorry, Tavi," Elise says resolutely. "I'm not."

But she isn't a violent person. She may have been born a mafia princess, but she's made of sterner stuff.

I reach my hand out to her knee. "I know, baby. I know."

This time, she doesn't tell me not to call her baby.

She rests her hand atop mine.

The entire time we're driving, I'm on high alert. I'm watching for signs of somebody following us, an ambush, or Santo not giving us the truth. I don't trust him for a minute. I secure his wrist the second we get in the car, hand Elise the gun and instruct her. "Keep this gun pointed on him, and if I tell you to pull the trigger, do it."

She gives me a nod. "Believe you me, I would be happy to."

Santo looks at me in surprise.

My voice is hoarse, merciless. "She knows about Piero." I sigh. "Start talking, Santo."

I want to beat the shit out of this guy for what he's done, but I also know that he's my direct line to the truth I may not get any other way. And I won't forget the signal he gave me. It appears he just killed my enemies, so it's entirely possible that he was undercover.

But without telling Romeo? Without telling Orlando? No matter what, he'll pay.

"Anna Regazza wanted to prevent your wedding. But you were supposed to be getting married weeks out. You threw a wrench into her plans when you got married early, which is why she tried to crash your wedding." His voice is hoarse and weak. He draws in deep breaths. I shrug out of my jacket and take off my T-shirt, ball it up and press it to his shoulder.

I'm bare-chested and shivering, my hands covered in blood. Elise stares at me before she looks back to Santo.

"My mother?" Elise asks. She looks a little stunned, but I don't blame her. She knew her mother didn't have her best interests in mind. I knew she didn't show up to give us a fucking wedding gift.

"Yeah. She was due money from your father's death that went to you if you married. She's been trying to plot against you getting married for... for a while."

I glare at him. How long has he known? "And how do you know this?"

He looks away. He's hiding something, obviously. I press my tee into his shoulder wound. His whole body arches and he swears out loud.

"Tavi," he pants. "I promise you I'll tell you every single thing I can. I promise. But there are some things I can't, not now, but I will as soon as I can. I promise, brother, you have to believe me."

I'm not gonna fight this battle now. I'm not even sure it's mine to fight.

"Tell me everything you can."

I can't help the note of resignation in my voice.

I'm exhausted. My wife hates me. I don't know what happens next.

"You're not gonna wanna hear this, Elise," Santo says. He's panting heavily. "Your mother was working with Piero." He scowls. "I don't regret killing him."

Her hand holding the gun shakes and she goes almost as pale as Santo. "What are you talking about?"

Santo closes his eyes and turns away from her. "Piero took you away from here. He stopped your wedding to Orlando, Elise."

I hate hearing this for her. I've never felt so much sympathy for someone else.

I ordered his death. He stole what belonged to my family. That doesn't mean she isn't hurting, deeply.

"He protected you, that's true," Santo said. "But he had ulterior motives."

She looks to me, as if I can help her, as if I have any answers to this. I only shake my head.

"He didn't want you to get married, because Anna promised him a percentage of the payout. You made it—you made it easy. It hurts to talk, Tavi. It fucking hurts to breathe."

"Keep going," I tell him. "Be brief if you have to. I don't know how much time we have."

If the Regazzas seek retribution, we'll have to protect ourselves.

"Jenoah knew. He overheard their plans at a bar in Tuscany before they relocated. Regazzas were sloppy." He grimaces. "Leo had him executed."

We'll find Leo, and we'll have to see what he knew.

The pieces are starting to fall into place.

Anna didn't want her to marry, because she wanted the money from her late husband. Leo betrayed our family, and was working with Luigi Regazza, Elise's father, from the beginning. Fucking rat. Jenoah was killed because he knew information he wasn't supposed to. The Regazza family has relocated to Lombardo because they want nothing to do with us. Piero took Elise because he wanted to prevent her marriage to one of us.

I did the right thing having him killed. I'm not sure Elise will see it that way. But there are still unanswered questions.

"Santo. Can you tell me anything, anything at all that will vindicate you? I don't want to be the one."

The one to punish him. The one to take his life. He knows what I mean.

Santo takes a deep breath, then lets it out slowly. "I hate not being able to tell you everything. I promise, I would die before I betrayed you. You know that, Tavi. I saved Elise because I knew they'd kill her."

I frown and shake my head. "When will you be able to tell us everything?"

"Soon," he says. "I don't care if you exile me. I don't care if you punish me. Just don't off me, brother. You'll know why soon enough."

"Will anything give us the truth?" He knows exactly what I mean.

Elise goes real quiet and lowers the gun, though it's still pointing at him.

"I think he's telling the truth, Tavi."

The fact that she's pleading for him means something. She wanted to kill him earlier.

She either knows something or suspects something I don't.

I stare at her. "What the fuck do you know you ain't comin' off of?"

She shakes her head. "I don't know anything that you don't, but I have suspicions. I'm not going to say anything until the time is right, because I'm not going to assign motives where there may not be any. But I think he's telling the truth, Tavi." She shakes her head. "I really do."

"It will be up to Romeo."

Romeo is loyal, and he loves his family, but if Santo betrayed us in any way, Romeo will have his head. Literally.

But Santo saved my life. Santo saved Elise.

Or did he?

"Ah, Tavi?" Elise says. "I think we're being followed..."

Santo heaves himself up. His face has gone even paler, and his eyes look almost bloodshot from straining. He looks out the window.

"I came here to end the Regazza threats against us," he says. "But they had many alliances."

But when I turn and look out the window, whoever is following is gone. I grit my teeth as our car takes the off ramp and heads to the narrower road that takes us back to the vineyard.

Elise shakes her head. "No. They're gone."

But I know better than to believe that. They aren't gone. They've only gone out of our line of sight.

I exhale and inhale slowly. Thinking.

Santo needs medical help or he'll be useless. Though I won't take him to the hospital, I've got a contact here who will come at a moment's notice. I make a quick call and give short, clipped instructions. I hang up the phone and look to see Santo's passed out. His head lolls to the side.

"Is he dead?" Elise whispers. Not an hour ago, I'd have thought she'd wish this on him. But now she looks scared at the very thought.

We're only several minutes away from the house now. Our driver isn't used to driving a getaway vehicle. If it comes to a shootout, it's me and Elise.

I look grimly at her hand trembling on the pistol, and wonder. Has anything changed between us?

"Will there be blowback from the Regazzas?" I ask Elise.

"I don't know…" she says with a frown. "I'm telling you right, Tavi, I may have married into your family, but I have goddamn clout with mine. And if they think for one minute that they're—"

She freezes when we pull up to the new house.

"What?"

"Thought I saw something just now." She shakes her head and shivers.

We have a large staff that mans the vineyard, but most of them should've gone home by now. I check her gun and hand it back to her, then check mine. My eyes focused ahead of me, I reach for Santo's wrist and check his pulse. The low overhead light from the house shines on his rose. I swallow hard and feel his low pulse.

He needs help. *Now.*

"Stay here," I whisper to Elise. "The doctor will be here any minute."

She nods. She may still hate me, but for now we're in this together.

I open the door. Santo's eyes open and he pushes himself up.

"Lay down," I tell him. "I've got this."

I feel Elise watching me from behind. I feel Santo's slow pulse, as he bleeds out onto my T-shirt in the back of the car. I feel the weight of the entire Rossi family on my shoulders.

My blood thrums hot in my veins, like a shot of adrenaline's been pumped into me.

I won't creep around this car looking for anyone. I won't cow in the face of fucking anything. I push the door open and yell, "Anyone out here, fucking face me. Don't be a motherfucking coward." Then I repeat the same thing in Italian, just for the hell of it.

No one comes. I look at every shadow, look behind every corner and in every crevice, but no one's there. No one at all.

I turn back to the car when headlights loom a good distance off. The doctor's come.

Just as I reach the car, I hear Elise scream. I turn to find someone in a hooded ski mask heading for us. But he doesn't reach for me. He goes straight for Elise.

She screams and kicks, shoots her gun but misses by a mile. He's got her around the throat, yanks her in front of him and puts his gun to her head.

"Come any closer," he grates in a voice that's familiar. He's trying to disguise his voice but doing a piss-poor job. "Come any closer and I kill her."

I call his fucking bluff and pull the trigger. He screams when I hit his shoulder, and his whole body jerks. Elise kicks him, and he rears back and slaps her with his good hand. She falls to the ground with a scream.

I don't remember lunging for him. I don't remember hitting him.

I'm aware of the fact that I'm taking every fucking bit of anger I've ever had out on whoever this masked attacker is. I slam my fist into his jaw, and his head snaps back. I pound my fist and snap his head the other way. I lay into him like I haven't beaten anyone in fucking *years*.

I pummel his body as he screams and writhes, then yank the face mask off. Leo's bloodied face looks back at me. He brings his hands to his face and blocks another blow, but he's no match for my fury.

"You motherfucking traitor." My fist slams into his broken jaw. "You fucking *asshole*." I hit him again, and again, every punch slamming harder than the last. My hands are slick with his blood.

I hit him for betraying us.

I hit him for going after my wife.

I hit him for ever making her afraid.

I hit him for fucking *everything*.

"Tavi," Santo grates. "He's fucking unconscious. You'll kill 'im. You don't want his blood on your hands."

I look at my hands covered in blood, a literal interpretation.

I hit him again.

And again.

And again.

Elise's sobbing, as her arms go around me from behind. "Tavi, no," she says. "You'll regret it. Bring him home. Let Romeo deal with him."

I stand and kick him, satisfied when I hear ribs break. He doesn't move.

The car door slams and the doctor I called stares at me with wide, terrified eyes.

"Who needs a doctor, Mr. Rossi?"

Half an hour later, both Santo and Leo, the motherfucker, are stable.

I call Romeo and fill him in.

"Thanks for leaving him for me, brother," he says. "But I promise I wouldn't have blamed you if you offed him."

I know he's talking about Leo. Santo's another story.

After Santo and Leo are resting peacefully in guest room beds, the doctor tries to tend to me.

"Le tue mani, per favore."

I shake my head.

"Check her first."

"Tavi, I'm *fine,*" Elise says.

I insist.

She is, indeed, fine.

I reluctantly let him check me out. He tends to some lacerations and a headache that won't quit. I put my guards on Santo and take Elise upstairs.

I don't know how things stand between the two of us. I don't know what to expect from her at all.

"There's a guest room on the top floor that we—"

She pushes me up against the wall. She's so much smaller than I am, a move like this would normally be laughable, but I'm so stunned, my back hits the wall in surprise.

"Kiss me," she whispers. "Fucking kiss me."

I'm so relieved, I lay my hand on her cheek and hold her gaze. "You want me to kiss you, baby?"

She lets me call her baby. My heart pounds.

So many words need to be said. So much needs to be explained, so much healed and mended between us, but she only says the one word I need to hear.

"*Yes.*"

I lift her in my arms and ignore the burning pain in my shoulders. I'd walk across hot coals for this woman. I can handle a little sting.

Her legs wrap around me, and she buries her head on my chest as if she's craved this, like she needs this.

"I love you, Elise Rossi," I tell her. "I love you. I'm sorry I hurt you."

She shakes her head. "I'm not healed from any of this, Tavi, and I don't know how long it will take. I won't lie to you about it. But I am telling you right now that I know this life is complicated, and I heard what you said."

"What did I say?" I ask, kissing her pink cheeks and remembering how soft she feels.

"You said it's… possible to commit terrible crimes, and still love someone." She rests her head on my shoulder. "And maybe that's true for all of us." She sniffs and repeats. "Maybe that's true for all of us."

I nod. "I think it is. For me. For you. For all of us."

I bend my head to hers and kiss her, relishing the sweet taste of her. The way she softens and yields to me, in a way she never would for anyone else. I'm honored by her submission to me. I'm honored by her forgiveness.

Our kiss deepens as we walk to my bedroom here at the vineyard. While not quite as big as the master bedroom in my main residence, this one overlooks the vineyard. The blinds are still open, the night sky out before us.

I'm so tired I feel as if my bones ache with exhaustion, but I know what we both need. I can tell by the insistent way her hands reach to take my jacket off that she needs this, too.

I've fucked her hard against a wall and in the shower, on her knees and on her back. Tonight, I want to hold her gaze while we make love. I want her to see all of me, and to know I see all of her. I want her to know I accept her just the way she is, and pray that she'll accept me, Ottavio Rossi, Underboss to The Family.

We reach the bed. I lay her down gently on her back, and she quickly takes my jacket off. I shrug, aiding her. Next comes my belt. The clasp quickly falls open, and she tugs it out and tosses it beside her. She makes a hungry noise in her throat as she slides her hands along my torso, moaning a little.

"Let me, Tavi. Please."

I put my hands out by my sides and nod to her. "Have at it, baby."

I love the way her small fingers move nimbly over the buttons. I love the way she bites her lip in concentration. I love the way her brow furrows when she slides the shirt off my arms. She helps me strip until I'm naked, my clothes piled haphazardly on the floor beside us.

"Now my turn."

I kneel in front of her and slowly strip her clothes off, each layer, bit by bit. I toss them onto the pile on the floor and take a minute to admire the perfection of her.

The gentle, graceful curves of her shoulders, her pretty pink breasts, the swell of her belly and curvy comfort of her thighs. I glide my hands to her ass and squeeze, holding her to me. "Thought I lost you," I whisper in her ear. "Thought it was over after this bullshit."

"I've been here all along."

"Yeah… but not in your heart, baby."

She closes her eyes only briefly before she opens them and nods. "I saw every woman I ever know wall herself off from true love," she whispers. "Until Angelina and Orlando."

I nod. I understand. Real romance in our circles is so rare.

"Speaking of Angelina…" she begins with a frown.

"We'll deal with that when we go back home."

I know she has no interest in discussing any of this now, but the time will come.

We won't discuss this now, though. Right now, I want this woman. Right now, I *need* her.

I lay her on the bed and lay kisses all over her beautiful, soft pink skin until she keens and moans with pleasure.

"Tavi," she says, moaning with every ministration from my lips. I brush my lips across hers, and her hips rise to meet me. She's so damn turned on it's an aphrodisiac. My own dick's hard as a steel rod.

I love the feel of her hands around my neck. I love the feel of her breath on my cheek. I love the way her body melds to mine as she gives herself completely, totally, irrevocably, to me.

I glide my stiff cock between her legs, and she parts them for me, silently begging for us to join together. I hold her to me, take in a deep breath, and slowly slide into her.

I groan out loud at the feel of her hot, tight cunt squeezing me. Her legs wrap around me as I seat myself fully within her, until we're as close as two people could possibly be. I lift my hips, pulling myself almost fully out, relishing the feel of the two of us skin to skin. Slowly, I work a rhythm that makes her moan with pleasure and close her eyes.

"I love you, Tavi," she whispers, as I thrust in fully again. She can take me, all of me, and doesn't balk or buckle. "I love you," she repeats, when I thrust in her, making her back arch in pleasure.

No woman's ever told me they loved me before. I love that Elise is the first, and Elise will be the last.

Our lovemaking goes on for hours or minutes, as time loses meaning. All that matters is Elise. All that matters is we're together. All that matters is what was once *me and her* has become... *us.*

Together as one.

We move in unison.

We come in unison.

One blissful wave of ecstasy washes over me as her own moans fill the room.

"I love you, Tavi. You ruthless, crazy, impossible man. I love you so much."

Her voice chokes up as she talks to me. She's overcome with emotion.

I love that she is.

The time apart from one another was brief but felt so much longer than it was. That's when I know... we're meant to be by each other's sides.

Her sweet, breathy moan makes my own need to climax skyrocket. I pump my hips and chase perfection. I'll never find it, but I'll die trying.

She comes when I do. Our fingers lace together as we come together. A rush of heat and ecstasy join as one. She groans and writhes, her grip around my neck even firmer than before. My seed lashes into her, and her pussy climaxes around me. The moment of bliss goes on so long, every muscle in my body's tense with anticipation.

And when I release a breath and touch my forehead to hers, she whispers something I didn't know I needed to hear until that very moment.

"I forgive you, Ottavio. Do you forgive me?"

I feel her sweet breath on my cheek. I draw in my own breath and release it slowly.

"I forgive you, Elise. Thank you. I forgive you. I love you. Be mine, baby."

We roll over together, a panting mess of arms and legs and beating hearts. But nothing's ever been so perfect.

CHAPTER 20

Elise

HE WAKES me in the middle of the night and reaches for me. I feel his strong arms around me and close my eyes. A warm feeling of contentment settles in my chest as he holds me. I know now that he does love me. Did Piero? I believed he did. And somehow, Tavi's helped me make peace with all that's happened.

I lean against him, his front at my back, his legs tangled in mine.

"I'll grovel if I have to, to make things up to you," he whispers in my ear. "And believe me when I tell you, I have *never* groveled for another person before in my life."

I smile, exhausted. "I'll take it." I roll over to face him and kiss him, and before I know what's happening, he's making love to me again, slow and sweet and unhurried, like a lover's stroll along a moonlit path. And when we're sated, we fall asleep again in each other's arms.

I wake the next morning to an empty bed. I feel around, wishing he was there. I hear him not far off, on the phone. Likely catching Romeo up to speed.

"First flight, yeah? Good. I'll escort Santo home."

He hangs up the phone shortly thereafter and fills me in. Romeo's men came to fetch Leo and have him in stable condition at Tavi's main residence. When he's strong enough, they'll fly him home. Santo comes home with us.

"And any word on Anna Regazza?"

He curses under his breath and finally hangs up the phone. When he comes to me, I can't help but smile at him. His hair's all tousled, and he's put the clear glasses back on. He gives me a wink.

"Get over here," I say, reaching for his hand. "What was that you said in the middle of the night about groveling?"

That gets me a teasing trip over his knee that warms me up well for when he lays me back on the bed and fairly worships me. My eyes flutter closed as he makes me come within minutes on his tongue, then pins me down beneath his large, sturdy frame while he takes me again.

"My, my, Mr. Rossi," I say, shaking my head. "You have incredible stamina. I love how you grovel."

He winks, reaches for his wallet, and slides out a plastic credit card. "Here, baby. You love to shop and my place here in Tuscany needs a feminine touch. How's that for groveling?"

My name, *Elise Rossi,* embossed in gold.

"Tavi," I breathe. "Really?"

"Really. You know we've got shit to sort out in America, but you asked if we could move here. How about we spend half the year in Tuscany when it's colder in Boston, then head home to The Castle so I can oversee the tourist boom at the bakery in the summer?"

"Oh my *God.* You are brilliant!" I frown. I'll oversee management and operations of my shop in Copley, but spending winter in Tuscany? *Heaven.*

We dress and head to the kitchen. Tavi gives his staff jobs to do, and I make him a simple breakfast of eggs over easy, hearty pieces of toast with thick creamery butter from a local dairy, and thick slices of peppered bacon on the side.

"If we weren't already married, I'd ask you to marry me," he says with a groan.

"And I'd say yes," I reply with a wink.

It actually feels like a real honeymoon for this small sliver of time. He has a few cuts here and there, but something tells me that won't be out of the ordinary in the long run.

He checks on Santo while I make a quick list of

things we need in the kitchen. Santo will be ready to fly home in a few days' time. He'll face interrogation from the Rossi family men.

I have my suspicions about why he's here, and it's the only reason I've forgiven him. The Rossi family eldest sister, Rosa, spent time here in Italy once. I've seen the way they look at each other. I'd bet money there's a story there.

But it isn't my story to tell.

I have enough of my own business to tend to, and if anyone should know how tangled relationships can become, it's me.

There's a pang in my heart with a different feel now when I think of Piero. It hurts that he had ulterior motives. But a part of him loved me, and I'll hold onto that. Tavi was within his rights to call for Piero's death. It hurt more that he didn't tell me after I came clean with him than anything. But people are complicated. Intricate and complex, as Tavi said, and we sometimes can only ask for forgiveness and try better next time.

He said he'll grovel. He asked for forgiveness.

And what is love, if not the blessing of forgiveness for the faults of the other?

We stroll in the garden after lunch, a simple meal of tossed greens, grilled chicken, and pressed panini with mozzarella and prosciutto. I asked the staff to bake fresh bread for dinner. I'm dying to get my hands on some of their own olive oil tonight.

Tavi doesn't bring me to Santo, and I'm okay with that. I want as little to do with any of *that* as possible.

He does spend lots of time on the phone, and several hours with Santo. When he emerges from where he has Santo resting—guards stationed at the door and in the room itself—he looks weary but hopeful.

"How long in Tuscany this time, Tavi?"

We're sitting on a patio overlooking the vineyard, drinking wine that's so delicious, someone should write poetry for it.

He sighs. "Few more days. Romeo hasn't been able to get any info from Rosa. She clammed up and packed her bags. He's pissed."

"Please, Tavi," I say, reaching for his hand. I give him a gentle squeeze. "Please don't let Romeo be too hard on her."

He frowns and strokes his thumb over my hand. "I can't make Romeo do anything, babe. I can try, though. Why are you pleading on her behalf?"

I sigh. "I don't know everything, but I have a few suspicions."

If Santo touched their sister, what he's been through will be *nothing* compared to what they'll put him through. Orlando or Tavi would beat the shit out of him before Romeo cut off his dick and shoved it where the sun don't shine.

At least, this is what would happen in my family.

I'll have to let them sort things out. For now, Tavi and Romeo are pleased enough with the intel Santo gave them that they've allowed him to live and will bring him back to the States.

So I'll leave well enough alone.

I know what it's like to be in love with someone you're not allowed to love.

We spend a few blissful days eating good, fresh food. I cook most of it but feel badly his personal chef isn't getting to do her job, so I enjoy a few meals made for me as well. But Tavi loves it when I cook for him.

And he eats more than any other human I've ever seen eat.

"Your mother must've fed you all day long when you were all teens."

"Babe, you have no idea," he says around a mouthful of ravioli. "No. Idea. You think it's bad *now*? Ha. We had three refrigerators, two chefs, and my mother had a personal shopper."

"Well, then," I say, impressed.

"You think it's an accident we own restaurants and bakeries?"

I smile around my glass of wine. "Uh, no."

He takes another huge bite of ravioli. "Babe, we practically bought those for the wholesale food discount."

In the evenings, we make love. Sometimes it's sweet, and sometimes it's rough. I like it rough, but there's an almost healing vibe to our sweeter love-making sessions.

On the morning before we're due to head home to America, I wake beside him.

"Tavi?"

His beard's grown into thick stubble, and his eyes are still closed. He's bare-chested and wearing boxers, one arm adorably tucked under his chin. I stroke the powerful swell of his inked bicep, lean in, and give him a gentle kiss.

"Mmm?"

He flexes his bicep for me, eyes still closed. With a giggle, I give him an obligatory squeeze.

"What happens if Romeo and Vittoria have no children?"

He shrugs. "He'll still be Boss, but those of us with children will have more sway than we would otherwise. It's in everyone's best interest for us to have children."

"Of course. And while I don't think you need to usurp the throne or anything, I think I'd like a baby, too."

I want to raise my children with my best friend. I like that we'll have children the same age.

He grins, eyes still closed. "Yeah, we couldn't usurp the throne if we wanted to, but I'm glad you have no interest. We can, however, strengthen our *own* small family with kids." He opens one eye. "How many do you want?"

"Oh, I don't know," I say, tracing his eyebrow. He gives me a funny look and chuckles. "Like three? Four?"

He nods. "Whatever you want, babe."

I smile and kiss him, and he pulls the blanket back up over his arm and yawns.

"Is this you groveling?"

"*Yup.*"

"Might a girl get another Pronovias dress during this groveling phase? I mean, wedding dresses are only a very small part of what they make, you know."

"Babe," he says, his lips tipping up. "You could buy a hundred of those dresses with that card."

"*What?*"

He only smiles. I am so going on the website today.

"Babe?"

I nod. "Yes?"

"You can get all the Pronovias dresses you want even when we're out of the groveling stage."

I grin, bend, and kiss him.

"I love you," he says. "I love you so much."

I sigh. I won't get tired of hearing this. My parents never told me they loved me, because they loved themselves above all. But Ottavio Rossi loves me. We've chosen each other, and that's what matters most of all.

"And I love you."

CHAPTER 21

Tavi

WE GET BACK to America on a private flight. Santo's stable and stationed between two armed guards. He's quiet but isn't brooding. He's more... melancholy.

"We need to make sure the Regazzas stop their attack on our family, once and for all," he says, as we take off.

As usual, Elise is holding my hand and doing her breathing. She has a small pill she'll take to steady her nerves as well, a sedative the doctor prescribed.

"Boys?" she says, while she takes in deep breaths through her nose and releases them from her mouth. "Allow me." She shakes her head. "I've had it. I won't let my dead father destroy everything. I'll make some phone calls. My mother doesn't hold

327

enough sway in our family to call any shots. She obviously was in league with Piero and his brother and one of our capos. But they weren't anyone that had any power, Tavi. I know people who do. Here. Phone, please."

I hand her her phone, and she makes a call. I watch as she purses her lips, and when someone answers the phone, she speaks in rapid Italian, then English, her voice tight and angry.

"Let me speak to Tony. *Now.*"

I feel my eyebrows hit my hairline. Santo mirrors my look of shock.

"Ascolta, amico."

Listen up, buddy.

She goes on a tirade about mistresses and money and theft and lies and finally finishes. "My name is Elise Rossi. I am married to Ottavio Rossi, one of the most powerful made men in all of America. Your stupid-ass attack on his family ends *now*. I'm bringing a baby into this family, and if you think for one goddamn minute that I'll allow you and your weak-ass shenanigans to cause one more *second* of stress to me or the baby or any of the members of the Rossi family, you are *sadly* mistaken. Oh, and Tony?"

I hear his voice on the other end of the line. "All that shit I just reminded you about? Your affair in Florence, the line of funds you intercepted from Switzerland, the way you lied to my family about it?

You think I didn't notice or I wouldn't do anything because I was a child. *Ha.* Think again, buddy. You guys step *one toe* out of line, and it's all coming down on *you.* I promise you. Got it?"

There's a brief pause on the other end of the line as Santo and I stare at each other. I look back at her when she continues. "Ah, good. Now that we've got that sorted, please tell me, how's Greta?"

Wow. My new wife can play hardball. She's just pulled out one of the biggest blackmail trump cards I've ever seen.

We arrive back in America by nightfall. I'm so exhausted because of the last few days, I want to go straight back to The Castle and go to bed, but there's a welcome party waiting for us at the airport.

Angelina, Orlando, and baby Nicolo wait for us beside the armored SUVs we often use for transport. Angelina looks white as a sheet. I give Orlando a quizzical look.

He only shakes his head.

But when Elise walks down the runway, Angelina hands Orlando the baby and walks straight to her.

"I'm sorry. Elise, I'm sorry," she begins.

Elise sighs. "I know why you didn't tell me," she says. I know they're talking about Piero. Now I understand. Angelina was sweating it out, afraid that Elise would never forgive her for not telling her.

Understandable.

"That was for Tavi to tell me," she explains. "It's all good now."

"Oh, thank God," Angelina says. She leans against Orlando as if she's completely spent.

"Is that all that was bothering you?" Elise asks. "You don't look well."

Angelina gives her a watery smile. "Ah, well, there's another reason, godmother. I'm pregnant again."

Orlando beams.

"*What?* I didn't even know that was physically possible!" Elise says. She gives Angelina a huge hug and I clap Orlando on the back.

"Good job, brother. Good job."

The news will be bittersweet for Romeo.

"Is Rosa talking?" I ask Orlando discreetly. He only shakes his head.

"Nah, man. But Santo will have answers for us." He scowls. "He'd fucking better."

It hasn't been long, but it feels damn good to be back at The Castle with The Family without wedding preparations looming or another trip coming up anytime soon. We won't leave for Tuscany for a while.

When we reach the front steps, the smell of garlic wafts through the air. I can hear streams of Nonna's favorite Italian opera singers filtering through the open window. Someone's baking fresh bread. The dogs nap peacefully by the front door, and someone's done fresh landscaping around the house. It's swept clean and brightly lit, with spotlights shining on Mama's rose plants.

"Oh, Tavi," Elise says, reaching for my hand and squeezing it. "It's just gorgeous, isn't it?"

"It is, just like you," I say, shamelessly flirting. "Welcome home, baby."

THE END

EPILOGUE

Elise

I LIKE LIVING in two places. It gives me a sense of wonder to arrive home at The Castle, where the Rossi family welcomes me with open arms. I love the old-fashioned feel of The Castle now that it's home and not my prison. I love having a place to gather with brothers and sisters and a niece and nephew. I love reading in the library, strolling through the garden, and swimming in the big stone pool in the courtyard.

And I love my job. The business is thriving, as we have the ideal location. Tavi says I have an eye for style, and three months after we open, I manage to score the deal of a lifetime—an actual partnership with none other than *Pronovias* themselves. They do a two-page spread on the store in *Vanity Fair,* and a TikTok video featuring my custom handbags that coordinate with the Pronovias spring line of dresses goes viral. Business is *booming*.

Rosa takes Santo's place as my assistant. She's a natural. I have no idea if she's ever given them any information about what happened to lead Santo to Tuscany, but I do know, because Marialena gives me *all* the gossip, that he's been exiled to do menial labor in Tuscany. It's odd imagining a strong, powerful, intelligent man like him watering grapes or something, but it isn't my business.

But I also love it when we fly to Tuscany. We go back and forth between the vineyard and our Tuscan home, and he does indeed enjoy my feminine touch. It's a joy to decorate the many homes that he owns, and an even greater joy to cook for him.

It seems fitting, then, that it's here in Tuscany, where we first began to fall in love, that I tell Tavi my news.

He's sitting on the covered patio with his evening glass of wine, staring out at the pale pink sunset. It looks like a postcard. I bring out a charcuterie board laden with sliced meats and rich wedges of cheese, rustic crackers, homemade jam, and olives. I slide the board onto the little table beside him. He looks down and his eyes light up.

"Looks incredible."

"Mm. Looks good to me, too." I smile and sit beside him. But I decline the glass of wine he offers.

"This is good, though, babe. The same Chianti that's won awards."

I smile to myself. "Well, Tavi, I have something to tell you."

His brows crease. He looks genuinely concerned.

"Are you sick?"

"Welllll…."

He sits up straighter. "Elise. What's wrong?"

"Well. Nothing's *wrong*…" I rest my hand on my belly. "But I think we should probably stay here for a little while until the nausea passes?"

He blinks. Then he blinks again.

I gasp when he jumps to his feet and sends his wineglass flying. Thankfully it doesn't break but only rolls onto the grass.

"Do you mean to tell me…"

I grin at him. He lifts me up in his arms and swings me around in a semi-circle. "Orlando won't be the only motherfucker with a baby?"

I laugh out loud. "Well, that's one way to put it, isn't it? But no, he will not. Easy, honey, you're making me a bit queasy."

He almost drops me, then realizes what he's doing and eases me onto the chair.

"Sit, babe. There. Do you need anything? Can I get something for you?"

I smile and shake my head. I only have mild nausea, but I'm exhausted. My eyes feel heavy already and we've barely eaten dinner. But I reach for his hand and give it a little squeeze.

"No, Tavi. Not now. And thank you." I kiss his knuckles and rest his hand on mine. "I have everything I need, right here."

We sit in silence, watching the sunset. I imagine hours from now, the sun setting in Boston where Angelina looks out over the water. And I think to myself... this, right here, is all I need.

PREVIEW

OATH OF SACRIFICE: A DARK MAFIA ROMANCE

CHAPTER ONE

Santo

A bead of sweat rolls down my back. I scowl at the landscape that most would find beautiful—rolling green hills that overlook the Rossi family vineyard, almost ethereal with the setting sun. The air's pregnant with the sweet scent of ripe grapes.

Fuck that.

I wasn't bred to harvest *fucking grapes.*

I yank at my t-shirt and pull it off, wipe it across my brow and ball it in my fist. A cool wind skates across my sweat-slicked naked chest.

September's usually the time of year they tell

tourists to come to Tuscany, instead of the hellish, stifling August heat, because the weather's begun to cool. But not this year. This year, September's started off almost as hot as August.

Others might see this as a gorgeous landscape, a little slice of heaven, really.

Not for me.

This vineyard's my fucking prison.

Bare-chested, glaring at the ripe vines that sprawl before me, I want to pound my chest and scream like motherfuckin' Tarzan. I want to claw at the rose tat on my forearm, the stark, vivid reminder of who I am.

Of who I try to be.

A reminder of the oaths I took.

All of them.

The ones they know about.

And the one they don't.

I turn my back to the vineyard and stare at the sprawling estate before me, only one of the number of places the Rossi family owns in Tuscany. I once had a place here in Italy, a place of my own, but I sold it when Romeo banished me to exile at the vineyard. It only mocked me with its vacancy and opulence.

Now I have an apartment here at the vineyard, where I oversee operations.

Motherfucking vineyard operations.

A part of me wonders if I'm here because Romeo wants me as far away from his family in America as possible.

Romeo, who's like a brother to me. My Don.

He knows I don't like to sit still and never have. He knows I like to get my hands dirty, whether that's changing the oil on one of my cars or breaking legs as punishment for a crime committed against the family. Romeo knows that the best way to really punish a guy like me is to take him away from anyone who matters and to make him do fucking *menial labor.*

As I head inside, a car pulls up the long drive. It's hard to see with the setting sun, but I cover my eyes to block the outdoor lighting and try to see. Ah. One of Tavi's, then. He's come to pay a visit. I wait, but he's busy on his phone so I give him space.

Tuscan homes are rustic and sturdy, many built centuries ago. The home set at the vineyard's no exception. Stone columns and benches line the walk to the main house, the most modern part of all the recessed lighting and spotlights in the garden. Here, the smell of ripe grapes fades a little.

Laughter comes inside from the kitchen Maurice, an older guy who's cooked for the Rossi family for decades, makes magic in the kitchen, unless Tavi's wife Elise is here. Elise can cook her ass off. But Elise is pregnant, and hates flying on a good day, so Tavi's got her home with The Family.

I wonder why he's here.

Another burst of laughter floats through the warm evening air. I clench my fists. It's been way too fucking long since I've had a chance to talk with brothers of my own, to feel like I had a tribe that actually welcomes me. I know what'll happen if I go to the kitchen.

I'll find Maurice regaling staff with tales of his many exploits from when he was a young guy in the Italian army. It's how he met Narcisso, the late Rossi family Don, and how he got the job here. Kitchen help in the army.

They'll be sitting around the large, rustic kitchen table with their pints of ale or glasses of wine, probably with a heavy antipasto plate at the center table. Maurice is famous for his antipasto boards—handmade cheeses, cured meats, olives cured from the Rossi's private collection, with jams and dried fruits. They'll drink and eat and talk in perfect amiability.

Until I walk in.

Tavi's still sitting in his car, probably catching up on emails.

I decide to test my theory.

I amble toward the kitchen. Sure enough, the whole crew's sitting around with their drinks and food, and Maurice is speaking animatedly in Italian, waving his hands for dramatic effect. He winks at me and continues his tale. Maurice has known me since I was ten years old, and he isn't afraid of me. That makes one.

I stand against the doorframe, leaning my hip against it listen to him.

"And the girl, she says, buddy, you want more than one tonight? I'm a triplet." Snickers and chuckles. Maurice waggles his eyebrows. "And I say to her, I'm glad you told me. Thought I was seeing triple. Still, I only got one dick, sweetheart."

The guys laugh out loud, slapping their knees.

"Ah, Maurice," I say from the back. "Don't sell yourself short, brother. You've got two hands and a tongue, too."

The laughter dies as the guys look back at me, their eyes wide with fear.

And then it begins. First one stands and feigns a yawn and heads off in the other direction toward staff headquarters. Then another, then another, until it's only me and Maurice left. Like a goddamn leper.

"Santo," he says warmly. "That hot, you take off shirt?"

"Yeah, sweatin' like a pig out there." In here, it's much cooler. I head to the laundry room off the kitchen where the housecleaner does our laundry and grab a clean tee. I pull it on, wondering what's taking Tavi so long. I won't invade his privacy, so I'll wait until he comes in.

"They scatter like ants when you come," Maurice says with a laugh. "They don't know the Santo I do. I remember you were just a boy, ten years old, the first one who ate everything. So thin I could see your bones."

I turn my back to him and close my eyes. I remember, too. The sleepless nights when hunger clawed at my belly until I cried. The way the boys at school made fun of me for my skinny legs and thin, emaciated body.

I remember how I beat the shit out of every one of them in high school, too, and how *no one* made fun of me then, not after Tavi showed me how to lift and Orlando showed me how to fight.

"Yeah, you could say I've filled out," I say with a laugh. I pat my belly. "Maybe even need to lose a few pounds, eh?" I've put on weight in Tuscany, but still workout, so I've bulked out.

"You don't need to lose weight, Santo," Maurice says. "Extra weight looks good on you."

It's extra muscle that looks good on me, I think to myself.

"Santo," he says softly. I turn to look at him. He's laying a hand towel across a ceramic bowl, probably covering the dough so it rises overnight. "Does it make you sad that they leave when you come?"

"Sad?" I laugh. "I don't give a fuck if they like me. I want them to do what they're told."

Maurice waves a wooden spoon at me. "And that's

one thing that hasn't changed. You still have the same trashy mouth you did when you were ten."

I laugh. "Only now you don't smack me with that spoon like you did back then."

He rolls his eyes heavenward. "Didn't do any good anyway, did it?"

He'd whack me good for my foul language, and Romeo tried to clean up my mouth a time or two, but it didn't work. The men of my brotherhood swear like sailors, and I always wanted to be just like them.

Always.

It never quite worked.

He takes the spoon, lifts the heavy lid on a pot in the back of the stove, and stirs. "They leave because they're scared of you, Santo."

I know. I know they do.

"Yeah."

"You should try... well, to be a little gentler with them."

"Maurice," I say dryly, turning away from him when I hear the side door swing open. "I don't fucking care."

I leave the kitchen to great Tavi in the living room.

"Hey, brother," he says with a grim smile.

Shit.

Something's wrong.

"Hey. You okay?"

Tavi brushes a hand through his wavy brown hair and heaves a sigh. He's got the Rossi family blue-gray eyes and strong, muscled physique. "Campanelle's calling foul, man."

Shit, shit, shit.

The Campanelles, one of the many rival families that give us shit, have been crying wolf for years. We never listened to them. Romeo assured us that he'd settled outstanding accounts and they had no claim on us anymore, but right after Tavi's wedding and my subsequent exile, the Campanelles provided evidence that the Rossi family owed them several million dollars, thanks to a deal their father made back in the day.

I sit down on one of the heavy sofas and cross one leg over the other. Tavi walks over to the sideboard and pours himself a glass of house Chianti, the very same that's won awards throughout Tuscany.

"What happened?"

He takes a sip of wine and exhales in contentment. "Fuckin' missed this. Haven't touched it at home because Elise can't have it."

Tavi's wife Elise is pregnant and can't touch wine for a while.

"How much longer you got? Like six months?"

"Nah, man," he says with a grin. "She's almost in the third trimester."

"Jesus," I mutter to myself. I'm missing goddamn everything being exiled out here. It's been longer than I thought.

I miss Boston.

"So what'd Romeo propose?" I ask. We don't want the Campanelles coming after us. We fought them before and won, but not without significant losses to both sides. We don't want to have to fight them again.

Tavi sits heavily beside me, his lips turning downward in a scowl. Before this conversation, I'd have told him that marriage was good for him. Eased his tight-ass ways a little, made him actually fucking smile every once in a while. But now, he looks older.

He looks up to me with haunted eyes and shakes his head. "He's promised Rosa, Santo."

I blink. A cold chill skates down my spine.

No.

No.

"Rosa?" I ask, my voice choked. I knew this could happen. I knew that Rosa, after the death of her husband, was considered eligible to be married. And in our world, the Rossi women are commodities.

They're treated with respect and protected at all costs, but all of us have known from the very beginning that they were never meant to stay here, that they weren't going to stay with us forever. We knew it was only a matter of time before they were given away in marriage to someone else.

I stand and somehow make it to the sideboard. I pour myself a glass of wine, but my hand trembles.

None of them know how I feel about her. If they did, I'd be a dead man walking.

I try to hide the way the wine sloshes on the table and pour more than I need in my glass. I grab a bar towel and swipe at the dark red liquid. I watch the wine stain the white towel. I've cleaned blood the same way, watching it seep into the terry cloth.

I swallow hard.

Tavi's phone rings, an obnoxious girly ringtone.

I give him a quizzical look. The wine's already dimmed my initial rage at the news, but my knuckles on the stem are still white.

"What the fuck is that?"

He rolls his eyes. "Elise gave me all these damn ringtones," he says and shakes his head. He snorts. "Wait until you hear yours." He hits a button. "Hello?"

Ah, it's not a phone call. FaceTime from Elise.

Her face takes up the whole screen. "Oh, hi, honey!" she croons as she blows him a kiss. "Is that Santo back there?"

She squints, and I wave, lean back on the arm of the couch and take another sip of wine.

Rosa.

Rosa.

My mind can't help but spin this around, to try to decipher meaning in the black hole of this intel.

I'm not paying attention to the FaceTime call until I hear my name again.

"Santo?"

I look to see Elise isn't home like I assumed, but in her store in Copley, the same I helped her prepare for retail.

I hate retail. I only helped with the store because Rosa likes pretty things, and I knew because she's friends with Elise she'd end up there as well.

And Rosa is safer in America.

"What's up? How're you feeling?"

All the Rossi women are like sisters to me.

Well, all but one that is.

"I'm good," she says, and she does look like she's glowing. She holds the phone back so I can see her hugely swollen belly. That makes me smile.

"You sure there's only one bambino in there? You can't trust a guy like Tavi..."

Tavi play-punches me, but it still hurts. I duck and laugh, rubbing my arm, when I suddenly freeze.

Elise isn't alone.

I swallow.

Rosa's bent over a display of leather handbags, arranging them artfully. She turns and looks over her shoulder at the phone when she hears my voice.

"Oh, hey, Santo," she says casually. Not a hint of familiarity.

I've been a member of this family since I was ten years old, and she greets me like I'm the guy that pumps her fucking gas.

"Hey," I say, an icy tone in my own voice. "How's business?"

"Oh, Santo, it's booming. Thank you. I think the marketing guy you found has really helped our exposure. You know how competitive it is in Boston, but he's put us on the map!" She beams. "And, Rosa's got the Midas touch, you know."

I swallow hard. "Yeah?" My voice is a little husky. I hope I mask it. I can feel Tavi's razor-sharp gaze on me. "How so?"

"Someone comes in for one little handbag, and the next thing you know, they talk to Rosa, and they walk out with *the entire collection.*"

I smile. "Well done, Rosa. How do you do that?"

Fuck, but I like the feel of her name on my lips. It feels like velvet and chocolate, soft and seductive.

She shrugs modestly and looks away from the camera. "I tell them they're worth it. I tell them they work hard, and that it's okay for a woman to indulge herself once in a while." She smiles. "And if it's a guy, I tell him his woman will be very, very thankful and be sure to show her appreciation."

Tavi laughs. "Well done, sis. Looks like you have a calling, eh?"

A calling to be the wife of one of our enemies. Yeah, she's got a fucking calling.

"Guess so," Rosa says. She walks back to her work, and Elise and Tavi chat it up again. She had a visit to the doctor today and fills him in on everything about the size of the baby, how healthy things are, and all the little details that matter. He eats it up like she's feeding him manna from heaven.

I turn my back to them and finish my wine, until he hangs up the call.

The room's silent for a minute, until the clock chimes eight. It's two o'clock in Boston, then. They'll be closing in only a few hours.

"Who's watching them?" I ask nonchalantly, as if I don't hold my breath waiting for his response.

"Amadeo and Tommaso," he says. Amadeo was once reprimanded by Romeo for drinking on the job, and ever since then, hasn't stepped a toe out of line. Tommaso is new, but trustworthy. I trained him myself.

"You've got two guards on them?"

He nods. "One per person. Not enough?"

He should have a fucking legion stationed out there.

"Need one for your bambino, man." I watch him grin and smile to myself.

I change the subject. "Rosa looks pretty good for someone who just found out she's betrothed to a stranger."

I try to keep the edge out of my voice but fail miserably.

Tavi looks away and doesn't meet my eyes. He twirls his wine glass between his fingers and frowns.

"Ottavio."

He still doesn't look at me.

Though technically Tavi's above me in rank, we're brothers. We've taken then same vows to The Family. Well. Most of them, anyway.

Any of us would give our lives for the other.

But I don't push him. I wait.

Finally, he releases a breath and looks to me. "She doesn't know yet, brother."

READ MORE

USA Today bestselling author Jane Henry pens stern but loving alpha heroes, feisty heroines, and emotion-driven happily-ever-afters. She writes what she loves to read: kink with a tender touch. Jane is a hopeless romantic who lives on the East Coast with a houseful of children and her very own Prince Charming.

You can find Jane here:

Jane Henry's Newsletter

Jane Henry's Facebook Reader Group

https://www.janehenryromance.com

bookbub.com/profile/jane-henry

facebook.com/janehenryromance

instagram.com/janehenryauthor

amazon.com/Jane-Henry/e/B01BYAQYYK

Printed in Great Britain
by Amazon